DAMNATION CORNER

Lee Johnston

This is a work of fiction. All dialogue and incidents, and all characters with the exception of Meg Matthews, are made up, and not to be confused with any other person, living or dead.

ISBN-13: 978-0-9938719-4-8

Thank you to my family for their support and patience with my preoccupation with prostitution in Owen Sound for the past four years. Laurie, you introduced me to your hometown and I fell in love with you both. Emily, you were gracious above and beyond in being my model.

Thank you to Deborah Johnston for taking such evocative pictures on a bitter Grey-Bruce winter day. Thank you to Deb's Girls for being the most wonderful group of women imaginable.

Thank you to April Bulmer whose feedback was precise and illuminating. Thank you to Marcie Schwindt who is scary-smart and good at everything. Thank you to Stan White for his wizardry with the cover. Thank you to Marianne Scott who walked this road before me and who is so generous with her experience.

Thank you to Cambridge Arts Connect for their financial contribution to this project.

Finally, thank you to the Cambridge Writers Collective, a small group that shines a big literary light.

Mistakes are mine alone.

DAMNATION CORNER

I am no heroine, but neither am I a villain.

I was born in 1884, and raised in Galt, Ontario. My family was of comfortable means. Daddy was a chemist, and sold a cornucopia of goods and medicines, some of the snake-oil kind, I admit. Galt was Scottish, mostly, and although we were of English stock, it was near to impossible to avoid the Calvinistic sense of sin, of brooding, dark guilt.

Even so, my early childhood was enchanted. Each Saturday, while Mamma was at her Temperance meeting at Trinity Church, I would walk downtown by the Grand River with Daddy, holding his hand, chattering happily, basking in the warm glow of his love. We'd reach his store, and he'd pass me the big iron key, which I fit ever so carefully into the lock.

I loved the bold red sign over the door: *Evans' Apothecary*. Daddy's full name was Joseph Jacob Evans, and Mamma was Edith Elizabeth. My own name, Charlotte Elizabeth Evans, I secretly found a little dull.

Once inside, Daddy would take inventory, order merchandise, unpack and stock shelves, and converse earnestly with customers, while I played quietly with my doll, or read one of my books. Mamma had patiently and lovingly taught me to read from the time I was three. From time to time, Daddy gave me an important job to do, such as count and sort buttons, ribbons, or other fripperies he stocked. After I was done, he solemnly presented me with a shiny, pretty penny. Bliss!

Mamma was a somewhat stout, strong, beautiful lady with soft brown hair framing her face. Her greatest sorrow was to be unable to provide me with a brother or sister. I didn't care, as my parents lavished all of their love and attention on me.

I went to the neighbourhood school, Dickson, and we lived in a two storey, beautifully furnished yellow brick house on nearby Aberdeen Road. I had a best friend named Emily, and a cat named Huckleberry.

One or two weekends every summer, we'd take the train to Toronto, and then the ferry to the Toronto Islands, which were full of picnickers, families, and courting couples enjoying themselves without a care in the world. I'd swim and splash at the beach. Daddy and I built tall sandcastles, while Mamma was engrossed in the book she always brought along.

One summer, when I was seven, we rented a canoe and paddled lazily along the shoreline. A large wave from a ferry came upon us without warning. Mamma and Daddy were not accomplished paddlers; our canoe tipped into the lake, and I panicked. I swallowed a large mouthful of water and felt the lake closing over my head, its green coldness inexorable. I sputtered and choked in my blind fear, but soon felt a pair of strong arms lift me from my watery fate.

I clung to Mamma, who was standing sturdily, waist deep, careless of the ruin of her brown silk dress. She smiled at me. She didn't say anything, and neither did I. I clung to her for a long moment, and she returned my embrace just as tightly.

Nothing more was said about my misadventure, and at the end of the day, as usual, Daddy bought us all an ice cream cone. My favourite was always vanilla. Daddy enjoyed lemon, and Mamma, chocolate. Life was safe, secure and happy. Life was good.

***

When I was nine, Mamma developed a cough, trifling to begin with, then worsening during an especially hard winter. I barely noticed at first, as I was busy enjoying my pampered life, but her cough became harsher, chestier, and her breathing more laboured. I asked Daddy as we were walking to the store one frosty November morning when Mamma would get better.

He looked at me with a scary intensity and said nothing. When we entered the store, he asked me to sit down and he sat opposite.

"You know that Mamma is sick."

"Yes," I said. "When will she get better?"

He cleared his throat. "That's what I am trying to tell you, Poppet. Mamma can't get better."

I looked away, swallowed, then lunged and pummeled his chest. "What do you mean?" I screamed.

He took me in his arms. I always thought those arms could fix anything.

"Mamma has consumption, my love. We have to do our best to make her happy, and comfortable. That means good behaviour from you, my darling."

"Can't you send her to Switzerland? They can fix her there." I had heard adults talk about the miracle cures available in sanatoriums in Switzerland.

"No, dear heart. Doctor Gordon says that she is too frail to travel. She would never make it to Switzerland."

"You're a chemist," I shrieked, and a couple of well-dressed ladies passing the store stared at me through the screen door with disapproval.

"Can't you cure her with some of our medicines? We have *Doctor Seth Arnold's Cough Killer.* You tell everyone that it has morphine in it and works like magic. Why can't you cure Mamma? She's your wife!"

I cried and cried. Daddy plied me with sweets. Twisted barley sugar and lime fruit were my particular favourites.

"Charlotte, you must stop carrying on so. What will our customers think?" Daddy begged me.

I despised Daddy then. Mamma was dying, and he only wanted to silence me, worried about what people would think. I cried harder, and I could feel my face go quite red. I began to almost enjoy my passionate display.

Daddy was desperate. He slapped me, harder than I ever thought possible, on the cheek. I don't know who was more shocked, him or me. We stared at each other in horror. I stopped crying and huddled into myself on my stool. When I gathered my courage to peek at Daddy, he had tears pouring down his cheeks and he was shaking. I got up slowly and went to comfort him. We hugged for a long moment, then, in the cruel, casual way of children, I allowed myself to be distracted, and soon immersed myself in my favourite book at the time, *Alice in Wonderland.* Alice's misadventures could be solved easily when she awoke from her dreams. She would emerge unscathed from the rabbit hole.

When Daddy walked me to school, I skipped ahead as usual, much to his dismay, I think. But when you are a child, the concept of death has little meaning.

That evening, I borrowed Daddy's favourite medical book, brought it to my bedroom and shut the door tight. *Tuberculosis has been with humanity since the beginning,* it informed me. *The disease has been found in native peoples of North America, Africa, Alaska, China, Japan, Russia, Corsica, Malaya, and Persia. It waxes and wanes, beginning unnoticed, then peaking in epidemic proportions, then waning again as the population acquires a collective immunity to the tubercle bacillus. This cycle takes approximately two hundred years.*

The lungs are the main focus of the infection, as with Mamma, I thought, *but it can also attack the meninges, bones, kidneys, liver, spine, skin, intestines, eyes*…the list went on. Opium was widely prescribed to control coughing. Many consumptives became addicted to opium. Despite my wild notion that a trip to Switzerland could control the disease, medical experts were in agreement that tuberculosis did not respond to any climatic condition. I closed the book and wiped my nose with the handkerchief Mamma ironed that morning. Daddy was right. There was no hope.

***

Mamma was fortunate that Dr. Gordon was a modern medical doctor, and did not attempt to bleed her with leeches, prescribe medicines laced with cocaine or lead, or use uncomfortable and entirely ineffective treatments such as plaster, poultices, cuppings or inhalations. He made her as comfortable as possible, and prescribed laudanum, which was opium based. He advised slow, frequent walks, plenty of fresh air, and a good diet.

Our family had always planted a garden and Daddy tempted Mamma with sweet carrots, fresh lettuce, corn, and peas, her particular favourite. In the winter, he cooked hearty, simple and delicious stews. We kept a store of root vegetables in our cellar and he incorporated these into almost every meal.

One of Mamma's favourite stews was from *The Early Canadian Galt Cookbook 1898*, by the Ladies of Galt. It was named simply, "Stewed Rabbit" (page 55).

One rabbit, one-fourth pound of butter, a little flour, one pint boiling water, a little grated onion, salt, pepper and celery. Sink and clean the rabbit, cut into pieces, put the butter into a stew-pan with the pint of water, the pieces of rabbit and several pieces of celery cut up fine; when this is cooked tender take half pint of cream or milk *(Mamma preferred cream)*, make a paste of the spoonful of flour with a little of the cold milk and add this to the stew (the onion grated should be put in half an hour before). Season, let it boil up well and serve hot. A little curry powder may be added. *(Mamma preferred it without.)*

Rabbits were in abundant supply in our neighbourhood. For a fee, neighbourhood boys were only too glad to procure them for us using methods I was more than happy not to contemplate.

I'd help Daddy measure, chop and stir. I grew so proficient that if he was tardy in returning from the apothecary, I could cook Mamma and me a wholesome dinner by myself, and Daddy would return to a fragrant, steaming meal.

Mamma's condition worsened slowly, and I grew used to her illness. I continued to attend school, play with my friends, and help Daddy in the store. I became accustomed to Mamma spending much of the day wrapped in blankets on her favourite rocking chair, with Huckleberry the cat curled up in her lap.

Listening to her cough was excruciating. It was particularly bad in the morning. It began as a soft rumble in her throat, and she'd try her best to suppress it. Sometimes she would have to spit, and Daddy bought her an antique silver spittoon which she used more and more frequently, with the utmost delicacy. She drank endless cups of tea that Daddy and I brewed for her. She liked it with lots of milk, and two cubes of sugar.

Sometimes, nothing would stop her cough, and she gasped for breath while Daddy offered her Beecham's cough lozenges that he ordered especially from Boston. She sucked on them obediently, her face flushed and beaded with perspiration. She did her best to protect me from the distress she felt every day, every hour, every minute. She'd smile at me brightly and rise from her chair to see me out the door as Daddy walked me to school.

"Have a wonderful day, Poppet," she called as I walked down our walkway, holding Daddy's hand.

Daddy would look back and blow her kisses.

"Make sure you rest," he admonished her.

"Of course. Don't worry about me. I have many books to read, and my quilt that I'm working on…" She coughed daintily into her now very thin hand.

She shut the door, and every day, I had a little worm of worry inside my belly - would she be there after school to greet me? Despite her brave pretense, I knew that Mamma's condition was getting worse.

After some months had passed, the only way to ease her hacking cough was laudanum. Mamma fought it for as long as she could. Temperance had been the cause dearest to her heart. Daddy walked slowly to the medicine cabinet, which was out of my reach, and returned with the little brown bottle in his hands.

"No, darling, you know I don't believe in stimulants of any kind," Mamma protested.

Daddy was patient but determined.

"I can't bear to see you suffer. And think of how difficult it is for Charlotte."

Mamma relented, taking the detested medicine, for my sake. I knew she was wracked with guilt at how her illness affected me, as well as being wracked with the illness itself. The laudanum did ease her cough, but it made her sleepy and distant as well. Daddy read me my bedtime story more and more often.

***

For the first time, I began to yearn for a little brother or especially a sister, but I knew now that this would never be. However, Mamma's sister, Aunt Esther, lived in nearby Preston, and I was able to visit with my cousins, Georgette and Jonny. They were close to my age, and as Mamma continued to deteriorate, I spent an increasing amount of time at their house.

Auntie Esther's husband, Uncle Gregory, was a tall, thin man who had a balding pate, wore spectacles, and walked with a limp. No one ever told me why he limped, but I don't remember him ever without his cane. The head was carved into the shape of a lion with protruding teeth. The teeth fascinated me, and I spent many long minutes staring at that rapacious face. My uncle, however, was mild-mannered, polite and kind. He worked as a lawyer and had an office on King Street.

Georgette, Jonny and I had grand fun and played together for hours at a time. They shared their hoops, marbles and skipping ropes. I was the undoubted skipping champion, but Georgette was not far behind. Jonny was not quite so dexterous as us girls. We passed long, happy hours playing chasing games such as tag and catch with balls. Georgette was particularly good at hopscotch, and Jonny excelled at marbles. The odd, sweet evening, a street musician would stroll down

King street, wheeling a barrel organ, which played tunes when the handle was turned. Heaven! Once, the musician even had a monkey with him.

"Can we pat him?"

Jonny and I were shocked at Georgette's temerity, but the organ grinder smiled. His teeth were yellowed, and a few were missing, and he puffed on a cigarette. *What an ugly man.*

"Sure, go ahead." He smiled, and I realized that he was not ugly in the slightest.

Jonny, as the only boy, reached out his hand, and gently patted the monkey's head. We screamed when the monkey reached out and gently patted Jonny's head.

"Can I try?" We took turns playing with the monkey until he tired of us, and the man fed him a banana. We felt like we had tasted paradise that evening.

Eventually, my mother's condition became almost too much for me to bear. Her coughing worsened, and now she could rarely leave her bed. All Daddy and I could do was to keep her warm and as comfortable as possible. She no longer read to me, so I began to read to her, and we moved slowly through Charles Dickens' novels. My favourite was *A Christmas Carol,* but it disturbed Mamma with its ghosts and intersection with the afterlife. I realize now that she felt like she had one foot already in the grave and wanted to cherish her remaining time on earth.

When Mamma began to cough up blood, any pretense that she would recover was dropped, and when I turned 11, she and Daddy sent me to live full time with Auntie Esther. I was relieved to leave that house of suffering. In particular, I could not bear to smell the tincture of laudanum dissolved in sherry that Mamma consumed in large amounts to keep her pain at bay. The sweetly alcoholic medicine seemed to pervade our entire house, and I was certain even my clothes reeked of it. It was the stench of death.

I transferred to the Preston school, and played happily with my cousins. However, all the time in the back of my mind, I worried about Mamma, and worried, too, if I would ever see her again. My uncle and Daddy met every Sunday morning in their buggies, to allow me to return home, attend church with Daddy, then spend time brushing Mamma's long brown hair, which seemed to be thinning now. I plucked the hairs from her brush, threw them away, then turned to the literature she adored. We enjoyed Browning, Tennyson, and a somewhat curious book called *Walden* about an antisocial gentleman who, to my unformed schoolgirl mind, preferred his own company to a ludicrous degree.

"What a frightful old bore!" I tried to keep my voice light and teasing, without any whininess.

"Mr. Thoreau has discovered peace of mind," said Mamma. I tried to be a little sassy, as I would have in happier times,

"All by himself? With no one to talk to?"

"Come here, darling. I don't want to argue." I cuddled up to her on the sofa, careful not to crush her. She was thin to the point of emaciation now, her skin almost translucent. She held onto me tightly, but her bony shoulder pressed into mine and I had to pull away. She looked hurt, so I took her hand in mine and stroked it gently.

"Shall I comb your hair some more, before I leave?"

"Oh yes, I would love that. Your daddy doesn't have the same touch with hair as you do."

"He's a man."

Our eyes met, and we giggled.

To my shame, there was a part of me that was always relieved to bid my parents good-bye, and return to my aunt's bustling, busy, happy home.

***

One day, I returned home from school, skipping and jumping, and enormously hungry. Aunt Esther looked like she had been crying, but she fed us some cake and milk. It was my favourite, fluffy sponge cake with a jam filling.

After I had enjoyed a generous slice, she said to Georgette and Jonny,

"Charlotte and I need to talk for a little while, privately. You must not disturb us."

I was a little alarmed at her serious tone. She took my hand and led me into the bedroom that she shared with my uncle, and closed the door firmly.

"Aunt Esther, you're scaring me. What's the matter? Is Mamma worse?"

"She passed away this afternoon. I'm so sorry."

"She was fine last weekend. A little tired, but her cough was a bit better. She enjoyed being read to. You must have made a mistake Aunt Esther. Let Uncle Gregory drive me home, and you'll see. You have made a big mistake…."

"No, Charlotte. I wish I were mistaken, but your Daddy came here this afternoon to tell me the sad news." Her eyes were red, and she looked at me with such compassion that I began to believe her in spite of myself. Still, I denied.

"No, you must be wrong. Daddy would tell me himself if my own mother died. He wouldn't leave it to you!"

"I tried to persuade him to stay, my darling, but he was dreadfully sad. He has to attend to the funeral arrangements…."

"Are funeral arrangements more important than his own daughter?" My voice rose. I was shaking. I turned to the wall and began to beat my head against its uncomplaining hardness.

Aunt Esther said, "stop this minute!" She held onto me, wrapping her arms around my shoulders, dragging me forcibly from the wall. I broke away and resumed my rhythmic banging. My cousins came in to see what the commotion was about and they all grabbed me then led me downstairs where I was set down on the sofa.

"Make tea, quickly," Aunt Esther said. She held me as I sobbed, huge gulps of misery. Tears and mucus ran down my face, and she gently cleaned me with her second-best lace handkerchief.

Aunt Esther stroked my head. "Your grief illustrates how much you loved your mother. You will feel sad for a long time; that's only natural. I sewed a pretty mourning frock for the funeral…" I was brokenhearted that I had not been present when she slipped away and had so cheerfully lived a separate life with my aunt and uncle. I cried and cried, and would not be consoled. Aunt Esther held me in silence. I remembered that Aunt Esther was Mamma's sister and must feel distressed too.

The funeral was a wretched occasion, mourning the passing of a young mother, and the weather was damp and chill. The service at Trinity Church was dignified and very long. I stared at the Reverend as he pontificated in the pulpit, something about Mamma being with Jesus now, and I felt hot rage. I didn't want her to be with Jesus. She belonged with me.

My black bombazine mourning dress, which Aunt Esther had hand sewn for me months before, was a little too tight. The hard, crinkly silk crepe trim dug into my wrists and neck, and it was scratchy. When we stood in the cemetery after a short ride up Blenheim Road following the service, my only thought was to strip off that hated garment and don a more comfortable, calico dress that had been washed too many times and was beginning to fray at the sleeves. But we returned home to Daddy's house, and I had to sit through the wake in my uncomfortable mourning clothes. I was forced to receive with good grace the comments of innumerable adults tripping over themselves to console me with reassurances that Mamma's death was for the best, that she was not suffering any more, that I must be strong for Daddy.

Finally, I could endure no more. I ran upstairs, slipped into the shabby, comfortable frock that seemed to welcome me like an old friend, grabbed an equally shabby shawl that belonged to Mamma and slipped out the door. The shawl smelled a little musty and of vanilla, Mamma's smell. The true grief that was a hard knot inside of me began to soften, and tears blinded me as I ran down Parkhill Road to walk beside the Grand River. I walked for a long time.

When I returned, I was dirty and exhausted. All the guests, including Aunt Esther, Uncle Gregory and my cousins, had gone home. Daddy's eyes were bloodshot, his hair was disheveled, and he began to cry when I tried to explain my absence.

"I was so worried I would lose you too…" his voice seemed thick and slurred. "I need you, honey. Don't ever do that to me again."

He turned and walked slowly into the study, glass of brandy in hand.

I followed and was dismayed to see him sprawled in his armchair in front of the fireplace, glass now empty, a half-full decanter on the round table at his side. I remembered buying that table with Mamma, before she got sick. We had taken the train to Toronto, and had spent a pleasurable afternoon perusing the shops, then had a lovely afternoon tea at Bay and Front Street. I remembered the crumbly biscuit, the clotted cream dissolving in my mouth, and the sweet, tangy jam. We had spotted the table shortly before we had to catch our train back home, and Mamma determined to buy it, despite the impracticality of transporting it home. Daddy had not been pleased at the additional cost to have it shipped to Galt, but as always, he could refuse Mamma nothing.

I swept the decanter onto the floor with one impulsive push. Daddy's jaw dropped. I was shocked at my own daring. I decided to brazen it out.

"You shouldn't drink so much. Mamma wouldn't approve. You know she didn't like you to drink. Why do you think she attended all of those Temperance meetings at Trinity Church?"

We were both shocked at my outburst. His face blanched and he began to weep, his body shaking violently. He was so immersed in his own misery that he did not notice me slink out the door. I stood on the front porch for as long as I could, willing Daddy to come out to comfort me.

He did not appear. It was raining and cold, and I began to shake from cold, so I went back inside and huddled in my bed for long, hard hours. Later, I tiptoed downstairs and found him passed out in his chair, empty glass beside him, snoring sonorously. I debated pulling a coverlet over him but decided to let him be cold and chilled. *It was his own fault, and he should have looked after me.*

***

The adults decided that I would continue to live in Preston until the school year was completed. Children are relentless at healing, and within a few months, I began to experience a ghoulish relish at my status as *the poor motherless dear.* Although my grief was raw and real, I would be a little too dramatic when playing with my cousins.

"You must let me win this game of Go Fish, because my Mamma died…."

My cousins, although good natured and kind, brooked none of this nonsense.

"You can't win on your own? Are you that stupid?"

They slapped me down with good humour, and I'd sulk in a corner with a cookie that Uncle Gregory slipped me. Not for long, though, as I didn't want to miss out on the next game of tag.

The September following Mamma's passing, I returned home to live with Daddy, and he let me adopt a puppy, a mongrel I christened Jack. He was part beagle, and part unknown, and had skinny, spindly legs, and the softest brown eyes. I had to keep him tied up at all times as he loved to roam, but he was enormously kind, patient and good natured. Even Huckleberry couldn't resist the puppy's charms, and he'd stalk with serene arrogance up to Jack and nuzzle against him. I spent hours reading to my new friend, patting him and dressing him up in frilly garments. He submitted patiently to the most absurd ministrations. When I looked into his soft brown eyes I felt a love so complete it healed.

Much to Daddy's dismay, Jack and I sometimes left without a word, to take long walks along the Grand River. One spring when I was eleven, we discovered a fox den. I returned without Jack the following week to sketch pictures of the tiny kits as I sat motionless for hours, using Daddy's binoculars to spy on the brood. The mother would bring the babies tiny rodents, some still wriggling in her mouth. I marveled at her patience and dedication and returned time and time again to the den. I yearned for my own Mamma.

Other days, I sat by the river, sketching in the sun. I enjoyed watching the otters as they frolicked by the shore, occasionally diving for fish. I was cheered by the comic stance of blue herons as they stood on one spindly leg, patiently waiting for a fat, unsuspecting trout to swim by. I grew talented at sketching, then painting orange day lilies, white morning glories, and the pink rose mallows that looked so like miniature hollyhocks. Sometimes I gathered the white and pink daisies, blue chicory and purple clovers, and brought them to the apothecary to try to cheer up Daddy.

Daddy and I limped along. He remained kind and good to me but he was consumed with grief and loneliness. Most nights after school, I'd join him in the apothecary and I became a dab hand at serving customers, and even gained precise knowledge about the various herbs and medicines Daddy dispensed. Apothecaries were almost like doctors. They treated patients, dressed wounds, and even performed minor surgeries for a fee. When Daddy was indisposed, I was able to attend to some very minor injuries.

One hot, sticky summer afternoon when I was 12, a group of children was wading in the Grand River. My best friend Emily began chanting "the red-head is dead; the red-head is dead" when Timmy McLean slipped in the mud and got his brand-new trousers filthy. He tried unsuccessfully to clean off the mud, which only smeared and spread. With a temper to match his flaming head of hair, Timmy kicked her viciously. He howled in pain, as his toe broke when it made contact with her boot. He had forgotten in his fury that he had no shoes on. I calmly ripped my cotton petticoat into thin strips and immobilized the toe. Doctor Gordon complimented me on my handiwork the next time we met in church. I flushed hot with pleasure.

***

I was left too much to my own devices as I matured into young womanhood. Daddy worked long hours, and on evenings when he returned early, would drink more than was good for either of us. Brandy was his favourite tipple. I tried pouring it out, hiding his bottles, and I begged and pleaded with him to stop or at least slow down his drinking. To no avail. He could not, would not stop himself from pining for Mamma. Drink blunted his sorrow, but also made it impossible for him to grow past it. I had no such solace.

I grew adept at covering up for Daddy when he had drunk too much, or was "indisposed," as he would mutter before slinking to his bedroom. I already hated the sweet smell of the sherry in Mamma's laudanum; now I found the smell of all alcohol repellent. Many mornings I opened the apothecary before school because Daddy was too ill from a previous night's drinking session. Sometimes I missed classes due to the necessity to serve customers, and keep the business going.

"Charlotte, you are a very accomplished apprentice," Daddy complimented me when he arrived at the store one spring morning, smelling deliciously of aftershave and looking fresh and barely worse for wear. "If only you were a boy. You could go to the University of Toronto and gradually take over the business."

"But as I'm only a girl, Daddy…I had better return to school."

"Thank you, my dear." His dark brown eyes, pleading and ashamed, conveyed his true gratitude.

"Best not to drink any more Daddy. You know it doesn't agree with you…"

"Yes, I know you are right. I will stop, my dear. I promise. Just give me a little more time…."

But his promises were hollow and I knew that even if he did cut back, within a month or so, another drinking session would find him passed out on the settee, and I'd have to open the store yet again.

In many ways, I was proud of my own efficiency. Here I was, barely 16 years of age, and a mere girl at that, able to take care of a professional man's responsibilities. Daddy was right about one thing. If only I had been a boy.

When I attended Galt Grammar School, I made a close group of friends, a family of sorts. We had some very distinct and strong opinions about how the world should operate. Following in my mother's footsteps, I became involved in our school's chapter of the Temperance movement. We handed out hand-crafted posters in front of the Hunter brewery, as well as in front of the Royal tavern on Main street. Daddy did his best to dissuade me from this mission.

"Charlotte, many upstanding members of the community enjoy the odd tipple. Reverend Braithwaite serves sherry at the dinner table."

"I'm sure you enjoyed that," I said, rolling my eyes.

"My customers frequent the brewery and taverns! What will they think of me?"

This made me ever more determined to vanquish the demon drink in our town. Of course, we had not the smallest success, but our ambitions were earnest. One day a group of us Temperance girls were handing out leaflets outside the tavern, much to the disgust of the patrons entering and leaving. It was cold and beginning to get dark, and we were muttering amongst ourselves that it was time to go home for dinner. Poor Jack had begun to shiver at my feet. Just then, the door opened, and I noticed to my horror that Daddy was emerging. He was walking unsteadily.

"Isn't that your father?" one of the girls asked, her voice dripping with phony concern.

"Yes. Come on, Jack."

I marched up to Daddy, took his arm, and walked home with my head high, burning with shame inside. I never attended the Temperance club again.

I met a young man in my third year of high school. He was most definitely not part of the Temperance Club. He was muscular, dark, and very Italian, although he spoke flawless English. I had never been friends with an Italian before. He had to shave twice a day, and by the time school was dismissed, his face was covered in a dark shadow. I found this impossibly exotic, and felt a small swoon when I was in his presence. Of course, I blushed furiously if he so much as glanced in my direction, which he would tease me about in his gentle way.

Not only was he attractive, but he seemed to be genuinely kind and witty. He had a sharp sense of humour and I was quick enough to volley a riposte in almost any situation. We enjoyed dissecting the quirks and mannerisms of our teachers.

"Mr. Miller's cravat was crooked today," he said as we walked out of math class together.

"As were his figures. He made a mistake in the algebra question he himself wrote on the board..."

"I noticed." He smiled at me, and his eyes crinkled, and my heart skipped a beat.

His name was Tony Rocco, and his family owned a small general shop on Water Street. They imported Mediterranean delicacies from Toronto and enjoyed brisk custom. My favourite treats were the Baccala, a dried, salted cod caught from the Grand Banks of Newfoundland, and a unique Mediterranean cheese made from goat and sheep milk combined. It had a strong, delicious and tangy flavour which I appreciated enormously given the blandness of the cuisine normally on offer in small town Galt.

"Baccala again for dinner?" Daddy asked.

"Yes, I bought it today."

"At the Rocco's shop?" He winked, then hiccupped.

As the female in our household, shopping mostly fell to me. Of course, once I realized that Tony helped out in the shop each Saturday, purchasing our staples took on a new and exciting allure. I spent hours preening before leaving to do the shopping. Fringes were the style, and I carefully heated my curling tongs early Saturday morning, and shaped them into the most elegant swirls to decorate my forehead.

Daddy always smiled at me when I left the apothecary with my basket to "pick up a few necessities." I think he knew exactly why I was so eager to depart. He had a very kind heart and always wanted the best for me.

Tony and I began to take long walks beside the beautiful Grand River, and I told him the names of the wildflowers, and showed him the fox den I still paid close attention to. I wore my nicest dresses for these walks, and although I sometimes had to stitch fine, careful repairs to rips from the brambles, I was determined to look my best.

Tony was two years older than I, and I knew that he was soon to complete his time at school. However, I envisioned us marrying and having glorious brown skinned, blonde children together. Our friendship intensified over a long winter, and we skated together on a nearby frozen pond. At times, we forgot our new adult status, and had great fun whizzing down the hill on a toboggan at Dickson Park, me clutching his waist. He had to pry my arms away when the toboggan finally stopped.

***

Spring came, and still our friendship was a delight to me, and I thought, to him as well.

"Charlotte," he looked at me with those dark eyes that at times appeared almost black, "I need to speak to you."

We were gathering up the remains of a picnic I had prepared. I brought my prettiest blanket and made beef sandwiches as well as packing strawberries, home-made lemon tarts, and a thermos of sweet tea.

My stomach turned a somersault. Was he about to ask me to marry him?

"What is it Tony? Don't keep me in suspense…." I stifled a giggle.

He looked solemn. He reached for my hand and stroked it tenderly. I noted how white my skin was compared to his, and I felt we belonged together forever.

"I have to go to Italy." His brown eyes were so soft and intense that it took a moment for me to understand.

"For a holiday?"

"No. I have to go to help my grandparents and my aunt and uncle with the farm back home. I'm going back to live, at least for a few years."

"But I thought your family was settled in Galt. You belong here!"

"No, not really. I'm the eldest son, and I have to go where I'm needed. You must have known this could not have gone on much longer. I'm Catholic. We don't marry outside of our own religion…I'm sorry."

I slapped his cheek as hard as I could.

He looked stunned, then angry. He turned on his heel and began to march down the path, back to Parkhill Road.

"No, wait, I'm sorry!" I started to run after him but my dratted long skirts caught on the brambles.

He turned around and came back. Carefully and slowly, he disentangled my skirts. He smiled briefly, took my hand and without haste, we walked together into the privacy of the bush.

"I don't want to have a baby," I mumbled. I couldn't meet his eyes.

"I won't let that happen."

He was gentle, and it was tender. Surely, he wouldn't leave now.

We did not speak again of his departure. Instead, he and I spent long, languid hours together until school ended in June. My dog Jack was delighted with our long walks, as we enjoyed ice cream cones while strolling hand in hand beside the river. I made us frequent, delicious picnics – chicken, fruit, cheese, apple pie. Furtively, I studied his beautiful face, trying to embed it in my heart, keep it permanent and inviolate. He noticed, looked away, then studied the slowly moving river. *He must feel a terrible guilt. How can he turn his back on a love such as ours? He'll change his mind.*

***

But leave he did. I begged him, but he did not, could not change his mind. Daddy took me to Toronto so I could wave him off when he boarded his train at Union Station, which would take him to Montreal, where he would catch a ship to Italy. I never ceased to be amazed at Union Station, built in 1873 by the Grand Trunk Railway, on Front Street, between York and Simcoe. It was modelled on the Illinois Central Station in Chicago, and had three domed towers, one containing a clock. "It's one of the most modern and striking stations in all of North America," Daddy told me as proudly as if he had had a role in its construction himself. It was imposing: the main entrance was a seven-storey Romanesque office building on Front Street, and an arcade over Station Street led to an eighty-foot square waiting room.

At the time of Tony's departure, Union Station was operating at capacity. The din was overwhelming, as people bustled about, people shouting for porters, newsboys hollering about the latest headlines, the clicking and clatter of trollies and wagons. Steam swirled across the platform, and I looked ruefully at my dress. *I should have worn the navy frock.* I felt angry with myself for wearing my favourite buttercup yellow, and I tried unsuccessfully to clean off the smut that had descended on my shoulder. *The first of many more*, I resigned myself, and thought of the long washing and careful stain removal that lay ahead. Anything to keep my mind off the impending farewell.

Tony's parents did not seem impressed that I was present to wave off their son. They barely smiled when I made awkward introductions. His mother was a small, sturdy looking lady with dark hair and fine features, while his father had snowy white hair and a matching beard. They nodded politely to Daddy and me, but then moved purposefully away. I hoped for a private farewell with my beloved, but to no avail.

He looked embarrassed to see me at all, and did not come over to say good-bye. When I heard the whistle, and the train rushed into the station, I walked to his side and asked, "Are you not going to say good-bye to me?"

He muttered a brief farewell, then shook my hand. He turned to his parents, and his mother took him in her arms. They turned their backs to me, and he boarded the train without another word. He did not look back.

***

I felt like Tony had punched me, hard, in the gut. I had hoped against hope that he would change his mind at the last minute, an ending worthy of the romantic novels I enjoyed. Daddy took me for tea and fine sandwiches, and he pretended not to notice my blood-shot eyes as he chatted about old times with Mamma, about the apothecary, and about the difference between life in Galt and Toronto. I paid him little heed. I still had a healthy appetite, and despite my true sorrow, I ate every last crumb of my delicious tea-biscuit and drained my mug of tea sweetened just as I liked it, with honey.

After this repast, Daddy took me to a chemist warehouse on Queen Street. We took an omnibus, and we sat on top. The breeze felt cool and cleansing, trifling with my hair as we followed the plodding horses. The ride was over too quickly. When we entered the warehouse, I followed Daddy's inquiries and purchases closely.

"I need an oversized, balanced, portable brass handled set of calibration weights," Daddy told the clerk. "I'm not certain mine are completely accurate any longer. I'll also need some cocaine tooth drops, as there seems to be a large number of colicky babies in Galt. I'll need toothpaste, castor oil, and I think I'll buy two of Dr. Scott's Electric Flesh Brushes…."

I continued to listen, although I felt like I was present and detached all at once. I had a good head for business, and no amount of heartbreak would change that.

We took the omnibus back to Union Station, and once again we walked through its imposing halls. Putting one foot in front of the other seemed an accomplishment by this point of the day.

Daddy and I said little on the return train ride home. I was weary and heartsick and so was he: that was his lot in life since Mamma had passed away. I am sure he was looking forward to having a good stiff drink. I shuddered. The mere thought made me feel queasy. I took some deep breaths and looked at the countryside whizzing by. This made me feel worse, so I put my head on Daddy's shoulder and closed my eyes. If only Daddy could solve my problems, the way I believed he could, before I learned of Mamma's consumption. If only.

***

I was young, and summer was particularly lovely that year. I worked at the apothecary, and my knowledge of herbs, potions and medicines grew ever more broad and deep. Daddy and I were working side by side one hot July day when Ethel Harrington came rushing in, carrying her infant daughter in her arms. "Help me!"

Daddy nodded to me. I took the baby who was about six months old, in my arms.

"What's her name?"

"Margaret. Help her for goodness sake."

"What are her symptoms?"

"She won't wake up! It's past time for her feed. She's barely breathing. She just won't wake up!"

Daddy came and stood by my side. He motioned again for me to take the lead.

"Have you given her any medicine?

"Yes, I bought *Bayer Heroin* in Brantford. I was helping my sister with her confinement, and Margaret was teething, and she would not stop crying."

My heart sank. Young mothers did not realize the potency of the medications that were so readily available, and many chemists did not bother to explain how dangerous the effects could be. Daddy and I were meticulous in this regard, but sadly, this was not always the case.

"How old are you, Mrs. Harrington?" I kept my tone gentle.

"I'm 19. I got married to my Bob proper, you know."

"Yes, I know. I think Margaret has simply been given too much of a potent and dangerous medicine. If I were you, I would take her to Doctor Gordon."

"Can't afford to pay no doctor."

I was not surprised. I looked down at the baby, who seemed to be breathing more deeply now. I was almost certain that a day or two of rest would remedy the situation.

"Well, take her home, and keep her comfortable. It is very hot today, so I would just cover her with a sheet. Talk to her gently, and check on her every hour, even through the night. And don't give her any more medicine without consulting with Mr. Evans or me. That's an order. Even if you don't buy the medicine from us, you need to speak to us about the proper amount to use. Are you still nursing her?"

She hugged her arms to herself and looked embarrassed. "Yes, I am."

"That's the best thing in the world for Margaret. Every hour when you wake her, try to get her to nurse. I think she will come around. But if she is not better by this time tomorrow, you simply must see Doctor Gordon. He is flexible about payment when it is an urgent case."

Mrs. Harrington retrieved her baby, thanked me profusely, and left. Daddy didn't say anything, but the look of pride in his eyes was reward enough. That evening, he suggested that I petition the University of Toronto for a spot to train as a chemist, and I began to seriously consider this. Women were admitted to the University for the first time in 1884, and I had some hope of being accepted.

"How would you manage without me?" I asked.

"I would have to, my dear. You deserve your chance at life. You are young, and clever. I don't have a son, so I would like nothing better than for you to take over the business."

I was ever so pleased and flattered. I thought of Tony working on a farm in Italy and realized the discrepancies in our backgrounds. I began to let go of my misery, and to enjoy my youth and rude good health.

***

The summer passed gently and uneventfully, and I missed Tony less and less. I joined a baseball team, and we played twice a week at Dickson Park. I chafed at the long white skirt I had to wear and looked at the grass-stained trousers of the men with envy. After each game, win or lose, the team walked to Main Street and enjoyed a soda and ice cream, then walked along the river, chattering and laughing loudly at silly jokes.

The only difficulty I had that golden summer was an increasing tendency to nausea. I would wake up in the middle of the night and have to run to the nearby basin. Daytimes were better, but every evening, I was ambushed by sickness. *At least it wasn't a cough*, I reasoned, *so I couldn't be consumptive like Mamma.*

I had a niggling suspicion then of the true nature of my malady. *No, Tony promised he wouldn't let that happen.* And I refused to consider it further. I returned to school and put my heart and soul into my studies.

One fine November morning after a particularly sleepless night, I finally felt I had to confide my indisposition to Daddy. Night after night he had slept through my bouts of illness having drunk himself to sleep.

"Daddy, I think I must book an appointment to see Doctor Gordon." I felt a hot blush on my cheek.

"Whatever for dear girl? You look glowing these days."

"I have been sick almost every night. I'm surprised you haven't noticed." I tried to keep reproach from my voice, but I don't think I succeeded.

He looked stricken. Then worried. He chewed his lip.

"Do you have any other symptoms my dear?"

"I can't talk about it Daddy." My voice was shaky.

"I'm going to take you to see Doctor Gordon's wife. Now. Get your cloak!"

His urgency cowed me, and I obeyed without a word. We strode in silence to the doctor's surgery on Grand Avenue. By the time we reached our destination I was quite out of breath and had the beginning of a stitch in my side.

The house was two storeys, made entirely from local limestone and granite. It was in the most picturesque spot imaginable, right beside the Grand River, and many summer evenings Mrs. Gordon and I had knitted on the back porch, our conversation accompanied by the gentle sounds of the flowing water. She tried to take an interest in me after the death of Mamma, and I often looked after her young daughter when she was busy on Saturdays, helping her husband with his duties. When we reached the door, Daddy stepped back.

"Go on, ring the doorbell."

"Are you not going to come with me?"

"Women's business." I could barely hear his mumble.

"Won't you at least stay and walk me home?" I wanted him to wait for me. I needed him.

"I have to get to the store. You can meet me there, or we can talk this evening at home."

He kissed my cheek. His eyes did not meet mine, and his eyelid flickered, a sure sign that he was upset. But still, he turned his back and walked down the front stairs. I took a deep breath, then rang the doorbell. Mrs. Gordon welcomed me warmly, and ushered me into a small room upstairs, overlooking the Grand River. I could hear it faintly in the background as it ran by, and I heard the squawking of the birds as they hunted for fish just below the surface. No blue herons, but I did see an osprey before I focused my attention on the task at hand.

"How can I help you dear girl?" Mrs. Gordon prompted me gently after she closed the door on the retreating maid who had just served tea.

"Um, well, I have had some peculiar symptoms…" I told her my concerns and my suspicions.

She looked grave, and her blue eyes gazed at me with a deep sympathy as I finished.

"I think you may very well be pregnant."

"What?" I had suspected, deep down, but had denied the truth, even to myself. I was an unmarried girl. I would be ruined.

"Have you been close to a boy?" Her tone was gentle but her eyes steely.

I looked at my feet, then looked out the window, then covered my face and wept.

We spoke for a long time. Finally, Mrs. Gordon stood up, signaling that it was time for me to take my leave.

"Would you like me to tell your father?" she asked.

"No, thank you, I need to tell him myself."

"Brave girl. Be safe, and take care of yourself. Drink lots of water and tea to help with the nausea. Plain bread and crackers may help."

Her kindness made it impossible for me to keep my composure. She held me a long time in her arms. How I wished she were my mother. How I wished for my own dear Mamma. I knew without a doubt that had she been alive, I would not have found myself in this shameful predicament.

***

I plodded home, and, as always, cuddled up with Jack in my cozy bed, under the quilt Mamma had painstakingly made me. She had sewed the quilt ever so carefully after her diagnosis. It was her gift of love to me, her final gift. It was fashioned in the latest, very fashionable "crazy quilt" style, a combination of wool, wool challis and velvet pieces with whimsical wool embroidery. She incorporated snippets from frocks that she no longer wore, and even a cutting from her wedding dress. She used a piece of Daddy's old silk shirt that he had torn after church one day, squares from day dresses and Sunday dresses that I had outgrown. Even a fragment of my baby blanket found its way into this quilt. Mamma had fashioned all these various materials into multiple dogs, birds, a lady bug, and a river, which had *Think of Me* carefully stitched in gold along its meandering path. The warm hues and careful stitches warmed me, comforted me, and broke my heart.

Finally, I couldn't bear to be in bed any longer, so Jack and I went walking beside the river. I did not take note of any wildlife that day. But as always, sweet, faithful Jack stayed right by my side. We walked for miles, until I tired myself out. When dusk began to fall, I turned reluctantly towards home. I knew Daddy would be back by now, and indeed he was, sitting by the fire, drink in hand. I couldn't meet his eyes as I mumbled a greeting.

The wonder is that Daddy had not noticed my wretched sickness each day, but I supposed the effects of heavy drinking rendered him impervious to my suffering. Ironically, I was doing better in my school classes than ever before, as the goal of attending university and following in my father's footsteps had made me ambitious and more focused.

I prepared a delicious dinner that evening. Boiled beefsteak pudding was Daddy's favourite, so boiled beefsteak pudding it was. I took extra care with the crust, and it was as light and fluffy as air. I wrapped a napkin around it and carried my creation with the greatest care to the dining room table on a bone china plate with a delicate rose edging. I thought of how many times I had witnessed Mamma do just this and sighed.

"This meal looks delicious. Did Mrs. Gordon put your mind at rest?" He spoke lightly, but his bloodshot eyes signaled concern.

"Let's eat in peace, shall we Daddy? Do you want some wine?" Over the course of the meal, he drank three glasses.

Finally, when he had finished the pudding, polished off the jam tart that I had baked earlier in the week, and was sipping the last of his wine, I cleared my throat.

"Daddy, there is something I need to tell you."

"Ok Poppet. I'm all ears." His voice was only slightly slurred. He leaned forward and looked at me with those blue-green eyes I had always loved. My eyes were grey, like Mamma's.

I pulled myself up short. No more ruminating about Mamma - I had no choice but to tell him.

"Mrs. Gordon is pretty sure that I'm expecting a baby." There, it was done. It was spoken.

"What?"

"I'm so sorry Daddy…."

"You little slattern!"

He got to his feet. His chair scraped the floor. His eyes were teary now. Spittle flecked at the side of his mouth. He walked unsteadily, like an old man, to my side of the table. Was he going to hug me? Before I knew what was happening, he slapped me hard on the back of my head. Then again.

It took me a moment to breathe again. "Daddy. How could you?" I ran from the room.

Jack was at my side. I attached his lead and for the second time that day, we walked together. The streets were dark, barely lit by the weak gaslights. It was icy, and I hoped against hope for a fall that would cause this unwanted child to die a natural death. Of course, I was completely steady on my feet, and no black ice caused that convenience.

Thankfully it was late enough that most God-fearing folks were eating dinner with their families, their curtains tightly shut. I pulled my cloak over my head, and walked for hours. When I finally returned home, exhausted, I let myself in as quietly as possible. I could hear heavy snores from Daddy's bedroom. I was certain that he had drowned his sorrows. I removed my outer-garments, performed my evening ablutions, and put myself miserably to bed, with faithful Jack at my foot. Daddy's snores were regular and sonorous; I did not sleep.

The next morning Daddy and I pretended that the previous evening had not occurred. Thankfully, if one could ever be thankful for a beating, Daddy had hit me on my head, and although I was bruised, it did not show under my hair. Brushing and pinning my hair in its customary style was a little painful, but I went to school as usual, and he left for the apothecary.

We maintained a polite, strained civility for the next couple of weeks. I knew Daddy was debating the best course of action for me. I could see him gaze at me when he thought I wasn't looking, puzzlement and pain etched in his face. His face was lined and weary. He was not shaving as often as usual, and his face looked a little grizzled, the stubble grey. This was surprising, as he was usually meticulous. Finally, when we entered into the month of December, I realized that I couldn't could hide the grim reality much longer. I let out the seams on my dresses, and covered myself with my shawls but one day when I was working at the store, my least favourite busy-body came in. Her name was Mrs. Beattie.

"My, you've put on weight, my dear. I hope you aren't ill." Her eyes glittered with malice.

"I'm a very good cook, Mrs. Beattie." I looked at her coldly and our eyes locked.

She suspects, and in a matter of weeks, she'll know for certain. All of Galt will know my disgrace, and the shame will break Daddy. We need to talk about this, no more pretending.

That evening, I forced it into the open.

"Daddy, I'll heat some water for you to have a nice bath tonight."

"Yes, I suppose it's time for me to have a good wash." We looked at each other and smiled, and for the first time since I told him of my pregnancy, I felt close to my father again.

"No need for you to lug the water, my dear, especially in your condition."

There. It had been said. I felt a twisted lump inside of me dissolve. We smiled at each other again. The tenderness between us was back. His hand shook slightly as he raised his cup of coffee.

"I have pondered what to do about your situation." He looked me squarely in the eye.

"I was obviously very angry with you for allowing yourself to sink to such a state. I'm still upset and disappointed. I take it Tony Rocco is the father?"

"Daddy - how could you ask such a thing? To what depths do you think I have sunk? I thought Tony and I were to be married. I loved him!"

"Now, Charlotte, let's not get ourselves riled up again. We need to be coolheaded about this. I have come up with a plan that I think is in your best interests."

"Do I have to leave you?"

"Yes, I'm afraid you do. But you can come home after a time, and we can write every week. Thankfully the mail service in Ontario has improved since when your grandparents emigrated here…."

He swallowed, sighed, then plunged ahead.

"You will have to go north, to Owen Sound." He seemed unaware of the tears slipping down his cheeks, which were scored with deep lines.

"I have written to my cousin, Bartholomew, and his wife Janie. They at least are delighted with the situation. They have been unable to have a child of their own. It's a good solution as they live on the outskirts of town on a farm and will keep you there hidden until you have the baby. After that, they will adopt and raise the child as their own, and you can return home, and begin your life again."

Following this brave speech, he put his head down on the kitchen table. His shoulders heaved. I sat beside him and cradled him to me as best I could, an unlikely source of comfort.

"Oh Daddy, I am so sorry…."

"We won't speak of it further, my dear. I blame myself more than I blame you. I should have let you live permanently with Esther and your cousins in Preston. Life with a sad, lonely man such as me has not been healthy for you. I can see that now.

"We won't tell anyone the real reason why you are leaving. I'll say that you've gone to Owen Sound to help your cousin with *her* upcoming confinement."

His kindness and understanding were worse than any amount of berating could have been. We embraced. When I looked up, I saw tears dripping from his nose. I handed him my handkerchief, and he mopped his face. We sat together for a long time in silence that evening, holding hands, watching the fire burn down beneath the mantle with Mamma's picture taking pride of place.

***

I wasn't quite ready to accept Daddy's plan. I wrote to Tony in Italy, explaining the situation to him. *We have to get married now, with a baby on the way. We can say the baby was born prematurely…. I know you said you were needed in Italy, but I need you here! The baby will need a Daddy…* The letter, neatly sealed in its brown envelope, was returned unopened. I was physically sick. How I wished I could purge myself of the baby too.

One fine Saturday, I arose and dressed myself slowly, with much thought. Daddy always insisted that I present myself with great care, and was very generous with me.

"You need to reflect my position as a successful businessman," he said more than once as he pressed coins into my willing hand. "In a small-town society like Galt, appearances matter."

Yes, and you don't want anybody suspecting how much you drink, I thought as I put the coins into my purse.

I yearned for Mamma. I had no one to teach me the appropriate attire to wear in different situations. I coped by being closely observant of the other girls my age and station. I liked to think I had succeeded. Aunt Esther was helpful too, taking me shopping to near-by Berlin and sometimes as far as Toronto to peruse the latest fashions.

I donned my most sober navy-blue silk with mother-of-pearl buttons down the front. I had ordered it from the new Eaton's Catalogue with Daddy's blessing the previous Christmas. The Eaton's Catalogue carried the most up-to-date fashions, copied from England. I spent hours poring over its pages each year. I pulled the strings of my corset extra tight, so that I could barely breathe. No hint of my condition was noticeable. I hoped.

I put on my best boots, carefully polished the night before. They had a charming heel which lent me extra height. I twisted my hair into the newest style, demure but most becoming as my mirror assured me. My hair was my chief glory, in my mind, blonde and curly. Of course, I kept it pinned up as decency and fashion dictated, but corkscrew ringlets constantly escaped, to my especial advantage, as I reassured myself that morning when I peered into the mirror.

I walked at a steady pace to the Rocco Italian Grocery store. I was apprehensive, but still dreamed of the look of surprise and delight on Mrs. Rocco's face when she learned she would be a grandmother for the first time. I imagined how gorgeous the baby would be with a combination of Tony's dark olive complexion and my own fair and pretty features. I began to plot our wedding. Tony was Roman Catholic of course, but we Anglicans were not so different. I imagined our priest, the Reverend Cahill, conducting a lavish service, and I dreamed of a fine reception in the church hall. If we acted quickly, no one need ever guess my condition. I imagined that I would help Mrs. Rocco in the store. I was an intelligent young lady, and could quickly learn to speak Italian.

I continued to dream about how beautiful my baby would be. I pictured a girl, with my big blue eyes, and his black hair, swathed in white, being baptized. In my mind's eye, the church was built on noble lines, surrounded by flowering bushes, embraced by roses in full bloom, awash with colour. We would push Baby ever so carefully in her pram, while holding hands. Tony would put his arm around me, look into my eyes…

I reached the store in what seemed like no time at all. I stepped inside and politely asked the nearest sales clerk for a private interview with Mrs. Rocco. She looked at me curiously, and called into the back. There was no answer, and the clerk disappeared for a minute or so. When she returned, she told me brusquely that Mrs. Rocco was too busy to speak to a customer.

"She will want to hear what I have to say."

The clerk looked surprised at my insistence, but once again walked into the back. She returned quickly this time. "No, Mrs. Rocco is too busy to speak to anyone now. You should leave."

I took matters into my own hands and marched into the gloomy back room.

The diminutive Mrs. Rocco was dressed in practical black silk with her hair scraped into a severe bun. She was seated at an old desk, doing figures. The room smelled of lemon furniture polish. She ignored my intrusion for a long minute, then looked up at me, and sniffed. She tapped her pencil on the desk.

"This area is for my clerks only, young lady. The store is very busy now, Saturday morning, as you can see. Have your parents taught you no manners?"

Her voice was deep and hard. Most of her Italian accent had been eliminated and she spoke carefully and deliberately.

"Too busy to speak to the mother of your grandchild?"

She put down her pencil and sat still for a long moment. Her face looked ghostly under the dark, slicked back hair. I reached down to touch her arm, but she slapped my hand away with scorn. Customers walked by the open door pushing their carts, oblivious to the sparking tension between us.

She stood up and grabbed my hand, practically shoving me into a further room, invisible from the store. Her grip was steel. I followed mutely, my mouth dry.

"What did you say to me?" Her black eyes blazed. I noted that she had a few grey tendrils of hair mixed with jet black escaping from her carefully pinned-back locks.

"I am going to have Tony's baby."

The slap resounded sharply. I cried out and she grabbed me by the shoulders and put her hand tightly over my mouth. I gasped for air. I was so upset and shocked that I couldn't breathe through my nose, and my mouth was covered. She held me in an iron grip for a long moment, until I gave up fighting. I was on the verge of passing out when she finally released me. I took a deep breath.

I looked at her in disbelief. How could someone so tiny be so powerful? I realized in that moment that she was truly the matriarch of the Rocco family, and that Tony would always be under her thumb.

"There is no proof that Tony is the father of your baby, you little slut." She was still breathing heavily, but her words sounded measured and determined.

I bowed my head but kept the tears at bay. "Tony is the only man I have ever been close to."

"So you say. How much money do you want?"

"If you are so certain Tony is not the father, why would you offer to pay me?"

She put her finger to her lips.

"Shhh you stupid girl. You do not want your shame to be known throughout Galt, surely?"

I breathed deeply, trying to calm myself. I clenched my hands into fists; my fingernails dug into the palms of my hands.

"You will be the baby's grandmother, like it or not."

"I refuse to accept that. You are a little whore. The father could be any boy." Her eyes were black and implacable.

Finally, I began to cry. My face was hot, and my nose leaked. She watched me with a little smile on her lips. As I grew noisier, however, she became impatient. She slapped me once more; quickly and smartly on my left cheek.

I stopped crying, stunned. I stared at her and the smile re-appeared.

She's enjoying this, I realized in amazement. *She is denying her own grandchild and enjoying my misery.* No wonder Tony was content to cross the ocean to escape this mother of his.

I dried my eyes as best I could, grabbed hold of my reticule, and stood up. My hair had become unpinned in our struggle, and I tidied it as best I could. I took my handkerchief from my reticule, one that had belonged to Mamma, and wiped my face. I felt sick and dizzy, but strove not to show any further weakness before this ghastly woman. She smiled, a mocking rictus.

"Good day to you, Mrs. Rocco. I am sorry to have troubled you with my difficulties."

"Don't come back here. You are not welcome; neither is the bastard you are carrying."

I moved towards the door I had entered only a few minutes before. She grabbed my arm.

"Don't even think of leaving though the front door, looking as like you do! There is a back exit, over there."

I mustered every ounce of dignity I possessed, and walked slowly out of the private rooms, through the boxes lining the back hall that smelled of fish, and out the door. I was burning with rage and frustration, as the realization that Tony would never own up to the responsibility of our baby fully sunk in. After my encounter with his mother, he would never be allowed to return to Galt.

The day became warmer, and I was thirsty, hot, and bedraggled when I reached home.

Daddy was at the apothecary and the house seemed empty. Jack welcomed me with happy licks. *What an uncomplicated and beautiful life dogs lead*, I mused as I lay in bed, Jack cuddled at my feet. *If only my own life were that simple.* I thought back to the days when Mamma was alive; happy, safe days of being cocooned in her love, and an immense fatigue washed over me. Why did she have to die? Why couldn't it have been me?

But my breath came steadily, in and out, and soon I felt hunger pangs that were insistent and greedy. I got up slowly, washed my face in cold water, and went downstairs. I reheated some beef and cauliflower soup I had made and made myself a thick roast beef sandwich. I topped it with a slice of pickle, and some mustard, and forgot my woes, for a little while.

However, nausea followed this simple meal, and I was plunged back into misery. I realized that Daddy's plan was best. Remaining here to give birth would mean I would be entirely ostracized from Galt society. Daddy too. Small towns did not forgive big social crimes. I flinched at the shame I would bring to Daddy, and to Mamma's memory…it did not bear thinking about. I made up my mind that I would go to Owen Sound and give these unknown relatives, Bart and Jane, the most precious gift of all. I touched my belly and felt an enormous sadness. I rose and looked in the mirror on the wash stand; my face was slightly fuller, but my complexion remained clear, my eyes a little too bright, but other than that, my secret remained mine. But not for long.

***

Daddy explained to Galt Grammar School that his cousin in Owen Sound required help with her forthcoming confinement, and aid in looking after the bairn. The easy way he lied both impressed and unsettled me. I had learned to dress in loose, bulky frocks that had been Mamma's (with subtle alterations to make them more modern, suitable for a young girl), so no suspicions were raised. I knew that Mrs. Rocco would never breathe a word of our conversation. I suspected that she knew the baby was Tony's, hence her extreme cruelty in her rejection of me. She would never admit it, and as a young, fallen girl, I had no rights. My predicament was entirely my fault, entirely my responsibility.

Daddy accompanied me to Toronto on a warm, sunny afternoon in June. We stayed overnight in the Black Bull Hotel, on Queen Street West. We smuggled Jack in in a big basket I had thought to bring for just that purpose.

"Jack, don't you dare bark or whine!" Surprisingly, he obeyed, and allowed me to carry him sitting regally in the basket, although he made it very plain by the disdainful tilt of his long nose that he did not appreciate this arrangement. He even tolerated being hidden under a small blanket which I draped over top.

The CPR timetable made for an early start the next day. We left Toronto at 7:20 a.m., reaching Orangeville at 9:50, Shelburne at 10:45 and Owen Sound at 1:00 p.m.

In Union Station, as we waited to embark, I was amused by the signs along the platform:

SPITTING
in Cars or Waiting Rooms or on Platforms
or other premises of the Railway
IS PROHIBITED

THE COMPANY'S OFFICIALS ARE REQUIRED TO ENFORCE STRICT OBSERVANCE OF THIS RULE.
Every person violating this regulation is liable to a FINE not exceeding FORTY DOLLARS
Approved by the Board of Railway Commissioners for Canada Sanctioned by the Governor-General-in-Council.

I had never seen my dear, ineffectual, kindly Daddy spit.

I had not hoped for the luxury of the Pullman car that I had read about in *The Toronto Globe,* but I was pleasantly surprised by how clean and sleek our more mundane carriage was. At the end of the train was a car, called an "observation car." This had an open-air platform at the rear, with a few seats. It was a bit chilly, but I insisted that Daddy and I sit outside and observe the scenery as it rushed past at a dizzying 30 miles-per-hour. We whizzed past ancient forests and some that had been harvested. In Orangeville and Shelbourne, some passengers disembarked and purchased a meal or hot tea from accommodating vendors. Daddy bought me a soda and a piece of vanilla cake in Shelbourne. It was light and fluffy and had a coconut icing. I ate the entire piece, and the familiar nausea surprisingly did not appear.

As we progressed further north, we tucked into the simple lunch of cheese and pickle sandwiches I had brought with us. We washed it down with a thermos of tea, and I pretended not to notice Daddy adding something from a flask that emerged from a pocket of his jacket. I was too happy and feeling too free to remonstrate with him today. The train zoomed north. I felt a real sense of release from gloomy, judgmental, Calvinistic, guilt ridden Galt. No more stout, smug matrons pursing their lips when I coughed in church. No more Temperance meetings. No more homework, at least not for a time.

I knew that Owen Sound was a town with few pretensions to gentility. It was populated by loggers, tradesmen, and fishermen, with a small sprinkling of Negroes who had fled slavery, heading north on the Underground Railroad. Daddy explained to me that Owen Sound had been the northern terminus of the Underground Railroad, and former slaves were grudgingly accepted. Mostly, they were allowed to live in peace.

For a time, I was able to put aside my anxieties and shame and enjoy the adventure. I had only met Cousin Bart once, and his wife, never. I had a hazy memory of Bart as being very big and having a large, very round head. He had been gentle with me at Mamma's funeral. I covered my burgeoning figure with a handsome, flowered shawl, that Mrs. Gordon, the doctor's wife, gave me before I departed. I don't think my fellow passengers suspected my condition. Today, I did not care. Gloomy old Galt was behind, and the excitement of my future ahead.

As I disembarked from the train, I caught my first glimpse of the deep blue sparkling water of Owen Sound. I felt like I was home. The Sound, which was in fact a very long bay that emptied into the much larger Georgian Bay, stretched out as far as the eye could see, embraced by rock and trees. Boats bobbed in the wind, and I could see merchant ships and ferries docked in the bustling harbour, awaiting their next cargo to be shipped to the romantic ports of my mind. Daddy told me that the destinations were indeed romantic: nearby Collingwood, Chicago, Montreal, the St. Lawrence River to the Atlantic Ocean, then Liverpool. I travelled to each in quick flights of fancy.

Cousin Bart came to pick us up at the station. He was bigger than I remembered and waved when he saw Daddy and me. He sported a large fuzzy beard that was dark, gleaming brown, and his head was nearly bald, shiny, with a ridiculous looking tonsure-like fringe. His trousers looked worn, patched at the knees, but scrupulously clean. He wore a checked shirt that strained to button across his protruding belly.

"Charlotte, this is your cousin Bart. Bart, this is Charlotte. She has grown a bit since you last saw her," said Daddy, after he shook Bart's hand. He reached for his flask.

Bart smiled, his mouth split wide. He offered his hand. It was huge, the fingers rough and thick. He had a sort of pungent, musty smell to him that I rather liked. Daddy always smelled of soap, and usually of alcohol. Bart did not smell of drink, but he certainly liked his food, judging by his girth. His eyes were brown, and his face had a weather-beaten look to it.

"I'm glad you can come for a long visit, Charlotte. We've been looking forward to meeting you."

His eyes travelled down to my belly, then he blushed and quickly looked me in the eye. He smiled again, pumped my hand then released it. *What a nice man.* I realized I was grinning foolishly.

Saying goodbye to Daddy at the train station was hard and sad. He could not leave the shop for long, and so was returning home on the next train. He held me for a long time, until I squirmed, worrying about watchful, prying eyes. He let go of me but kept my hand firmly in his. With his other hand, he reached into his satchel, and removed a piece of paper covered in his distinctive, spidery hand.

"Your Mamma left a diary.... I copied out a page that I would like you to have. Never doubt her love for you, my dear, nor my own..."

A tear ran down his face, and I watched in fascination as it dripped from the end of his nose. His spectacles were foggy. He hugged me once more as the whistle blew, then leaped back aboard the train. I folded the paper carefully and placed it in my reticule. I did not want to read my beloved Mamma's thoughts in such a public place.

I was a little disappointed that the chariot to my new home was a horse-drawn cart, pulled by two mammoth workhorses. The cart was rough and I had to sit on a bale of straw, which was prickly and uncomfortable, but it smelled surprisingly sweet. After twenty minutes of a jostling ride, we pulled into a long lane which ended at a tiny log house. It was embraced by sweet peas and wild roses growing promiscuously all around.

A dog ran up to the cart and my uncle scratched his ears and ordered him to sit. The dog was medium sized, black and white, and was called Toby. Jack, who had behaved impeccably up to this point, strained to meet Toby, and I released him. The dogs sniffed each other, growled a few times, then their tails began to wag, and they jumped playfully on each other. I let out a sigh of relief.

I dismounted heavily from the cart and looked in bemusement at the cabin that was to accommodate me and my baby for the foreseeable future. It was a sturdy and square. It was entirely constructed of logs. It was tiny.

"Our house has three rooms," Bart had said with great pride on the bumpy ride. "There is even a bedroom for guests. That's where you'll sleep. When the baby gets bigger, that'll be his room. I built the house myself, with the help of other farmers near-by when Jane and I moved here ten years ago. There's a woodstove which keeps us warm all through the winter. Plenty of wood in these parts."

Cousin Bart and Jane were unable to have children of their own, Daddy had reminded me on the train. The plan was for me to give birth, nurse the child until he could be weaned, then I would return to Galt, Daddy, my friends and complete my schooling. Bart and Jane would raise my baby and we would sever contact once I returned to Galt. It was a solid, well- considered plan, to which I had resigned myself, after the disastrous encounter with Mrs. Rocco. I had few thoughts of any attachment to my child, who would arrive within the next two months.

Jane ran out of the house. She was wearing a worn calico apron and she rubbed her hands on it with such vigour that I wondered if her skin would peel off. She embraced me, and spoke so quickly that she was close to stuttering,

"Nice to meet you Charlotte. I hope you will feel welcome here." She hugged me again, and I noted how chapped and red her hands were. Mine were soft and white. Her eyes slid down to my belly which was draped in shawls. I pulled my wraps closer around me, uncomfortable about the intrusion of her sharp glance. It was clear that the forthcoming child motivated her welcome. I swallowed down my uneasy feeling. She was squat, and quite plain. Her face was weather beaten, and her hair was a fine, mousey brown. She looked well-fed from the bounties of the farm. In the coming days, I came to appreciate that she worked tirelessly, gardening, cleaning, cooking, plucking fowl, salting meat, and in the evenings, sewing and darning by candlelight.

She ushered me into the house, which was dark and even tinier than it appeared from the outside. It was spotlessly clean however, and Jane had prepared a huge lunch of salted pork, potatoes, carrots, and an apple pie.

"These apples are from our own tree," she told me. "Feel free to eat as much as you'd like." I obeyed with enthusiasm. The food was delicious. We did the washing up together, then I asked,

"May I take some time to walk around the farm?"

"Of course. Be careful not to wander too far or twist an ankle."

I tried hard to keep any trace of contempt from my voice as I bade her goodbye and whistled to Jack and Toby.

"No, Toby stays here," said Jane.

"But wouldn't he like a walk?" I asked.

"He's not a pet. He's a farm dog, and he stays here with me." There was no sense in arguing, so I gave Toby an apologetic shrug, and Jack and I set off.

We tramped for a while, Jack happy to be free of the travelling basket. Then I sat beneath a graceful apple tree far enough away from the house to escape Jane's watchful glance. I took out the letter Daddy copied for me. I had hidden it in a pocket of my dress. Sometimes I could barely remember what Mamma looked like and other times, it was as though she were beside me, hidden a little, as if behind a curtain. Today, I smelled her tangy scent.

1897

Dr. Gordon came today about my persistent cough. He looked grave after he examined me. His dark eyes were shadowed, and the skin underneath looked papery.

He cleared his throat, then said,

"Edith, I'm very concerned that your cough has not gone away. Have you taken the drops I prescribed you?"

"Of course. My husband is the apothecary. He would not let me skimp on my medicines!"

"No, I realize that. However, you do not seem to be improving. Are you coughing up much phlegm?"

"Yes, a fair amount. I try to hide it from Joseph and Charlotte. Especially Joseph. He frets. His latest worry is that I have lost a good deal of weight. I myself am delighted not to be so plump..."

My voice trailed off, as I realized I was babbling, trying to forestall the Doctor's diagnosis. In my heart of hearts, I knew what it was.

"Do you have a history of consumption in your family?" His voice was gentle.

I looked out the window for a long moment. I glanced at the clock, Charlotte was not expected home from Dickson school for another hour.

"Yes, I do. My cousin passed away from consumption three years ago. But surely...she was thin and pale, and I have always been plump. I was always plump and healthy. I am perfectly fine, surely, it's just a catarrh that has not healed as fast as it should. It has been such a long cold winter, and the air is damp, blowing over the Grand River as it does. Why, I've seen the sea smoke so thick some mornings I swear one could cut it with shears."

"Edith..."

He put his hand on mine.

I tried not to cry, but some tears escaped. Dr. Gordon handed me his handkerchief. I noted that Mrs. Gordon had ironed it carefully and the corners were folded neatly and precisely.

"How long do I have?"

"There is no guarantee, but with care and lots of good food and rest, you should be able to live for another year or two."

"But Charlotte! I won't see her grow up and marry. And how will Joseph care for her on his own? She is such a spirited girl, and Doctor, he

drinks sometimes more than is wise. He depends on me...."

"I will send the Vicar to speak with you my dear. Would you like me to break the news to Joseph?"

In a moment of weakness, I almost said yes.

"No, I shall tell him myself. I will shield Charlotte for as long as I can."

"The disease will progress..."

"I know that Doctor. I watched my cousin fade month to month. I shall handle this in my own way."

My face was hot and I knew I had flushed. The cough ambushed me as it does always when I am excited or overtaxed.

Doctor Gordon waited until the cough had subsided then he said good-bye, walking slowly, a little stooped, out the door.

I opened my Bible to soak in the beauty of the psalms, to calm myself before Charlotte skipped in from school.

I was careful to ensure the tears did not smear Daddy's spiky writing. Jack and I sat for long hours under that apple tree, until the day dimmed, and became so cool I had little choice but to go in. Jane looked at me with raised eyebrows when I did return, but I ignored her and picked at another excellent meal she had prepared.

***

At first, life on the farm was enchanting. I helped Cousin Jane in the kitchen and learned to cook and bake simple and hearty fare for Bart, as well as for the farm hand. They both seemed hungry all the time. Bernie lived on the next farm but one. He was tall, skinny, unmarried, and painfully shy. He'd blush bright red when he saw me. He had few teeth, and fewer words. I was not sure that he bathed with any frequency, if at all, but as he worked outside and I lived mostly inside, our only interaction was at mealtimes, and I made sure to sit at the opposite end of the table.

Bart taught me how to milk the cows and although I did not relish awakening at 5AM, the sweet smell of hay, and the earthy aroma of the livestock made me appreciate the value of physical labour. I loved the splash of the milk as it squirted into the tin cans, and I soon made friends with the two milk cows, named somewhat improbably Merissa and Larissa. I suppose Jane had a romantic streak that the stern life of a farm woman could not totally obliterate.

My pregnancy was an easy one, and as corsets were not necessary on the farm, I could pretend it was not happening for most of the summer. I went for walks with Jack and explored the beautiful countryside. My favourite destination was Inglis Falls which spilled down the rocky Niagara Escarpment. Sometimes I could cajole Bart into dropping me there for an hour or so while he attended to business in town. It was a grist mill, so I had to stay well back of the men going about their business, but at 20 yards high, the water poured down with a satisfying, hypnotic roar. Before I became too unwieldy, Jack and I would walk along the rocks and admire the potholes. It was fall now, and the maples and oaks framed the falls with orange and red hues. I had never experienced such craggy beauty in Galt.

Whenever I could, I'd accompany Bart to town. I'd shield myself with shawls and walk along the shore of Owen Sound. I never tired of sitting on a dock, bare feet immersed in the water, watching the boats bobbing in the waves, sails sometimes nearly touching the water as they tacked and raced. Steamships were vitally important, and I would watch their progress too, the big plumes of dark smoke as they chugged self-importantly to and from Owen Sound, carrying basic supplies to the small town, and taking lumber from the Bruce Peninsula to be sent to bigger ports, Toronto, Chicago, and even Europe.

When the harvest commenced in earnest, I learned how hard a farm woman truly worked. Jane and I cooked endless meals for the men, we raked, tended the garden, put away produce for winter, canned vegetables, and salted pork. Butchering was my least favourite part of farm life. Pigs know when they are about to be slaughtered and let out a wrenching squeal. I know that Bart tried to be humane, slitting their throats as quickly and economically as possible, but I had fed those pigs for months, and looked deep into their eyes, and sometimes scratched behind their ears. However, pork was a mainstay of farm diet, as they were happy to eat scraps and reproduced easily every spring, so the butchering was inescapable. Gathering up the bloody straw was a job I left for Jane every time.

I was becoming bulkier too, and getting ever more tired, but the work was unending. I laboured from 5 AM to dark, and even then, I was expected to mend clothes, tablecloths, darn socks, wash floors, by candle light. I was grateful that Mamma had taught me to be a patient and careful seamstress. My stitches were tinier and stronger than any of the new sewing machines could manage.

Needless to say, this life was not what a pampered, indulged 17-year-old city girl had envisioned. I gritted my teeth and worked as hard as I might; soon, I would have my baby and leave him in Jane and Bart's safe care. I'd return to Galt, back to helping Daddy in the apothecary, back to school, with my reputation unblemished, my trim figure restored, and no one the wiser.

***

Daddy visited me at Christmas and although I was quite large by this time, we ignored my predicament and had a happy celebration. Winter time was the easiest on the farm - it was simple to get about when roads, lakes and even rivers are frozen, and sleighs glide smoothly over the snow. Daddy brought us each an orange, and we marveled at the juicy tanginess of the fruit, eating it slowly, savouring each crescent piece.

"Where did you find an orange?" I asked. Bart and Jane gaped as they held their treasure, stockings discarded beside the woodstove.

"I went to Toronto and stayed the night before taking the train here. There is a small grocer on Front Street - I often buy my medical supplies from him. I asked him in October to make sure to save me four oranges…."

He had to stop speaking as I hugged him too tightly around his neck.

He and I went for a long walk by the moonlight, along the paths the horses and sleighs had trampled down, and as my dear Jack ran and sniffed beside us, it felt like old times. "Do you ever think about Mamma?" I asked.

Daddy looked at me, his eyes piercing under his bushy eyebrows. "I never stop thinking about her. I miss her every hour of every day. Often when I wake up, I reach over to hold her hand, and the emptiness of my bed…" His Adam's apple bobbed.

"I miss her too Daddy. I have wondered time and time again if she were alive, if I would have gotten myself into this predicament."

Daddy took my hand but did not meet my eyes.

"It is not your fault, my dear. I blame myself entirely. He pointed to the flask in his pocket. "I am too fond of the drink. When your Mamma was alive, I could keep it in control, but when she died…I suppose I was full of anger and self-pity. I did not raise you as I should have."

"I'm the one at fault, Daddy. I knew right from wrong. I just was so lonely, and Tony seemed to love me…"

We embraced, holding each other for a long moment.

"Do you remember Christmas when Mamma was alive?" I asked.

"Of course. She was so particular about finding the perfect tree…I had to borrow the biggest sleigh possible, we'd go to the woods, and your Mamma would spend close to an hour trying to decide which tree would fit perfectly in our parlour."

"I remember that! Then we helped you bundle it into the sleigh, and we'd be crammed in trying not to get scratched by the boughs."

"Do you remember your mother's allergy to pine needles, the way her skin would get blotchy?"

"Yes, of course! You would give her a salve to soothe the rash…what was in it, Daddy?"

"It was mostly just coconut oil. I think she enjoyed the attention…She did love us so Charlotte."

"Yes, I know."

We were quiet for a while, then we spoke of the wreath Mamma hung carefully on the front door each December. She and I carefully decorated it with pine cones and pretty ribbons Daddy brought us home from the store. We stood year after year shivering in our thin day dresses while struggling to attach it to the door, to make sure it was centered and hanging exactly in the right place.

"Do you remember the red dress she made for me when I was nine?"

"Velvet, wasn't it?"

"Yes, and she spent hours embroidering tiny flowers along the collar. Don't ever throw it out, Daddy. And never give it away. I want to keep it for…."

I remembered my predicament and fell silent.

"I have a new friend, Charlotte," he said, and reached for my hand.

"Oh yes, who is he?" I asked absently, just happy to be spending time with my father. I had missed him.

"She, my dear. My friend is a lady. She's the widow of Mr. Harrington, who used to own the bookstore across from our store."

I froze. Try as I might, I couldn't remember her at all. I remembered Mr. Harrington, though. He was short, fat and smoked a pipe. I used to smell its acrid smoke as I walked past his bookshop. I remained silent, then he rushed to speak,

"She has agreed to marry me, my dear. The nuptials will be quiet and private. We will marry at Trinity Church, then travel to Niagara-on-the-Lake for our wedding trip."

"When?"

"New Year's Day," he said. His shoulders were hunched, his words rushed. "Please try to accept this, dear heart. With you gone, I am so lonely…"

"But I am going to return! Was going to return! I'm going to leave the baby with Jane and Bart…" I said. My throat felt like it was full of gravel.

He flinched. "Now, honey, this doesn't change our plan…Mrs. Harrington, Lavinia, will be more than happy to welcome you back to our home, your home…" He spoke so softly that I strained to hear. His eyes were fixed on the ground. Suddenly, I despised him.

"No wonder I'm in trouble with a father like you. If Mamma had survived, my life would be wonderful! Why did she have to die and not you?"

His face looked sunken and grey. He turned away from me. After a long moment had passed while I stood in sullen silence, he spoke in a choked voice,

"Don't you think I wish that too? I know I'm to blame. But what can I do? She's gone, and you are going to have a child, and we need to move ahead in life as best as we can."

"You disgust me. Mrs. Harrington is probably too good for you." I stamped away back to the farmhouse and didn't look back.

Daddy left later that day. Bart readied the horses to drive him to the train station. I stood in sullen silence, refusing to hug him or even say goodbye.

"You are a good girl," he said quietly. "I will pray for you, and I'll come to visit you again when the baby is born and bring Lavinia. I'm sure you will grow to love her…you'll have a new Mamma."

"Never!" Jack flinched and hid behind my skirts, looking guilty. Jane, who was peeling potatoes in the tiny kitchen, hurriedly put on her boots and grabbed her shawl, muttering about milking the cows.

Daddy hugged me, the bulk of the baby awkward between us, and left. I peered out the window and saw that he walked with a stoop, like an old man, although he was barely fifty. Shame rose hot in my breast, but I turned resolutely away and finished peeling the potatoes Jane had left on the counter. I ran once more to the window, but he was gone. I longed to chase after him, beg his forgiveness and tell him that I'd accept Mrs. Harrington, *Lavinia,* but my feet remained rooted to the rough pine floor. I poured boiling water into the sink and washed and scrubbed until my hands were raw.

My insides were still churning, and my head had begun to ache. I grabbed a glass and hurled it at the wall. It shattered into twisted, jagged shards. Jane, who had crept back into the house, began to scold, but I ran to my attic room, screaming obscenities over my shoulder. Jack jumped on the bed, and I pulled him close and he licked me gently. After a time, I quietened down, and Jack rolled over for a belly rub. I obliged - it was the least I could do for my faithful companion. The sight of his big, soft ears splayed on either side of his long nose made me giggle. A little.

When I returned downstairs, the glass had been swept up, and Jane was busy in the kitchen.

"How was the milking? I'm sorry I didn't help you," I said.

"It was fine. I enjoy that chore. Do you want to help me peel these apples for the potluck at the church? They are tart, but I think they will taste fine in an apple pie."

"Yes, of course. Can we make two pies, so I can have some too?"

We did not delve deeper. Jane kept darting quick, inquisitive glances at me, but I looked away, and hugged my swelling belly. This made her flinch, as I know she had never stopped mourning her own inability to conceive. I gloated inwardly.

***

In a few weeks' time, I was overtaken with pain as I raked the barn. I doubled over, coughing and hollering, and Cousin Bart ran for Jane, who sent him for the doctor. Jane supported me to her own bedroom, which was only slightly larger than mine. Bart had made a maple cradle during the long winter nights. Jane knitted baby blankets and clothing in the most expensive ivory wool she could afford and had even stitched a quilt made from every day rags she had saved over the years: Bart's old work shirts, a piece of the lace from her wedding shawl, and a calico work dress. She had asked me if I would like to contribute to the quilt one long winter evening.

"Yes," I replied indifferently. I gave her a snippet from a shawl Daddy had bought for me a few Christmases ago. I had never liked the colour - a pale yellow, which I thought did not complement my curly blonde tresses. She sewed it dutifully into the quilt.

Jane sat with me through a long, painful birth. I was young, which worked in my favour, but I had never experienced pain such as this. I screamed the house down and Jane was amazed at the expletives I knew and used. I had visited many poor families with Daddy, helping to dispense medicines and basic care; I had listened and picked up an entirely new vocabulary. Sometimes even Daddy's language turned blue when he had been drinking heavily. When I wasn't in the throes of agony, I took a perverse delight in shocking her. She was such a goody-two-shoes.

The doctor arrived, and finally, around noon of the following day, I cradled a lusty young son. He weighed an impressive eight pounds - all that farm food I had enjoyed, I suppose. He had a shock of dark hair, just like Tony. He was perfect. I counted his fingers and his toes carefully. Ten of each. Jane took him from me and rocked him gently. He began to cry, at first quietly, then with a loud, unholy shriek.

"You must feed him now," she said. Her voice shook slightly and I knew that she wished with all her heart that she could perform this function.

I held him, and again marveled at his tiny perfection. He looked back at me, and I noticed that his eyes were a dark blue, with an indigo ring around the edges. I put him to my breast. I held him gently as he suckled. It hurt, but surprisingly for one as selfish as I, I didn't mind so much. When he had finished, after a thorough wash, and after Jane carefully tied the umbilical cord following the doctor's instructions, we placed a small flannel pad over the cord, smeared his bottom with lard, and swaddled him, to keep out the cold drafts.

I fell asleep, exhausted as soon as Jane took him from me. When I awoke, at first I did not remember the baby Tony and I had created. However, I winced as I moved to rise from bed to let Jack outside, and then reached into the cot and pulled Baby to me. I stroked his tiny hand which was curled loosely into a fist. He mewled a little then fell back asleep.

I had tried my best to block all thoughts of Tony, but now they came rushing back. I pictured his muscular shoulders, toned and honed by hauling boxes of groceries to stock his mother's shop. I thought of his warm brown eyes, and the slight crinkle at the corners when he laughed. I remembered the way his shirt smelled tangy and a little bit spicy when he held me in his arms, and I thought of his hands, thick and muscular, our fingers entwined.

I had not imagined that Baby would resemble his father to this degree. I held him to me more tightly. No matter the bitter ending to our love, neither Tony, nor his mother, could take the result away from me. Baby began to stir, and I realized I was holding him too tightly. I relaxed a bit, then stroked his head, and began to croon a little ditty Mamma had sung to me many times,

Hush ye, my brainier
Bonny wee laddie
When you're a man
you shall follow your daddie.

Most likely, my baby would never meet his Daddy.

I made my way downstairs, attended to Jack's needs, then returned to my chilly attic bedroom. Baby was stirring, fussing a little, and Jane was leaning over the crib.

"Go ahead, pick him up," I said.

"No, I think he is hungry…"

She retreated to a pine rocking chair by the window and Baby and I fumbled. He was not nursing properly this morning.

"You're holding him wrong. You need to cradle his head up higher. Be careful to support his neck."

"Why don't you take over then?" I snapped, stung by her criticism.

She sat back in her chair, picked up her knitting, and the needles clacked furiously.

Finally, it was time to give the baby his first proper bath. Jane heated some water on the woodstove, and I tested it carefully, dipping my elbow into the basin. Jane lifted Baby, and lowered him into the water gingerly, wiping him with a soft rag she had put aside for this purpose. Next, she dried him with the thickest towel she owned, and smeared lard on his diaper area, "to protect from the dreaded rash babies are prone to develop," she lectured me. I watched sullenly. *I should be the one to bathe my own child.*

Jane and I had prepared 15 diaper cloths during the long nights of my pregnancy, and Daddy had mailed me five safety pins from the apothecary. "They were invented in 1849, he wrote solemnly, "and ensure that babies are not pricked." I had shrugged off the gift at the time but was now grateful for his foresight. I fastened the diaper covers, which were made of a tightly woven and glazed cotton. These helped prevent leakage. This time, it was Jane who looked on.

Next, we put on the binder, a simple strip of cloth that we carefully wrapped around Baby's ribcage and belly. This was made of a soft cotton and provided warmth and structure to support the newborn. The firm binding also helped the umbilical cord heal quickly and cleanly. We quickly put Baby's shirt on, made from the softest cotton Owen Sound had to offer. Jane and I had spent hours stitching these garments during my pregnancy. Over the shirt went the flannel, sewn to a long skirt, pleated around the waist for fullness.

Next, we tied Baby's cap on snugly to keep his head warm, although my baby was far from bald…With all these layers in place, Baby was ready for his cotton petticoat. Lastly, we put the frock on. This was made from white cotton, and Jane had carefully embroidered rather fussy patterns upon it. I thought they looked silly but bit my tongue. We laid him down in his crib and tucked him in with a soft quilt and left him in peace to sleep.

Jane and I began preparing lunch for Bart and Bernie.

"Will you please cut the bread?" Jane handed me the knife.

She cleared her throat. She always did this when anxious or uncomfortable, which was frequently the case in my company. I looked at her.

"Bart and I have decided on a name for Baby. We can't keep calling him Baby!"

"You decided without even talking to me about it?"

"Charlotte, he is our baby now."

"He's my baby. Always will be. What name did you choose?" I made no attempt to keep the sneer from my voice.

"Thomas, after my father."

"I hate the name Thomas! It sounds like a king, stuffy and boring…" My face grew warm, my head felt swollen and pounding. "I will choose his name! I'm the mother here!"

"Charlotte…we have an agreement…"

I used words that shocked even me. When I saw Jane's disgusted reaction, I repeated them, louder. I turned, with the sharp knife in my hand, and moved towards her. Some evil part of me enjoyed the frightened expression on her face. She began to inch slowly towards the door.

Hot, sweaty, shame coursed through me. I put the knife down and said, "I'm thirsty. Would you like some tea if I make it?" My voice was shaky.

Slowly, she relaxed, realizing that the moment of danger had passed. She was breathing hard, and her hair had escaped its usual tight bun. Her eyes were bloodshot, and a few tears ran down her chubby cheeks. My shame only grew deeper, but I donned an insouciance I did not feel.

"You baked the bread yesterday. If we don't eat it, it will get too stale, and Jack can't eat an entire loaf…! I'll toast it over the fire. I'll finish the housework when we have eaten."

I picked up the knife again. My hands were shaking, and I hoped Jane didn't notice. I cut the bread into two thick slices, toasted them carefully, and spread the butter on thick.

"Do you want jam?"

"Yes please." Jane's voice was barely audible.

"Oh Jane, don't be so silly. I would never hurt anyone. You don't know how hard this is for me, I miss my friends, my Daddy has married a silly lady I don't even know. I've asked him to come up to see his grandson, but he refuses to come without Lavinia, and I don't want her here. Now I have to give up my own baby…"

Suddenly, I was crying in earnest. Jane held me. Her plumpness felt comforting, maternal. A few wispy strands of her thin hair itched my face. This made my anguish worse: I pictured my Mamma's long braid, from which hair rarely, if ever, escaped.

***

The three of us sat by the woodstove that evening, after Baby had fallen asleep, discussing his name. Jane offered me a shot of whiskey, but I refused. She looked surprised, no doubt thinking that no debauchery was beyond me, but I never dabbled with spirits of any sort. I learned and lived Daddy's lesson. So, she and Bart had their tipple, and I had milk and honey.

"What do you think to call him, Charlotte?" Her voice was soft and shook ever so slightly.

"Tony." I didn't think twice.

Bart looked at me for a long moment. "Why that name?"

"I just like it, that's why."

They both tried and failed to wipe their faces clean of an identical look of exasperation. "Is that the name of his natural father?" Bart's voice shook just a little.

"I want to name my own son." The words were louder than I wanted. "I know I can't keep him but I love him. He'll always be mine. Can't you let me name him? I haven't given him to you yet. Maybe I never will."

I scooped Jack up and ran outside. My hasty exit was slowed down by the necessity of pulling on my boots and the warmest shawl I owned; the nights were cold.

Jane came running to the door, and she called, "Stop, Charlotte! We can talk more…We didn't mean to upset you."

It was too bitter to make a grand statement such as running away, so I slunk to the barn, and huddled into a bale of hay with Jack. I stroked him for a long, cold, dark hour, and he cuddled his warm little body into me. I calmed down and began to shiver. I also remembered Baby needed to be fed, and as I was his nourishment, I returned to the house.

It was dark when I went in, and I lit a lantern that we kept by the door. I moved to the kitchen to pour myself a drink of milk and saw that Jane had left a short note on the table.

I'm sure we can come to a compromise. Baby is tucked in and sleeping in our room tonight. If he wakes up, I'll bring him to you. Cordially, Jane.

I thought bitterly that the only reason that she was willing to compromise was that my son was her dearest dream come true. I cudgeled my brains; how could I keep him? I could bring him home to Daddy and we could move to another town and inform the gossips that my husband had died of consumption…but wait, Daddy had just married *Lavinia.* I spat mentally. Why did Daddy abandon me? How could I abandon this innocent babe? I knew how lonely and desolate it felt to be motherless, and now I was fatherless too. I put myself to bed. Dear Jack lay in my arms and listened graciously to my quiet distress. I had caused Jane and Bart enough suffering for one day. Even I could see that.

The following day, the three of us were scrupulously polite to one another and for the following three evenings, we discussed in a dispassionate, almost emotionless manner, the naming of the child.

Finally, I accepted Thomas, and Bart and Jane insisted that his middle name be Anthony.

To me, he was Tony. His colouring was so much like his father's. I followed my Daddy's advice and refused Bart's offer to pay a local doctor who was known to be shady and a heavy drinker, to fudge the birth certificate so that he and Jane could be officially named as Thomas' parents. The birth certificate listed me, Charlotte Evans, as mother; father unknown. However, I did agree to Jane and Bart's demands that he be known by friends and family as Thomas Anthony Cooper, which was their surname. I accepted this with fairly good grace, as I grew to realize day by day what a huge responsibility it was to raise a child, and I began to yearn increasingly for my freedom.

Raising a baby on a remote farm was boring. I could have screamed at the relentlessness of the routine of Thomas' first six months: sleep, work around the house and farm, nurse, then relinquish. I stubbornly continued to call the baby "Tony." When I called him by that name, Jane frowned, but she needed my nursing capabilities.

"It's your job to empty the chamber pots," Jane said every morning without fail. This I did, taking them to the outhouse in every kind of weather. Full chamber pots are heavy as well as revolting. I then cleaned them outside, with snow in the winter, and with water we collected in barrels when the snow melted.

Jane's energy was boundless. "Today's Monday, we need to begin the laundry." I groaned, giving Thomas one final kiss after he finished nursing. We gathered and sorted clothing and linens on Saturday, so I was prepared for the drudgery that lay ahead. We gathered wood for the outdoor fire, hauled 20 gallons from the well to the giant copper pot, and filled several other barrels with water.

Laundry was a four-stage process. We first soaped and rubbed the clothes until they were clean. We had to wring each item individually. We then turned the clothes inside out, and using fresh water, repeated the soaping, rubbing and wringing. Next, we boiled white cottons and linens in soapy water. Jane and I wrung each garment again. Finally, we thoroughly rinsed all items in fresh, clean water, then hung the whole lot to dry. When it was too cold or rainy, the house was full of drying racks, and the humidity inside was nearly unbearable. Thomas' napkins had increased our load enormously.

"How did you manage without me?" I asked Jane one day after we finished pegging the clothes on the outdoor line that Bart had carefully strung between two trees.

"Quite well." She marched inside and tended to Baby while I began to prepare the mid-day meal.

The plan was that I would return home to Galt as soon as it was safe for Thomas to be weaned. Sometimes, I'd toy with the idea of taking my son with me. I imagined the shocked looks of Galt's matrons, the tittering behind gloved hands, and the looks of disdain I would endure at Trinity Church if I brought him to services. These imaginings were delicious and relieved the dreary tedium.

Jack took to the baby, and he was the first to run to the cradle to investigate when he cried. Jack would turn and fix me with his big brown eyes if I was tardy getting to Baby's side, and begin to whine softly, then with increasing urgency if I was not prompt enough in his eyes in caring for the infant. How I loved that dog. My fear was that I had begun to love Thomas nearly as much. *I must avoid getting too attached.*

***

"Thomas is getting so big," Jane commented one day. I looked down, and realized she was right. He had adorable little rolls of fat on his arms, he was capable of kicking strongly when being held or changed, and his appetite was beyond robust. My milk wasn't enough for him anymore, and we had begun to introduce some solid foods into his diet.

"Yes, but he still needs his Mamma's milk," I retorted, and held him so tightly he squeaked.

"Charlotte, you're hurting him. Let me take him." She held out her arms and glared.

I handed him over, and sulked.

The following morning, I left the house and walked the three miles to town. It was a brisk, cool day, and a breeze flowed from the water, messing with my hair. I opened my cloak to embrace its coolness and strode quickly. I felt wonderful. I had lost the weight I had gained with the pregnancy, and I knew I looked as though I had never had a baby. Thomas was beginning to drink cow's milk and eat some solid foods, which Jane would prepare, mashing ever so proudly every evening after she put Thomas down for the night. I had some hours to spend doing what I wanted to do, for a change.

I considered letting Jane have her own way over the baby's name as

I savoured my new freedom. *Let her have the responsibility. Let her get up in the middle of the night and feed him.* I wandered around town and bought a few ribbons with money Daddy had pressed upon me before our unhappy leave-taking. Jane kept herself occupied with constant sewing and knitting in the evenings, creating a durable and thoughtful wardrobe for my son. The idea of purchasing new material for him didn't even cross my mind. Yet I thought of him again with great fondness and giggled slightly at the thought of his chubby perfection.

I bought myself an ice-cream cone and went down to the harbour to eat it. I plopped down on a bench, soaking in the late afternoon sunshine, and surveyed the hustle and bustle. The harbour had been dredged in the 1860's and regularly welcomed a variety of vessels. The *Frances Smith* was a 182-foot paddle steamer that was built in Owen Sound. It was the finest passenger steamer in our area, and regularly serviced a route connecting Collingwood, Owen Sound, and Port Arthur on Lake Superior. I admired its sleek beauty and watched as people disembarked, anxiously scanning the harbour side for loved ones or for a buggy or wagon to take them to their destinations.

I watched, fascinated, as the *South American* cruise ship lumbered slowly towards the dock on the opposite side of the harbour. Passengers stood on the decks, throwing pennies into the water. I knew that local children often jumped in to retrieve them. I hoped that Thomas would not be so foolish when he grew older. I continued to lick at my ice-cream and watched the stevedores as they unloaded and loaded goods. The men were tough and muscular from the labour they performed, and I enjoyed the view.

I left the farm as often as I could as the weather improved, to Jane's stifled contempt. However, I also think she was happy to be rid of me and enjoy Thomas to herself. Bart was busy with work on the farm, and in the way of most men, tended to avoid domestic conflict or any overt commentary on my behaviour.

The spring folded into summer, and I continued to luxuriate in my newly regained freedom. One day as I sat enjoying my ice-cream cone, a slim young lady around my age of seventeen, dressed entirely in black, walked slowly towards me, and sat down by my side. Her movements were dainty, and I looked at her with interest. She had a lush figure, despite her somewhat dowdy clothing. Her face was pretty, then I realized with astonishment that her cheeks were rouged. I couldn't believe it. Women of my class did not enhance their looks with cosmetics, although I knew a few covert tricks to augment beauty due to my time helping in my father's apothecary. I had often rubbed beeswax on my lips to make them darker and shiny, and in the winter when I was unusually pale, I had at times rubbed a little beet juice onto my cheeks. But rouge? Never.

"May I pat your dog?" Her voice was deep and husky, unusual.

"Of course. His name is Jack."

"Oh, I've known some Jacks…" Her voice trailed off and she stared at the harbour. She stroked his silky ears, and he gave a little grunt of pleasure.

"I'm Charlotte. Originally from Galt, but I'm here helping my cousin with her baby. She needed some help, first baby and all…"

"I'm Felicity. Felicity Ross. I lived in Preston for a time, so we were practically neighbours."

"My cousins live in Preston, and I spent months there when my mother was sick."

She smiled at me.

"It's so nice to meet someone my own age. I've been stuck on a dull farm, milking cows and looking after a baby," I said.

"I'm stuck too at times. Would you and Jack care to walk with me?"

"I'd like that."

I treated her to an ice-cream cone, and we walked slowly beside the harbour, then ventured to the downtown area, peering into shops. I bought Thomas a leather ball which was dyed in multi-coloured hues. I pictured his look of delight when he would grasp it in his chubby hands and felt a pang. He had a tooth now, and his smile was enchanting.

I looked sideways at my new friend. *Why did she dress so dowdily, and in unrelieved black?* I could restrain my curiosity no longer. "Have you been bereaved?"

She flinched. "No, as far as I know, my family is in good health."

"Sorry." I could have kicked myself at her sad expression. "I'm always too curious."

"No, it's fine. I haven't seen my family in almost two years."

"Do they live far away?"

"No, they are still in Preston. My father died when I was young, but the fact is that my mother has disowned me." Her voice was low and sad.

"Disowned you?" I couldn't believe it. "Why would she be so

cruel?"

"It's due to my line of work."

I gave her a searching look, which she ignored, gazing at the ground. I spotted a brightly coloured shawl in a store window-front and grabbed Felicity's arm.

"Look at the colours. That shawl would look fetching on you, and really accentuate your dark hair. Let's go in and you can try it on."

She stopped still and looked at me intently.

"Charlotte, I will not be welcome in that shop. Don't you realize what I am?"

I gaped. "No, I truly have no idea what you're talking about."

"I'm a whore, Charlotte. A dollymop. A harlot. I sell my body for money to men I don't know and could care less about. Now are you satisfied? No respectable shop keeper would allow me entrance, and you really should not be seen with me. I never should have sat beside you."

I stood still for a long moment. I felt a little sick. Finally, I reached out, and touched her arm. She was shaking, but dry eyed. We stood for a long moment. Neither of us spoke. What was I to say? I was astonished, as prostitution was not something a polite young lady from an affluent Galt family knew much about. Daddy had mumbled an explanation to my question when I had once read about the oldest profession in the *Galt Reporter,* and I had never considered the matter further, despite my own fallen state.

"Let me buy you some tea."

She shook herself, almost like a dog coming out of the water, and nodded.

I had plenty of money to buy Felicity a treat. Daddy was always generous, and cheques arrived each month with reassuring predictability. I opened my reticule. It was beaded, made by the local Newash woman who peddled her crafts by the harbour. The constabulary usually turned a blind eye to such exchanges, and white women such as myself were delighted by the brightly coloured, handmade goods she sold. The vendors had to vacate Owen Sound promptly by late afternoon to be back on their Indian reserve by their strict curfew of 10PM. If Indians were found outside the reserve after that hour, they could be summarily executed by the constabulary. Executions occurred with distressing frequency. One gentleman was hanged by an over-enthusiastic officer *before* the curfew time simply because he had no chance of making it home in time for 10PM. Bart had told me this story on the one long evening at the farm, in part to pass the time, and in part to relieve my sullen boredom.

"You can't be telling me the truth." Bart had certainly cured my boredom. "That's a travesty. We're in the 20th Century now! Why would you tell me such a horrid story?"

"It's the way it is here Charlotte." Bart's voice was gruff, as though he was fighting his own battle against despair. I liked him so much more than Jane. We sat for a long time that night, in front of the fire, while Bart smoked his pipe, and we mourned for a man cut down in his prime for no reason at all.

I reached for my wallet, and felt my hand instead caressing a photograph of my son, that I had had taken when he was two months old. I did not remove it from my reticule, but instead caressed the photograph's leather covering, remembering the sweet smell of my baby following a bath. I released the photograph, blinked hard, and then scrabbled for my wallet. My fingers slid over the ribbons I purchased for myself this morning, and I felt a pang that I had not taken the time to buy Thomas material for new clothing, as he was growing so rapidly. *That's Jane's responsibility now.* I extricated my wallet, grabbed some money, then closed my reticule tightly.

I walked into the nearest teashop and purchased two steaming beverages. We carried the tin cups to the banks of the Sydenham River, and sat on a bench. I didn't know what to say, and somehow, I was wise enough to say nothing at all.

The river was dark and rather muddy, and it swirled relentlessly. Ducks floated downstream in their endless search for sustenance, occasionally diving and presenting their backsides to the world. I thought of how I would bring Thomas here when he was a bit older, to enjoy this comic sight. I would have to teach him about nature, birds, and flowers, I mused, thinking of my many wanderings beside the Grand River home in Galt. I stopped myself: Thomas would not be mine to teach.

"I expect you won't want to have anything else to do with me after today." Felicity's eyes were still red.

I reached for her hand. "Nonsense." I surprised both of us with my rash promise. "I'd like to be your friend. In fact, I'll return tomorrow, and buy you another ice-cream cone if you will allow me."

Her eyes watered again, and I passed her my lace handkerchief. It had been a Christmas present from Daddy. I thought of Lavinia and shuddered. Jack stared at me, wagging his tail. He looked so cute that I obliged, offering him a piece of my tea biscuit. He snapped it up without any grace at all.

"Shall I walk you home?" I strove for a casual tone, but I was burning with curiosity to see what a house of ill-repute actually looked like. I was sure we did not suffer such homes in Galt.

"Are you sure you wish to walk with me?"

"Yes, of course."

The house looked ordinary, even a little bourgeois. It was on 3rd Avenue East.

"The corner you see ahead is known as *Damnation Corners,"* said Felicity. "It has a tavern on each corner. Of course, the next intersection is called *Salvation Corners,* as it has a church on each corner." She shrugged her shoulders. I grinned to myself at the complexity of human nature.

The brothel was large, built of the orange brick that is peculiar to the Owen Sound area, and had a very ordinary mansard roof. Two wicker rocking chairs graced the front porch, and the door was a respectable, boring black. I hid my disappointment and bade goodbye to my new friend. She did not invite me in.

***

I returned to the farm, and my smothering routine of farm work, feeding the baby, and the endless evenings spent conserving candlelight, knitting or sewing. When the weather and the mosquitoes and the blackflies obliged, I'd sit outside, reading my beloved Tennyson, Dickens, and my favourite, Anthony Trollope. Daddy sent me as many novels as I requested, and I requested many. I'd put my book down and daydream; I was Eleanor Bold, wealthy widow in *Barchester Towers,* being pursued by the oily chaplain Obadiah Slope, the dissolute Bertie Stanhope, and the brilliant young churchman from Oxford, Mr. Arabin, while bouncing my cherubic baby son on my knee…

"Where's Bart? The plough broke down." I opened my eyes to see not Mr. Arabin, but Bernie, the farm hand, whose fingernails were black with dirt, and who needed to shave.

My escape was to the harbour. Throughout the long, hazy summer days, as Thomas relied increasingly on solid foods and cow's milk, I was needed less. He began to turn to Cousin Jane for comfort, rather than to me.

"Thomas, eat your potatoes," she coaxed one evening as I was washing dishes.

"Mamamamama," he burbled, turning to her. I wanted to run and snatch him from her arms, but I restrained myself, wringing the tea towel until my hands felt raw.

It slowly became easier to relinquish nappy changes and feedings to Jane.

"You'll be returning to Galt soon," she remarked hopefully to me one Sunday after she and Bart returned from church. My heart felt heavy as I thought of living with Lavinia and my father. How could someone with such a ridiculous, frilly name take the place of my Mamma? How dare she even try? I tried hard to remember what she even looked like. I had not paid much attention to a middle-aged widow; I only had a foggy picture in mind of a stout lady with stubby hands and thick fingers. However, I wasn't even certain that this hazy memory was indeed Lavinia. I knew I was being unfair to my new stepmother, but I didn't care. I glared at Jane, then muttered an excuse and once again left the farm with Jack in tow.

The weather was becoming cooler, and I knew that in a few months, snow would fall. Walking the three miles to town would not be as easy. I had some decisions to make, and not much time in which to make them. I walked again to the harbour. The water danced and sparkled in the weak September sunshine. I was happy to see Felicity perched on her habitual bench, delicately eating a doughnut and watching the hurly burly of merchandise being loaded onto a ship, the passengers queuing to board. Jack chased a leaf to the steep edge of the break-wall. I called to him sharply as the water was colder now and I had no desire to jump in to retrieve my pet.

We strolled the short distance from the harbour to 3rd Avenue East. Felicity hesitated. "Would you like to come in?"

I felt my cheeks grow warm. I knew I should return home, but I was buzzing with curiosity. I paused for a long moment while Felicity waited patiently.

"Do you want me to come in?" I asked.

"You probably should go home."

"I'll come in just for five minutes, then I'll leave."

She nodded, and my heart thumped as she opened the door.

The madam, or keeper as they were called in Owen Sound, was named Mrs. O'Hara. She seemed pleased at our introduction. She was a big-bosomed, big-boned lady well into her fifth decade. She wore a tight-fitting gown of unrelenting black. Her hair was jet black, surely helped by the bottle. She wore it scraped back so tightly I wondered that she did not suffer from perpetual migraine.

"I'm delighted to meet you, Charlotte. Felicity, get her some tea. The kettle is hot on the stove."

"I shouldn't. My dog is waiting outside." I said.

"Bring him in. I love dogs." She whistled, and an elderly, plump, black poodle waddled into the room. "He can meet Barney."

I obeyed. When I opened the door, I looked out and felt like I should run away as fast as I could. Instead, I whistled for Jack to come inside. Felicity served us tea and some cookies, and we exchanged small talk, while Mrs. O'Hara looked at me intently, and patted Jack, who was delighted with the attention. Barney curled up on a pillow, and fell asleep, snoring softly. When Felicity gathered up the dishes, Mrs. O'Hara said,

"You have such lovely skin and hair. Will you unpin it for me?"

I felt a worm of anxiety, but obeyed. It spilled down, curly and unruly, but splendid. She pinched my cheeks, and even asked me to smile for her.

"Your nose isn't too big, and your teeth are straight. That's very good."

I squirmed.

In the next fortnight, I found myself drawn time and time again to the orange brick house on 3rd Avenue East. I enjoyed the easy camaraderie with the girls, who made the most of their leisure hours, curling each other's hair, exchanging cosmetics which I had never dreamed existed, and gossiping about the men who paid for their services. I was a lonely, motherless girl, and the female attention and sense of belonging was joyous for me. I knew in my heart I was not ready to return to Daddy, his drinking, Lavinia. I was relieved to throw off my burdens and responsibilities and feel truly young for the first time since learning I was pregnant with Thomas.

One evening, I returned to the farm after sunset to find Jane seething. "You eat our food, but barely help with any of the chores. Thomas hardly knows you anymore."

"No, that's not true." I ran to Thomas' cradle and swooped him up in my arms. He had been sleeping and yelped with surprise.

"See what you've done?" I had never heard Jane's voice so harsh. "I spent an hour rocking him, trying to get him to sleep. He's teething now and really cranky. You are completely useless Charlotte. Utterly useless." She took Thomas from me, and his crying intensified. I had really scared him. I felt a hot shame, and I knew she had every right to be angry with me.

The next morning, Bart asked for my help in raking the barn. I agreed without argument, and Jane fed Thomas. Usually I fed him his first meal. I looked forward to waking up just to see his bright eyes and greedy rosebud mouth gobbling his food.

We walked in silence to the barn, then Bart said,

"I think you need to return to Galt. Jane is upset all the time, and you aren't happy here. The tension can't be good for the baby. Our baby," he said.

I breathed hard, but kept my temper, and raked the barn until I had big blisters on the palms of my hands. I was angry, but mostly with myself. I never wanted to hurt Thomas, and I knew I was doing just that. If I were to avoid returning to Galt, Daddy and Lavinia, I needed to find a place to live, and an independent income. I didn't see that I had many choices.

I walked slowly to the farmhouse, packed my clothes, and Bart drove me to town.

"Drop me off at the harbour, that's fine."

"Here, take this." He pressed five whole dollars into my hand as he passed me my bag.

"That's too much money. You and Jane will need it for Thomas." But he had already pulled away in the cart. I waved goodbye to his retreating back, then walked with slow and heavy steps to 3rd Avenue East, where Mrs. O'Hara was extremely pleased to invite me in.

Mrs. O'Hara was something of a martinet, and did not suffer any disobedience from us girls, or ladies, as she insisted on calling us. However, she treated us with scrupulous fairness. The only real tenderness she showed was to her poodle, Barney. Woe betide the girl who stepped on his tail or failed to pat him when he jumped up on the sofa beside her as she rested after a long night.

"Take off your clothes my dear," said Mrs. O'Hara on my second day. "I need to ensure you are not blemished."

I was taken aback at the suddenness of her request, but I did as I was asked. I felt almost nothing as I disrobed. Almost.

"Your body is fine. Have you had a child?"

"Yes."

"Will the child present entanglements? I need you to concentrate on our gentlemen."

"No, it's taken care of."

"Good." She smiled at me and motioned for me to dress myself. "There are two things people will always pay for Charlotte," said Mrs. O'Hara when I was fully garbed once more, "good food and sex." She smiled at me as an indulgent mother would smile at a not particularly bright child who had just memorized her times tables.

"What about my dog?" I was clear that I would not commit to anything without Jack.

"I love dogs." She smiled at me, and her face lit up. "He is a well behaved little fellow, and as long as he stays that way, he's welcome."

I smiled back at her, and the deal was done.

I had one more concern. I cleared my throat. "I don't want to fall pregnant."

She looked at me, then smiled again.

"I don't want that either. So brave of you to be so blunt. I provide all my girls with the latest in contraceptives: sponges, the cap, and of course I supply condoms for the men, the very best, that are made from vulcanized rubber. No need to blush Charlotte. There's no place for false modesty here. You'd best return to the farm if you can't face these things."

I nodded but did not reply. I wished that I could turn back time and use these methods when I was in love with Tony. Then I thought of the sweet baby smell of Thomas, his endearing smile, and chubby little legs, and wasn't so sure.

I felt sick to my stomach on my first night working in the house. We greeted the men in the parlour, dressed brightly and fetchingly in the most daring, up-to-date fashions possible in Owen Sound. We poured the men drinks, then circulated, as if at a party. The men would then confide their choice of girl to Mrs. O'Hara, who'd facilitate the pairing with a meaningful glance, or a whispered word in the girl's ear. We always had some choice in terms of the men we were matched with and could refuse if we wished. She knew how to keep the loyalty of her girls.

There was plenty of interest in me on my first evening, due to my newness, and of course to my blonde locks which I wore loose, draping my shoulders, covering a somewhat risqué pink silk gown with a plunging décolletage. While the men were enjoying their drinks, I noticed one fair-haired young man looking at me with open approval. He seemed clean and reasonably well groomed.

Mrs. O'Hara came over to me. "Ezekiel would like to spend time with you tonight." Her voice was barely audible.

I nodded and looked away.

Ezekiel had been watching our exchange. He crossed the room, smiled at me, then reached for my hand. I looked closely at his teeth, and was relieved that they were only slightly stained, and fairly straight. I blushed, but I also giggled as we moved towards the stairs, holding hands.

***

I returned to the farm every ten days or so and could never get Thomas entirely out of my mind, no matter how hard I tried.

"I've made some friends in town, I'm living with them for a time," I told Bart and Jane on my first visit back. I had written Daddy the same story. They all seemed relieved to accept this explanation and declined to probe. Jane and Bart's busy lives on the farm gave them little time to come to town; I was hopeful they would not find out about my descent into prostitution any time soon. I slipped them a generous portion of my earnings; it helped relieve my guilt. A little. *Thomas is their son now; he might not even notice that I've moved away.* Sometimes, in the early hours of the morning when our house finally put itself to bed, just before I drifted into a dark, dreamless sleep, I'd remember how soft Thomas' dark hair felt, and the sweet baby smell of him. I'd fight these memories and hold them tight.

My figure was trim, my features were pleasing, and I was in demand with the gentlemen callers. Thus, I was treated with favour by Mrs. O'Hara. Despite Mrs. O'Hara's strict and forbidding demeanour, she was surprisingly fair with her girls. Room and board was 10 dollars per week. Once that was settled, half the money we made was our own. Girls were supposed to pay her half the standard price of the house, but if a man gave a girl more, she was free to keep it.

"In most houses, the landlady demands half of whatever the girls receive, period," Felicity explained to me. "This leniency is wise on Mrs. O'Hara's part, as we girls don't have to dissemble and conceal extra earnings. We have a good morale in this house, and we can spend our money however we please. At the other houses I've worked at, when girls are compelled to lie about their extra earnings. The temptation is to buy drink, which leads to bad behaviour, trouble with the police, and the townsfolk trying to run us out of town."

The citizens of Owen Sound largely ignored Mrs. O'Hara's house. We girls dressed modestly and neatly, were rarely seen drunk around town, and went about our business inconspicuously and with as much decorum as possible. Oddly, her one demand was that we wear black when we left home, and for the most part we were pleased to obey. We were loath to draw attention to ourselves, as all upright citizens spurned and reviled our profession.

I remained on good terms with Felicity but became closer to Eliza Ryan. Petite and thin, her blue eyes sparkled under her black curly hair.

"Where are you from?" I loved her soft accent.

"Dublin, Ireland. My parents were forced to the edge of starvation by the greedy English landlords during the potato famine. We fled to Canada when I was 11." Her tone was bitter. "They died here of influenza when I was only 15, and I had nobody. Mrs. O'Hara took me in. She knows what the Irish went through; she's Irish herself. She has treated me fairly, and sometimes she's even kind. I'm lucky to have met up with her."

We'd work into the early hours of the morning, fall asleep exhausted, then woke up to a time of leisure mid to late afternoon. There was only one girl in Mrs. O'Hara's household that I took a real disliking to. Her name was Vicky Sander, and she hailed from Toronto. She was indolent and plump, and had very thin brown hair, which she disguised with hairpieces and clever hairdressing.

"Vicky is short for Victoria. You know, like the Queen…? My darling mother saw her once when she was in England, shopping for the latest fashions across the pond." Her voice was whispery and affected.

Her parents had died in a fire when she was 17, and after she spent her inheritance, she became mistress to a very wealthy gentleman.

"Really, my dear girls, he owns a simply fabulous factory where they make simply delicious fur coats and stoles. In Toronto, of course."

He paid for Vicky to have her own living quarters in Parkdale, one of Toronto's most fashionable neighbourhoods, with charming brick houses, and easy access to Lake Ontario. She enjoyed this life of luxury to the hilt, until she became pregnant, and his wife discovered her husband's activities outside of the home.

"He paid for me to have the very best of medical care, girls, and then he arranged for one of his friends to adopt the baby. But his wife, that jealous she-wolf, insisted that I leave Toronto, and so my dear, darling Mr…" and here she paused for effect, as though we were hanging onto her every word, just dying to hear the name of her former patron, "Jones, arranged for me to live in Owen Sound. He gave me a scandalous amount of money to begin my life here, and promised me that we would be reunited once he could calm his wife's suspicions."

She sighed and reached for another chocolate. Mrs. O'Hara frowned, as Vicky was growing decidedly plump, as she enjoyed nothing more than indulging her sweet tooth and gossiping about her gentlemen, who were always the most handsome and affluent, and poised to marry her, "if only they could persuade their parents." There was always a barrier in the way of the course of true love and Vicky's eternal happiness.

"Sadly, his wife is such a suspicious and paranoid creature that my dear Mr. Jones has never been able to renew our love." A fat tear rolled down her plump cheek. I had no doubt it was genuine, but probably in sorrow at the lost luxury Mr. Jones provided, rather for the gentleman himself.

"Charlotte, be a dear and pour me some more tea." I shot her a rebellious look, but obeyed. I was too new at the house to engage in feminine warfare. I brought her the cup, and noticed that she took a little bejeweled flask out of her pocket and poured something into the tea. Mrs. O'Hara had left the room. I held my tongue, wondering if the madam was aware that Vicky drank inside the house, which was strictly against the rules.

Eliza and I would eat a small meal, then more often than not, don our sober black clothes, and wander about the town. Often, we shopped for Mrs. O'Hara. She wrote us a list in black, spidery handwriting. We pulled our hats over our faces, covering ourselves as much as we could.

If one of our clientele passed by, he was only too happy to let us pass unrecognized. Very few men admitted to frequenting a brothel.

Mostly, I saw a brief jolt of recognition, then the gentleman would invariably avert his eyes, and then slink away. We let them be.

"Look, there's your favourite Friday evening gentleman, Mr. Christopher," Eliza whispered to me, the lilt in her voice more pronounced than usual. "Did he give you ribbons last week?"

"Yes, and the week before he gave me jam that his wife preserved."

Mr. Christopher was a haberdasher, meticulous in his dress, walking just now beside his wife who was buxom and had a gentle face, with her greying hair styled in an elaborate chignon. We chuckled at the cowardly ways of our gentlemen callers, but I was careful to show Mr. Christopher no sign that I had recognized him. Not a smile, not a wink. We knew the rules, and we abided by them as strictly as some folk did to their religious tenets. It was our life, our livelihood and strangely enough, our pride. The rules sustained us, comforted us and upheld us on our crooked path.

I was in my bedroom late one afternoon, when I heard someone playing the piano. The sound was exquisite, fluting and delicate. I ran downstairs, and saw a dark young man entirely focused on the instrument at hand.

"Stop gawping," said Mrs. O'Hara. "That is Damone Barrett. He provides the music here. He's a valued employee." She stared at me, and I looked away, my face flushed. Eliza reminded me later that Owen Sound had been the terminus of the Underground Railroad in Canada and had a sizeable Negro community.

When the song was over, I moved towards Damone. He seemed shy and a bit hunched into himself but took my hand and gave it a squeeze. His skin felt warm and soft, his fingers long and slender. I smiled broadly, and he responded with a matching grin. His smile lit up his face.

I later learned that some gentlemen have very strange tastes, after I saw one climb the stairs with Damone in his wake. Damone angled his face to the wall, and the gentleman pulled his hat far over his face. Nevertheless, I recognized him as a shopkeeper who sold shoes and dry goods such as ribbons and lace on 10th Street. I noted that he sported a thick gold wedding band when I shopped for ribbons one day the following week.

Nothing was ever spoken about this, and I grew close to Damone. He wasn't really that much younger than I was, as he was sixteen, but he was slight and small of stature and seemed younger, more vulnerable somehow. We began to spend some of our free time together, wandering along the shore of Owen Sound. One icy winter day, we rode in a farmer's wagon to Inglis Falls, a four-storey mill that produced flour, bran and shorts (feed for animals). Damone, who was enchanted by all things mechanical, ran to the barrier and leaned over, watching the huge wheel turn.

I ran as fast as my heavy wool skirts would allow and grabbed his overcoat in both my hands.

"You silly fool, you're leaning over too far. If you fall in..."

He shook me off impatiently, but I maintained my steady grip as he continued to stare.

Finally, he stepped away, and I let go. My teeth were chattering, and I was furious. I had been that afraid. But Damone was oblivious.

"Charlotte, didn't you see the power of the wheel? To think this waterfall provides that much power..."

"Come with me and we'll watch from a safer vantage point." I took his hand and steered him non-too gently to the side. The water poured over the falls, which were poised high on the Niagara Escarpment. Jagged pieces of ice were suspended, frozen seemingly in mid-air. It was spectacular. Church was not a place to welcome one such as I, but that day I felt a rare sense of communion with a higher power, maybe even God.

We caught a ride back to town with a farmer. "Shall we buy some candy for the girls and Mrs. O'Hara?" Damone helped me down from the wagon.

"Yes, good idea," I replied.

We went into a small store which sold everything: fabric, ribbons, candy, dry goods, and even medicines. We spent a long time debating our choice of goodies. When it came time to pay, the portly shopkeeper refused to take the money from Damone's hand. I noticed that his apron was filthy. *Grubby, small-minded excuse of a man...*

Damone tried to press the cash into my hand.

"No, forget it." I took the bag and dropped it with a satisfying thud on the wooden counter. I was pretty sure some of the candy broke as I stalked out the door. Damone followed, more meekly. I slammed the door. It shut with a satisfying bang.

"Charlotte, it's just the way it is. Best not to make a fuss."

"It's not right. I won't accept it." I said.

We walked silently home.

***

We enjoyed the rest of the afternoon curled up on the couch with Jack, laughing and gossiping with the girls. A few months had passed since I joined the house, and I had trained myself to separate my emotions from my work, and to put it from my mind in my leisure hours. The time I spent with the girls was precious. *They are my family now.* Eliza Ryan remained my best friend. I found Felicity too limp. Eliza had spirit. She was a few years older than I, steady, and mature. Some of the girls resorted to liquor or wine following the evening's work, despite Mrs. O'Hara's prohibition. Eliza was a teetotaler, as was I. I just couldn't stand to lose control, and Eliza had to abstain for medical reasons. She would get physically ill if she drank spirits.

"Let me twist your hair into a French knot." She waved a hairbrush at me.

"It hurts too much when you comb it." My hair was thick and curly, and tangled from one moment to the next.

"Her hair is too messy for that style," Vicky chimed in. "You can work on me."

"Some other time, Vicky." Eliza wrinkled her dainty nose which was dusted lightly with tiny freckles. Turning to me, she said, "I'll be gentle, and the style will really suit you."

I let her experiment with my hair, enjoying the female attention. I slept soundly that night, after entertaining my share of men callers. The benefit of the fresh air and exercise from our trip to Inglis Falls, I supposed.

In the early hours of the morning, I was awakened by an unholy shriek. I ran from my room into the hall. Matilda, well built, and twenty-four, was standing in her flimsy nightgown. The flicker of her candle revealed that her hair was disheveled, escaping in spider-like tendrils from the long black braid down her back. She had a wickedly serrated knife in her hand. I stared at it. *I used that knife at lunch yesterday to cut a fresh loaf of bread.* It glistened, wet in the flickering candlelight. She was shaking so violently I feared she would drop the guttering candle. I grabbed it, put my arm around her, making certain to stay far away from the knife, which was still vibrating in her hand.

"I found it." Her voice was barely audible. Fluid leaked from her nose.

"I heard a noise, and then a dull thud. I opened my door and began to walk down the hall. It was dark." She began to wail, rocking herself back and forth. The other girls and Damone emerged from their bedrooms, awakened by her keening. Their eyes were puffed with sleep, their mouths open. Vicky came out of her bedroom, pulling a very gaudy pink silk robe bedecked with feathers tight over her ample frame. When she saw the knife, she began to scream at the top of her lungs.

Eliza marched up to her and slapped her hard on each of her cheeks. The slaps resounded; her face must have hurt like the devil. Vicky was so shocked that she stopped her scream mid-breath, mouth wide open. Eliza then pushed her back into her bedroom, slamming the door behind her.

"Can we lock her in?" I asked my friend. Eliza smiled at me slightly, shaking her head.

I bent down and peered at the knife. It was indeed wet, covered in a thick liquid substance. Was it blood? I didn't want to know.

"What on earth is happening?" Mrs. O'Hara had arrived unawares. "Why are you ladies not in bed? Who is screaming? Go back to your rooms!"

I moved aside, and she fell silent as she gazed at the knife in Matilda's still shaking hand. Mrs. O'Hara was a strong, tough lady. She peered nearsightedly then said, "Is anyone hurt?"

"That's what we're afraid of, Ma'am." My voice was calm but quiet.

"Well, what are you waiting for? Call the constabulary, then search the entire house, top to bottom. Charlotte, you and Rose start looking in the cellar. Felicity, you take Matilda to the kitchen. Make her a strong brew of tea." Her tone brooked no disobedience. We girls were relieved to have her take such strong command. Her very harshness was a comfort.

Damone bolted out the door to alert the constabulary. Rose, a girl of twenty-five, who looked careworn, and older than her years, came with me. We walked down the stairs slowly. I wiped a cobweb from my face. It stuck on my hand. The cellar was cold and damp, dominated by a huge cistern which collected rain water. We used this water for everyday chores such as washing and bathing. In silent consent, Rose and I linked hands. I held a candle, and its light flickered.

I moved ahead and stumbled over something. It was soft, substantial yet squishy. I cried out, and nearly dropped the candle. Rose grabbed it and swore at me.

"Charlotte, you must stay calm," she said, although her voice was quavering. I swallowed and began reciting the Lord's Prayer over and over in my head, while she leaned down and shone the candle on the heap at our feet.

The man's waistcoat was bunched at his chest, leaving his flabby white belly exposed. I noted with horror the tufts of hair sprouting close to his navel. His stomach looked so exposed, so vulnerable, and yet curiously unremarkable. How many men had I seen thus naked? But his skin was cold, as I found when I touched his wrist gingerly, tenderly, to check for a pulse. Marble. Still. Dead.

"Do you recognize him?" Rose's voice was barely audible.

"No, I've never seen him before. He must be a gentleman caller. Who else would be here in the middle of the night?"

"I'll run upstairs and tell Mrs. O'Hara. You better stand guard over the body." Rose bolted up the stairs before I could open my mouth to protest.

Mrs. O'Hara walked down, carrying herself like a queen, lighting the way with an expensive beeswax candle. She faltered only slightly when she saw the body. She looked carefully at his face.

"This is Reverend Crudden, of Calvin Presbyterian church." I had to strain to hear her. "He was not a client here. But this will bring grave trouble to this house. Mark my words."

***

She turned and walked in a stately manner upstairs. I was close enough to note that the candle she held flickered as she ascended.

We waited a long thirty minutes. Still, the police did not arrive.

"Has Damone returned?" I kept my voice low.

"No," Mrs. O'Hara said.

"Something must have happened. I'll leave and search out the constable. May I bring Eliza with me?" I asked.

"Yes, I don't want you walking alone."

Eliza and I donned our cloaks and hurried out into the darkness. It was cool, humid, and foggy, with a faint breeze heavy off the water. I reached for her hand and she gripped mine. My lantern barely pierced the gloom. I tripped over a stone, and Eliza grabbed me even more tightly. I could see the ghostly outline of a steamship moored in the harbour. No animals stirred; the silence was eerie. *Is the ship tied up for the winter?* I envied its safe harbour.

I thought about the time I had sailed to Collingwood for the day with a man who asked me to pretend to be his new love interest in the hopes of making a lady jealous. (He was not successful and felt he could take unwanted liberties with me on the return trip). After I escaped from his advances with a sharp kick at his shin, I stood at the rail, enchanted with the waves, the rugged and lonely uninhabited islands off the coast, and the rocky shoreline which I knew had cost innumerable sailors' lives.

"Georgian Bay is an unforgiving water," another sailor had confided in me. He went on to tell me about the wreck of The *Asia*, in 1882, which foundered in a storm near Byng Inlet, taking with her 123 people. It was the biggest loss of life ever on Georgian Bay.

"My mother was one of only two survivors," he said. "She and a gentleman clung to a swamped tender for hours, until it made landfall at daybreak near Pointe au Baril. She hates the water to this day, and came close to disowning me when I told her I'd signed up to be a sailor. His affection and pride were evident in his grin.

I dragged my attention back to the distinctly unpleasant present, and we walked as quickly as our long skirts would allow towards the police station, located in the center of Owen Sound. Eliza rapped impatiently on the door with her gloved hand, and we waited in the frosty air, stamping our feet to keep warm, our breath smoky.

A beefy man of about forty-five ambled to the door, looked at us, and smirked. His breath smelled of gin, and his shirt was half untucked. He licked his lips, and I noted yellow, crooked teeth.

"How can I help you *ladies*?" The word "ladies" dripped with irony.

His blue eyes were small but piercing. He looked us up and down as we stood before him in our gaudy nightclothes which were not entirely hidden by our plain black cloaks. Both of us had untidy hair, mussed from sleep, and although it was the early hours of the morning, we were still marked by the remnants of rouge and other beauty enhancers. His leering was no more or less than we deserved, yet I felt a stab of anger. We were human beings who needed help from the constabulary. He was paid to do his job.

I drew myself up to my full height. I was a tall girl, 5 feet 7 inches, and I made every inch count. I squared my shoulders, jutted out my chin, and said, "We are here to report a crime."

"Of course you are…" He licked his cracked lips. I could see a white crust at the corner of his mouth.

"No, you fat lout, we have a dead man in our residence!"

"Overexertion?" He smirked.

"Stabbing." To my dismay, I began to giggle. Eliza pinched my arm, hard. I swallowed. My mouth was dry.

"If you *ladies* are fabricating a nuisance complaint, I'll have you." He licked his lips again.

I looked at Eliza. "We have a death at 3rd Avenue East. Mrs. O'Hara's house. Please take note that we were here. We need to return home. Goodnight." Eliza was splendid, her voice clipped and cultured. She flicked her skirts and I followed her meekly out the door.

We did not look behind us, but the Sergeant soon caught up with us on his bicycle, pedaling past us furiously. I stared at his retreating figure, his trousers straining over his thick legs. He wobbled a bit as he drove by, and I recalled the smell of drink on his breath. Would he even know how to begin investigating the disaster that had befallen our house? And where was Damone?

As we walked along, a statuesque Negress approached us, and tapped me on the shoulder. Her touch scared me more than it would have on a more ordinary day. When I looked at her closely, however, I realized by her remarkable, thickly lashed eyes that she must be Damone's mother. She looked at me with an odd mixture of pleading and fury.

"Eliza, I need to speak with this lady. Are you fine to continue back home on your own?" I asked.

Eliza looked at me with surprise. She was a kind and thoughtful girl. She had my best interests at heart, always. "Yes, of course. Will you be safe?" She looked at me with concern.

"Yes," I whispered in her ear, "I'm almost certain she's Damone's mother. I don't think she'll hurt me. I'll catch up with you back at the house."

Eliza gave my hand a squeeze and continued on her way.

Damone's mother grabbed my elbow and pulled me into an alley. Despite my brave words, I felt scared. She was a big lady, and the expression on her face was grim.

"Let go of me! I'll come with you willingly." I tried to keep my voice calm.

"You're nothing but a whore," she said, and pinched my arm, hard.

A splash of moonlight from behind the clouds revealed the whites of her eyes. She smelled fresh, like soap. I began to shake, but I gathered up my courage and said boldly,

"Don't touch me! You have no right to call me names. Do you have any idea what Damone gets up to? Let me go now. I'll not stay here to be vilified!"

To my consternation, she began to cry, big croaks that seemed to expunge her very soul.

"I know exactly what Damone gets up to, you stupid child. I know what you all gets up to. Do you think my family escaped from slavery risking being lynched so my boy could end up like this?"

I didn't know what to say. "What do you want, Mrs.....?" In the heat of the moment I forgot Damone's last name.

"*Barrett.* We had to take the name of our slave owners, and my husband and I belonged to Joshua Barrett of South Carolina."

"Why didn't you change your surname to evade detection?" My curiosity overcame good manners.

"No one cares what our names are in Canada. Why don't you change yours?" Her eyes flashed.

"Where is your husband? Will he be coming here?" I felt alarmed once more. Would he threaten me with physical violence?

"He moved away, long ago. I think to Halifax." She said more gently, "No need to be afraid of me. But I need to know where Damone went. They'll pin the murder on him."

I stopped her. "What? He told you about the murder? He said he was alerting the police. But, I'm sure that the murder will be investigated properly…"

"You know nothing. Of course he told me. Who else does he have to turn to? But then he ran away. I'm certain they will pin it on him."

"Why did he run away if he's innocent?" I asked.

"You're the innocent here." She looked at me, her eyes flashing scorn. "One Negro boy in a house of white women. Who will the police blame? Did my family risk everything to come here for this?"

She wailed once more, her big shoulders heaving. I moved to hold her. She pushed me away, then grabbed onto me and I tried my best to support the weight of her grief. Somehow, I forced myself to remain still, and I rubbed her back gently.

I held her for what seemed forever, then she finally quietened. We were still hidden in the alley, and for that, I was grateful.

"If you find him, tell him I'll help him get to Halifax. I know some sailors..."

"I bet you do, whore!"

"Do you want me to help or not?"

She looked away, then raised her eyes to mine. "Yes, I do. If you talk to him, send him home to me." Her big brown eyes were red and still leaking tears. Her body, which had been rigid, seemed to soften.

"You're not such a bad girl. Why are you living this life? You could change, repent, come to God, and live decently. You're young, and you still have your pretty looks and hair."

I stared at her for a long moment. I thought of Daddy, and the apothecary. I could almost smell his boozy breath as though he were standing right beside me. I squeezed her hand, then turned on my heel and walked as quickly as my skirts would allow back to 3rd Avenue East.

***

The house was in turmoil when I arrived. Mrs. O'Hara looked uncommonly flustered. Her hair was askew, with hair-pins sticking out higgledy-piggledy. I even spied a hint of grey. Her usually neat attire was a little crooked and I noted that one of her buttons had been overlooked. I couldn't stop myself from grinning.

"Charlotte, what could possibly entertain you about this situation?" Her voice was icy, each word enunciated.

I felt the heat of my blush. "Sorry, Mrs. O'Hara, I'm being stupid. I've just never seen a body before...."

"Yes, well, be that as it may, we have a right situation on our hands now. We need to comport ourselves with utmost decorum, do you understand me? It is possible now that the constabulary will shut down our house and along with it our livelihoods..."

I had less reason for concern than the other girls. I could return to Galt at any time, to my father's loving embrace, as long as I could stomach my new stepmother. But I thought about my friends, who had no one to turn to, and I became instantly sober.

"Did the detective arrive?" I asked.

"Yes, he is in the basement, examining the body. Do any of you ladies know what happened?" Her voice was shaky.

We all looked steadfastly at the floor. I thought of the hair on the

Reverend's flabby belly. The picture in my mind was obscene in its vulnerability and intimacy.

"Matilda, how did you come to have hold of the knife?" the keeper asked.

Matilda was an Ojibway girl who had drifted to Owen Sound from Cape Croker and fallen into bad ways. She confided to me one evening that her father died of exposure one winter while out trapping, and her mother found it nearly impossible to cope. When Matilda arrived in Owen Sound, she hoped to work as a maid, or a serving girl, but no one would hire a friendless Aboriginal girl. Mrs. O'Hara had snapped her up, as many men hankered after Native girls, and Matilda was a beauty. Her hair was a blue black and it shimmered. She carried herself like a princess.

Her eyes were red from weeping but she responded with great dignity,

"I was not able to sleep and went to make tea. As I walked down the hall, I noticed something silver stuck into Charlotte's door."

"What?" I couldn't stop myself from shouting. I'd had no idea.

"I pulled it out and when I saw it was coated with blood, I lost control and began to scream. You know the rest."

"Why was the knife in my door?" I struggled to breathe.

Mrs. O'Hara looked at me. "Do you really have no idea Charlotte?" Her voice was hard.

"No.no…." I stuttered. "Are you sure it was in my door?" I looked at Matilda. She nodded.

Mrs. O'Hara asked again, "Do you have any idea of what brought all this about?" Her black eyes bored into mine.

"Of course not! I'm Anglican. I've never been to a Presbyterian church in my life! I certainly never will after today!" I felt the hysteria burbling up again and turned away and gazed at the flowers on the wallpaper. I began counting the petals. Each rose had ten; the lilies had five.

When I calmed down, I turned to face the girls.

"Does the detective have any notion as to who killed Reverend Crudden?" I tried to keep my tone respectful but thinking of that fat, insolent copper made my blood boil. I turned to the keeper. "Is he that detective I've heard you complain of so often? The one who expects payment every month to look the other way?"

"Yes, his full title is Detective Sergeant Murray Craig. He was transferred to Owen Sound a couple of years ago from Collingwood. He was involved in some shady business in Collingwood. One of the prisoners he arrested died in a cell in the early morning hours. They transferred him here to hush it up, and a month following, he showed up on my doorstep demanding money. Said if I didn't pay him, he'd shut my establishment down. I've had to pay him ever since."

I felt sick. "Will he be able to discover the truth?"

"I very much doubt it," she said. Her voice was dull and heavy. "And until the truth is discovered, the press, the gossip, and the holier-than-thous will not leave us alone. It is possible that this house will not survive this disaster. Prepare yourself, girls."

Her hands were shaking, and her eyes were red. I had never seen her look remotely vulnerable before. I began to wonder about her as a woman. How had she become a madam? What was her life like that would lead her into such a sinning and shunned existence? And why despite her forbidding demeanour was she so scrupulously fair and humane to her girls? Most madams exploited the vulnerable sources of their wealth and were nothing more than pimps in frocks.

We all looked downwards, affecting not to notice her tears. She still held enormous power over us. If she threw us out on the streets, where would we go? Once again, I realized that I was luckier than most, as Daddy would be overjoyed to welcome me back home. Most girls were disowned by their families, if they were lucky enough to even have a family. They would have to move to another city and start again, or hope against hope that the Meg Matthews, the keeper at Branningham Grove, would take them on. No self-respecting housewife would employ a former prostitute for even the most menial job, and it was most unlikely in such a small town that our profession would remain un-noted, despite our quiet ways.

"Detective Craig wants to interview us all separately. I have given him the use of the front parlour. I expect all of you to co-operate fully with the man. The sooner this is cleared up, the better for us all." Mrs. O'Hara's hands were still shaking.

"What about the body?" I asked. "Is it still downstairs?" I could smell the sweet, cloying stench of rotting flesh. I knew it was in my imagination, but I shuddered nonetheless.

"The coroner is still examining it. They pulled some men into the basement for a quick jury; they'll find death by person or persons unknown."

I gulped and looked at the other girls. Vicki had her mouth open and was twiddling with a strand of hair. I saw her take a sip from a flask she kept stowed in a pocket in her skirt. Felicity was crying silently, big tears running down her round cheeks. I wanted to shake her, to make her stop. Matilda looked at the floor and didn't meet my eye.

"Let me make tea," I offered.

"Yes, that would be good. Make sure to offer a cup to the detective. Offer him sugar in the fine china bowl. Give him some biscuits as well."

Mrs. O'Hara offered nothing for free in the ordinary course of events. She was truly shaken.

***

I made the necessary preparations, then knocked quietly on the mahogany office door. I entered in response to a muffled invitation. Detective Craig did not look any better in the weak light of the oil lamp, which gave off a smoky, acrid odour. He did not smell much sweeter, either. He had removed his jacket, and his blue shirt was stained at the armpits. I tried not to look as he picked his teeth with a wooden toothpick that appeared to have seen much use. His nose was squashed, *probably broken in a fight. He must have trouble breathing.* The detective wore a pair of half-moon spectacles which perched on the end of his nose. He adjusted them self-consciously, and I wondered if his eyesight was indeed poor, or if they were an affectation. I noticed with a grim fascination that a drop of moisture was poised to drip onto the desk from the tip of his nose. Not an appealing gentleman.

"I've brought you tea and some biscuits." I worked to keep my voice friendly.

"Put them on the desk." He grunted and did not bother to look at me. I wondered what it was he was studying before him.

I banged the tray down with a satisfying clunk. Detective Craig did not look up. Nor did he thank me.

"Get out." Finally, his tiny, piggy eyes met mine. "Tell the redskin bitch who had the knife I'll talk to her first."

"How can you talk like that?" I was outraged.

"Vermin like you lot don't deserve courtesy." He stood up, and began to unbuckle his belt, in an unhurried manner. "Why don't you come here and I'll thank you properly. The desk will be more than adequate for a slut like you." He held his trousers up with one hand, walked across the room, and grabbed my arm. It hurt like the devil, his thick fingers pinching me hard.

I picked up the scalding hot cup of tea and flung it at him. We looked at each other, equally shocked at my recklessness. As if in slow motion, I could see the dark liquid dribble down his face, onto his blue shirt, then pool down onto his loosened trousers, creating a darker stain on the dark indigo of his uniform.

He yelled, spewing the vilest curses imaginable. He threw a chair against the wall, and in an almost graceful movement, arced his arm over his shoulder, and punched me on the side of my head. I cradled my head in my hands, appalled at my own temper and the violence it had provoked. Oddly enough, I had rarely encountered physical violence in my very dangerous work.

Detective Craig shoved me hard and I fell heavily to the ground, still clutching my head, striving to maintain consciousness. I noticed his trousers bunched around his ankles; he had obviously let go of them in his fury. He pulled them up, buckled his belt, then began to kick me. He kicked me methodically, again and again.

***

As if from a great distance, I heard the door open and Mrs. O'Hara shout in a harsh, guttural tone,

"Stop hurting her this minute. She is only a girl. Stop! Get away from her at once."

I looked up and to my amazement, saw Matilda, Eliza and Felicity, as well as Mrs. O'Hara, all holding onto the detective's beefy form, struggling to restrain him. Detective Craig knocked them back as effortlessly as a cat batting at a few pesky flies, and then resumed kicking my prone form with renewed vigour. I cradled my head in my hands and curled myself even tighter. He kicked my back and the top of my head, aiming to inflict the maximum damage. The pain was worse than when I had birthed Thomas. Mercifully, after a few moments, I blacked out.

I awoke to a vicious, sick throb in my stomach. My head was pounding, and I felt sick to my stomach. Eliza passed me a basin, and I retched. I looked around, and realized I was in my own bed, and someone had tucked me in under my beloved quilt. Jack was cuddled up to me in a ball at the foot of my bed. He licked his paw as if oblivious to what had taken place, but his presence comforted me.

"Here, have a sip of this cool water," Eliza said, passing me a small tin cup. I took it gratefully then groaned as even the smallest movement hurt damnably.

"How did you get that thug off of me?" My voice was a croak and I kept to a whisper, unsure if the thug in question was still in the house, within earshot. If anything, speaking made the pain worse.

"He stopped," said Eliza. "We all tried to hold him back. It was like he was in a trance or something, but he just seemed to collect himself, and he turned away and began barking orders to the girls. He is interviewing Matilda now. There's something wrong with him. Mrs. O'Hara says the only way he knows to get results is to beat confessions out of people." I groaned.

"He wants to speak to you next Charlotte." I had not heard Mrs. O'Hara enter the room.

I pulled the covers over my head in despair.

"Hasn't he done enough damage?" Eliza said.

"There is no way to stop him." Mrs. O'Hara pulled the covers from my face and stroked my forehead gently. "We have no recourse. The doctor has allowed him ten minutes with you."

"What doctor?" My voice remained a croak.

"I summoned Doctor Forsythe when you were unconscious. He is downstairs, waiting for you to wake up, to make sure you've suffered no lasting damage. He'll see you before Detective Craig is allowed in. Either he or I will sit with you during your interview."

I marveled that Mrs. O'Hara would spend a not inconsiderable amount of money on doctor fees to care for me. For a moment, I let myself to feel cared for, as if by a mother, but then I thought *I'm her investment. I make her a great deal of money.* I slipped back into my habitual emotional numbness and closed my eyes.

I could not rest because of a raging thirst. My voice sounded thin and papery when I asked for more water. My throat was on fire. It was Mrs. O'Hara herself this time who brought the cup to my cracked lips. I closed my eyes again, only to be awakened in an obscenely short time to a strange man entering the room.

"Hello Charlotte, I'm Doctor Forsythe."

His voice was smooth and pleasing. He looked at me closely, then said to Mrs. O'Hara, "Do you not have a balm for her lips? They are so terribly cracked and dry."

She actually blushed an unappealing beet red which spread up to the roots of her hair that was scraped back relentlessly, as always. I knew why she was embarrassed. We girls had no simple lip balm, but rather an enhancing product we made ourselves. At least once a month, we would scrape some paraffin wax from a candle into an old saucepan, along with beeswax, lard and beet root to give it a red colour, to add to our allure.

When Mrs. O'Hara only nodded, Doctor Forsythe said, "Well, fetch it, woman!"

She did so and rubbed the gaudy mixture carefully and even tenderly on my lips. I can only imagine what a sight I appeared, disheveled, bruised and in great pain, with painted beet-red lips. But at that moment, I hardly cared, and Mrs. O'Hara's ministrations were soothing. Dr. Forsythe poked and prodded me gently, and said,

"She's got a number of broken ribs, and probably a concussion. Plenty of fluids, plenty of rest, and keep her away from that detective if you can!" He gathered up his black medical bag and marched out the door, his back ramrod straight.

I fell into a fitful sleep to be awakened by a slamming door. I heard heavy footsteps climbing the stairs, and Detective Craig came to my bed and sat down. The four-poster swayed with his weight, the bedsprings groaned, and the jarring hurt parts of my body I hadn't known existed. I hoped the chamber pot had been tucked discreetly away. Of course, ordinarily a man would never enter a lady's bedroom, but I suppose I no longer was considered a lady.

"Really, Detective…" Mrs. O'Hara began.

"So, what's the matter with this filly?" His breath smelled like dead fish, his teeth blackened. I noted that a couple of them were missing. "Are you playing sick to escape answering my questions?" He poked me non-too-gently in the ribs. I screamed in pain.

"Stop at once!" Mrs. O'Hara shouted.

Detective Craig leaped from my bed and slapped her hard, once on each cheek. I could see tears in her brown eyes, but our keeper was made of steel. She did not make a sound, merely drew herself to her full height and glared at him.

"Now…" and Detective Craig set himself down once more with a thud on my bed, "you need to tell me why the murder weapon, the knife, was found in your bedroom door Miss Evans. Do you keep it there to keep your customers in line?"

Here he chuckled at his own cleverness, then began picking at his teeth. I wished I had the knife then and there to plunge into his porcine belly, which spilled over his belt as he sat on *my* bed, fat thighs spread comfortably. I lowered my eyes so he could not see my fury. I did not want to further antagonize him as I was still in agony from the first beating.

"I truly do not know how the knife came to be stuck in my door. I think it must be one of our kitchen knives…"

He banged his fist on my bed and my stomach lurched with dread as I bounced a little.

"Of course, it is a kitchen knife! How did it end up in your bedroom door? Did you kill the Reverend?"

"Me?" His shouting had made my head pound harder. I could barely think. "I have never seen Reverend Crudden before in my life! I'm Anglican!"

"You filthy harlot." His voice was so loud that the picture on the wall vibrated. Specks of spittle flew out of his open mouth, some landing on my face. I dared not wipe them off. I felt sore and weak, but some of my fighting spirit flashed back.

"I know what I am. But that does not change the fact that until today, I had no idea the Reverend even existed."

"Your sort doesn't attend church?" His voice was grudging.

"Well, generally, we are not very welcome in any kind of church." My calmness seemed to disconcert him.

"Can you prove that you didn't know him?"

"Of course not!" I raised one eyebrow.

"Don't be uppity with me, Miss. I know what you are."

"Everyone knows who and what I am! I still have never seen the Reverend alive. He was not one of my men. As far as the knife…I honestly do not know why it was in my door."

I was exhausted, and lay back on the pillow, distressed to show any weakness in front of this detestable oaf. But he was quiet now, even downcast; he seemed to have run out of steam.

"Don't leave Owen Sound. I will need to question you again."

"I can barely get out of bed thanks to you. I can't leave."

I flinched as Detective Craig clenched his meaty fist, but he restrained himself. He expressed his rage by bending over my bed, and pinching me so hard in a very tender, intimate area. My eyes teared up but I swallowed my pain, determined that he not see any further humiliation. He laughed, and I turned to look at him. He picked his nose deliberately, and flicked the result at my bed, then departed.

I turned to the wall and huddled into the extra quilt Mrs. O'Hara had brought me. The tears rose, but so did a bitter determination to never allow myself to be so humiliated again. I was grateful that one of the girls or perhaps Mrs. O'Hara herself had had the foresight to hide Jack while Detective Craig interrogated me. I could only imagine the sick joy it would give him to torment my beloved pet while I lay prone and helpless before him.

The man is beneath contempt I muttered over and over, but really, the only contempt I felt was for myself.

Mrs. O'Hara moved closer. She sat down gently on my bed, her weight barely registering. She was always tightly corseted but now she seemed to droop a little.

"Doctor Forsythe says you will recover fully. You have at least one, perhaps as many as three broken ribs. No corsets for you for at least six weeks."

I was shocked. Every decent woman wore a corset as a matter of course, to support her spine and internal organs, not to mention the flattering effect it had on one's figure. I knew that I could no longer be considered a decent woman, but the loss of my sculpted waist was painful to contemplate.

"Is that acceptable to you Mrs. O'Hara?" I felt little, and I sounded little.

"You are a lovely girl with or without a corset Charlotte."

Her head turned sharply to the door, then I heard it too, a shrill scream. Mrs. O'Hara rushed from the room and I lay back in frustration, straining to hear what was happening down the hall.

Long minutes passed, then Rose came hurrying in, her hairpins askew, her usually neat attire hanging awry, as if she had been pulling at her dress.

"He pushed Matilda, hard, and she fell and hit her head on her dresser. Her forehead is bleeding and she fainted!"

I forced myself to shut my mouth.

"Detective Craig tried to force a confession out of her. He decided as she admitted to knowing Reverend Crudden that she's the killer," Rose explained.

"How did she know him? Why did he think she had killed him?" I asked.

"She had a terrible time when her mother died. Her mother was white, very poor, and had never attended church in Owen Sound. She was too busy living from day to day, probably didn't have nice enough clothes to wear, and no money to put on the collection plate. Besides, folk would look down at their noses at her, having an Indian husband. But she had been raised as a devout Calvinist in the Old Country, and never lost her faith. After she died, Matilda begged Reverend Crudden to give her Ma a Christian funeral and to bury her in consecrated land. He refused because she had not attended his church. Matilda cursed him then."

"How and where, did Matilda end up burying her Ma?" I was incensed at clergyman's lack of Christian compassion.

"She was that desperate. She went from church to church, until finally the Methodist minister, Reverend Blythe, took pity and buried her in a quiet, decent service in the churchyard. She was laid to rest in the far corner of the Methodist cemetery, backing onto a field. It's close to the small town of Tara, I don't know if you know it? I accompanied Matilda, and he did his best to make the funeral as reverent and respectable as he would have done for his richest parishioner. Indeed, a few church members even complained at the time and trouble he lavished on a pauper. But Reverend Blythe quoted Jesus: *Verily I say unto you, Inasmuch as ye have done it unto one of the least of these my brethren, ye have done it unto me.* The most vocal protester, Mrs. Hendricks, stopped complaining but she skewered him with a look. He pretended not to notice." Rose smiled at the memory.

"How did Detective Craig find out about this?" I asked her. She just looked at me, and comprehension dawned.

"Vicky." It was not a question. Rose just nodded her head. What was there to say?

Matilda staggered into my bedroom, which was becoming hot and stuffy. Her right eye was swollen and puffy, and her nose was bleeding. Mrs. O'Hara caught her when she stumbled, supported her weight, then settled her into bed with me.

"No sense getting blood on more than one set of sheets," said Mrs. O'Hara.

***

Matilda, Jack and I rested for a long while in my crowded bed. Matilda snored softly, and I noticed that her forehead was still bleeding a little. I asked Rose for an old towel, and I cleaned her as gently as I could. Rose propped the window open slightly, and we could hear the odd bird chirp, horses clopping on the mud street below, and peddlers shouting out, trying to sell their wares. As much as I wished for oblivion, sleep escaped me.

The detective forbore from assaulting any more women, and within a couple of hours, he was ready to depart. He entered my room on his way out, buttoning his coat. I was not quick enough to hide Jack, who was resting contentedly on the bed between Matilda and me, licking his paws. I flinched when the brute approached, fearing the pain he would inflict on my sweet pet. I was amazed when he simply scratched Jack behind his soft ears, and gave his rump a gentle pat.

"If you girls can think of anything at all to help me solve this murder, it will be best for all of us. Me included."

"Yes sir," Matilda mumbled. We were both tense, waiting for him to thump us again. He gave Jack one last surprisingly gentle rub behind the ears, then stomped away, slamming the door behind him.

Matilda and I looked at each other in amazement while an oblivious Jack continued to carefully groom his paws and nether regions. The noise filtering in the window intensified. There seemed to be a commotion of sorts at the front door. We looked at each other in frustration. What was going on? I heard Mrs. O'Hara's shrill voice but couldn't make out the words. A man yelled back. "Begone to you," she screamed. A wagon pulled away.

About five minutes later, Mrs. O'Hara came into my room and sank onto the bed with a sigh. Her hair was escaping from her usual tight bun, and deep lines scored her face, which seemed paler than usual. She was breathing heavily, and her face was flushed dark, unbecoming.

"The coroner has removed the body. The reporter from the *Owen Sound Times* is lurking outside. We will be the talk of the town."

"Maybe the scandal will attract more business." I tried to be hopeful.

"No, Charlotte. Men will be afraid, and wives and mothers will be reminded of the very existence of houses such as ours. Women will pay extra close attention to men's comings and goings."

Her words proved prophetic. Business dropped off precipitously for the next few days. I was relieved, as it gave my corset-free body a chance to heal. However, in a trickle, men began to return, some sheepish, others openly curious. "Where was the Reverend's body found?" More than one man asked me that. One gentleman spent his entire hour with me entirely clothed, demanding every detail of the murder I could remember.

"Will you show me where the body was found. Is the floor still bloodstained?" he asked finally. I was fed up, and snapped, "Mrs. O'Hara would never allow guests in the basement. Besides, your hour is up." I couldn't wait to see him go.

The fact that a man of the cloth was found stabbed to death in a house of ill-repute proved to be titillating in the extreme. We had many middle-aged matrons out for an afternoon walk stalk by, tut-tutting in delicious, excited disdain. Mrs. O'Hara kept the curtains in the front window closed.

Our house filled a real need in the little city, and within a fortnight, she was pleasantly surprised at how her business bounced back. Damone returned with no explanation as to where he had gone, and I came upon the keeper one evening in the parlor humming rather tunelessly to his exquisite piano playing.

If Damone had been born white, he'd be playing to audiences in Toronto, Montreal, Chicago and maybe even New York City. Carnegie Hall... As it was, we were treated to music that seemed to trip from his slender fingers as they flashed up and down the keys. I don't remember ever hearing him hit a sour note.

Detective Craig returned often, appearing more and more anxious as the days passed with no arrest in sight. His cheeks seemed pinker and were sprinkled liberally with broken veins. He'd lost a button on the shirt that strained over the belly that seemed to have grown in girth from even the previous week. I looked in fascination at the dark hairs poking through the hole. His nose was bulbous and red, and his breath stank of old, digesting alcohol. I couldn't stand the smell of him but gritted my teeth and smiled. I took a deep breath and my still healing ribs stabbed. My eyes teared up but still I smiled.

"You dollymops are holding out on me." His eyes darted back and forth at us girls, then he plopped down on the most comfortable sofa in the parlour.

"What about the Reverend's wife?" Felicity asked. She picked at her fingernails and looked down, smoothing her dress.

"Yes, why don't you pursue her?" I said. "If the good minister was betraying his marriage vows, his wife would have a strong motive to rid himself of her husband. It'd be the only way she could get free of him."

"Do you really think I haven't already been looking into this?" Detective Craig's tone was scathing. "I thought of that a long time ago, and I'm making inquiries in Toronto." His face was getting flushed and he had large sweat stains on his shirt, although the house was cool.

"Why Toronto?" I asked.

"None of your God-damned business!" he roared. He raised his fist, and I cowered into the sofa.

"Would you like some tea and biscuits?" Mrs. O'Hara motioned to me to fetch them from the kitchen. We employed a local lady who performed most of the heavy chores each morning, scrubbing and blacking the woodstove, sweeping and cleaning and emptying the slops, but after mid-morning, we girls fended for ourselves.

"Would you like a shot of brandy as well?" I offered.

The detective made a show of considering the offer. It was not quite 11 AM.

"Yeah, make it a double."

I moved with caution towards Mrs. O'Hara. My ribs were healing, but I avoided sharp motions. Mrs. O'Hara could trust me with the keys to her liquor cabinet as I remained steadfast in my determination not to drink spirits. She passed me the key, unhooking it from her belt.

When I returned, the detective accepted the refreshments without a word. He polished off the brandy in one gulp, ate the four generously sized shortbread cookies, and wiped his mouth on the back of his hand, disregarding the napkin I had supplied.

"Detective Craig has informed us that his superior officer, Inspector Conall McLaughlin, will be taking over the inquiry into the Reverend Crudden's death." Mrs. O'Hara looked at me, her black eyes boring into mine. *Keep silent.* Her lips moved almost imperceptibly.

I can't show how happy this makes me. I tried to keep my delight from leaking out of my very pores.

"My boss has returned from Toronto where he was training," said the detective. He sounded morose.

"What was he training for?" I asked.

"The latest in fingermark identification, and how to file fingermarks so we can look them up and match them to criminals quickly. It's pretty complicated. Girls like you wouldn't understand."

Detective Craig wiped his nose on his sleeve. He looked defeated, and he sat slumped, staring at his black socks. One sock had a large hole. His big toe brazenly poked through, and I stared in fascination at a tuft of coarse hair and a yellowed toenail that badly needed clipping.

"Do you have a wife, Detective?" I swallowed, then wished that I could eat my words.

He scowled, but his anger had been blanketed by his obvious depression.

"I was married, but my wife left me and returned to Toronto to live with her parents. My son is with her. What business is it of yours?"

His snarl seemed to re-energize him, and the sofa vibrated as he lurched around to face me.

"None at all. I just noticed your sock has a hole in it. I can darn it for you, if you like."

Everyone in the room seemed to catch their breath, waiting for his reaction. Why I would feel any kind of compassion for the brute who had broken my ribs was beyond me, but compassion I felt.

The detective slowly removed his sock. I fetched my sewing kit, moving carefully. The sock was nearly stiff with dried sweat and the old, dirty wool emitted a pungent, musty smell. However, I was quick and efficient at darning after all of those never-ending evenings on the farm spent honing those skills.

My mind slid from mending to the farm, to Thomas, and I realized that it had been nearly a month since I had visited him. He was nine months old now, and his hair was plentiful and a rich brown. He looked dark and exotic, with almond eyes almost exactly like Tony's. He had my pert chin, and his hair curled in ringlets like mine. Jane kept it long, and for this I was grateful.

As I finished repairing the sock, I vowed to make the trek to the farm to visit the next day. I was healthy enough to manage the distance now. Although I had been unable to work my usual long hours since my beating, I still had a healthy savings in the bank from my earnings from the past six months. My dream of lifting myself from my situation and gaining admission to the University of Toronto and one day taking over the apothecary was not entirely dead. That reminded me – I should write to Daddy. His last letter had been full of unwanted details of his wedding trip with Lavinia to Montreal. I had torn it up and burnt it.

I put thoughts of my fractured family aside, and handed Detective Craig the still smelly, but now whole sock. He bent over clumsily to put it on, and I noticed how thin his foot looked in comparison to his swollen belly. Another button looked ready to pop, *I may have to sew that on too.*

He hits and bullies people because he doesn't know any other way to do his job. Look at the mess I've made of my life. Who am I to judge? He's still a brute though. I did not like the detective any better, but I disliked him a little less.

"When does Inspector McLaughlin take over?" Mrs. O'Hara asked.

"Next Monday. Gimme another shot of brandy."

This time Rose got up swiftly and poured him another generous measure. The detective drank it greedily, then sat the sweating glass down on Mrs. O'Hara's finest cherry table. The glass rocked a little and I hoped it wouldn't spill. Mrs. O'Hara grabbed a coaster, and wiped the table with a swipe of her black serge skirt. Her skin was white.

Detective Craig drank until he was almost incoherent as he tried to probe into the murder. He asked the same old questions and received the same old answers. None of us had any new information to tell him. Despite his clear frustration, his previous violence seemed to have evaporated into a cloud of defeat. When he had finally polished off the brandy bottle, he shifted on the sofa. The springs made a loud creaking noise.

"More brandy." I had to strain to understand what he said.

"I'm sorry Detective, but we have no more." Mrs. O'Hara's lip curled, but she kept her voice neutral. "Perhaps you'll be so good to walk Detective Craig home, Rose. It appears he's feeling a little under the weather."

"Yes," Rose agreed. The police had the power to shut establishments such as ours down, and their goodwill was of paramount importance.

"Charlotte…walks….me home."

"Are your injuries healed enough Charlotte?" asked Mrs. O'Hara.

"Yes Ma'am. The fresh air will be good for me." Escorting a brutish, drunk officer of the law was the very last thing on earth I wanted to do. But he could close us down.

Rose steadied him and kept him from falling while darting back and forth to avoid his wandering hands. He was trying to pinch her. I put on my cloak and bonnet. Jack sat at the door, looking eager.

"No," I said, and he slunk to his bed.

I took the detective's arm, which Rose relinquished with alacrity, and he leaned heavily on me. His weight was a real burden, and his breath was even worse. We made our way slowly. He made a few advances towards me which I tolerated without a word. Once he pinched my cheek so hard it brought tears to my eyes, but I refused to give him the satisfaction of taking any notice. We made slow progress and passed over the bridge by the harbour. He stopped, leaned over, holding onto the railing and was sick.

I turned away, leaving him to it, and stared out over the gleaming water. It was dark, and chunks of ice floated haphazardly on the surface. The water was never the same two days in a row, and some days, it looked different by the hour. The sight of it lifted my spirits. I thought of Mamma's description of sea smoke on the Grand River, and realized the water was a comfort and joy to her as well. I felt a closeness to her I'd not felt for a long time.

When Detective Craig was finished, I took his arm once more. Not a word passed between us. I deposited him in the front room of his boarding house on 2nd Avenue West. He didn't meet my eyes, but mumbled a "thank you," then clumped up the stairs to his bedroom, holding on heavily to the railing. The house smelled of boiled cabbage and stale human sweat; I couldn't leave fast enough.

I walked home with heavy steps. My ribs throbbed, and I was unable to forget the smell of alcohol, which seemed to permeate my very clothes. It was that smell that I especially hated about my new way of life – intimacy with men who had been cooped up on a ship on the Great Lakes for months on end, drinking themselves stupid at one of the numerous taverns that Owen Sound had to offer, then arriving at our house for a different kind of solace. As a ship came into harbour, we girls would hear the deep throb of its horn, then we'd quickly clean house, and get ready to receive the excited sailors, relieved to be on dry land again, appetites lusty for all sorts of physical pleasures. Often Mrs. O'Hara would stand on the widow's walk, looking over the bay, binoculars in hand, waiting.

I thought of my Daddy and hoped Lavinia would be better equipped to wean him off his love affair with the bottle than I had. As I turned back onto 3rd Avenue East, I couldn't stop thinking of Thomas. I resolved to go to the bank bright and early to withdraw money to give Jane and Bart to help with his care. They regarded him as their own son and were fully prepared to support him, but he was mine as well, and I was resolved that he should lack for nothing. I wanted Jane and Bart to be able to purchase good quality clothes, toys and eventually education that the hardscrabble life on a farm could not provide.

***

I awoke first thing the next day. I scrubbed myself vigorously at my washbasin. It was similar to Mamma's, which I cherished in my bedroom at home in Galt. The china wasn't as fine as Mamma's, but the roses were the same delicate shade of pink. I sighed, remembering the countless times she had washed her face as I looked on. I brushed my hair until it gleamed, then fastened it into a loose chignon.

Jack accompanied me to the farm. It felt wonderful to be free of the house and its atmosphere of excess. I realized that I had exchanged one type of mind numbing prison on the farm for an entirely different, more lucrative one. I could leave at any time, but where would I go? I could not bear to return to the farm, and Jane and Bart patently did not want me. I was well enough known in Owen Sound that any hope for a respectable life in town was gone. If I were to take Thomas back to Galt, the secret that forced me leave in the first place would be out in the open. I shuddered to think of the shame it would bring to Daddy, and I cringed at the idea of taking up residence with my dear drunk father and the unknown Lavinia.

I could see no way out, but still the walk in the open countryside lifted my spirits. Jack scampered ahead, also rejoicing in the brisk air and freedom from the house. Poor Jack had seen too much, but his spirit, unlike mine, remained unburdened.

I knocked on the door of the little farmhouse. Jane's hair was scraped back, and her face was smudged with flour. She did not smile when she saw me. Thomas was on her hip. I held out my arms in joy to see my son but he clung to Jane in alarm. Thinking that he was afraid of my stylish black hat, I carefully removed the hat pins and hung it carefully on a wooden peg just inside the door.

"It's me, Tommy. Your m…"

"Charlotte!" Jane's tone was so harsh that Thomas began to cry. She said quickly, "Look at the nice lady, Thomas. This is your Aunt Charlotte. Say hello."

Thomas was having none of it. He clung even more tightly to Jane and began to whimper. She clutched him closely, stroking his dark curls with an infuriating smugness as she looked at me straight in the eye.

"Thomas does not take kindly to strangers, my dear cousin Charlotte."

"Stranger! How dare you?"

Thomas sensed the tension between us and began to cry in earnest.

"If you have that money you owe us…we need it sorely. Thomas is growing out of his clothes so quickly, and I need to buy him leather shoes the next time I go to town."

"I could have picked them up today."

"You wouldn't know his size." She smiled sweetly, then looked at my reticule.

I wanted to throw it at her. I wanted to stalk out the door without giving her a penny. I swallowed down the red mist that was enveloping me and stared at my baby. He was bigger than the last time I visited. He was clean, his hair neatly combed, and he clearly loved and trusted Jane.

Slowly, I opened my reticule, withdrew the little beaded purse, and counted out a generous sum for Jane. She took it without thanking me, lip curled, large nose wrinkled. I worried that somehow, she had learned how I was making the cash that surely went a long way towards providing for the three of them. The money disappeared into a pocket in her calico dress. I noticed it was frayed at the cuffs.

"I'd like to spend some time with Thomas." I handed her my cloak, not giving her a chance to make excuses.

She scowled, but I was Thomas's birth mother, and I had just handed her ten whole dollars. Thankfully, Daddy had counselled me before I gave birth to make sure the birth certificate named me as Thomas' mother. He had foreseen the bitterness that could ensue from an unorthodox arrangement such as ours, and his advice gave me the option to one day reclaim my son. Silently, I thanked my dear, ineffectual, drunk parent for his occasional wisdom.

"Could I have a cup of tea please? I'm quite chilly. The air has a dampness today…" I was just as sweet as she had been.

I held out my arms for Thomas, and she reluctantly passed him to me. My ribs stabbed. I didn't care at all.

I sat him on the pine floor, which appeared spotless, took off my gloves, and sat down beside him, careless of my skirts.

"See what I brought you!" But Thomas' eyes were on Jack.

"Yes, this is our dear doggie Jack, do you remember him?"

Thomas's face lit up, and I passed him a small bread crust I kept in my pocket.

"Jack loves a treat. Can you ask him to sit, and he will take it from you?"

"Sit." His voice was adorable.

Jack sat down in a flash and presented his paw to a delighted Thomas. He squealed with laughter as he threw the crust to the dog.

I remained seated on the bare floor throughout my visit, sipping my tea absentmindedly, while soaking up the joy of being with my boy.

My tea seemed to vanish, and Jane crossed and re-crossed her legs while knitting in the rocking chair. She cleared her throat.

"Charlotte, I believe it's past Thomas' nap time."

"Surely not yet."

"He usually has his nap just before noon, while I prepare lunch for Bart and the farm hand."

"I can mind Thomas while you deal with the food." I did not want to leave the enchanting being who was my son.

"Charlotte."

I looked at Jane and saw the terror in her grey eyes. We both knew that I could take my son at any time, and she was powerless to stop me. *She loves him, and she gives him a good home. I can't do that, at least not now.* But I knew that if I left him with Bart and Jane much longer, he would never be mine. They were a family, and I was the outsider, no matter my biological status.

My ribs throbbed. I got up slowly and pulled one last small gift from my pocket. It was a tiny wooden locomotive which I had bought from one of my men. He had carved it especially for my son. I bent down, and Thomas squealed once more in delight.

"Goodbye sweet boy," I said quietly, but Thomas was so entranced by his new toy that he didn't notice that I was leaving. I wrapped myself in my cloak, nodded to a smiling Jane, and departed, my faithful Jack skipping ahead, sniffing at the bushes.

***

When I returned to the brothel, it was almost dark. I was surprised that the house was unlit, which signaled that we were not open for business. When I walked in, Rose, Matilda and Felicity came and took my cloak and scarf and led me to the sitting room.

"The new inspector is here," said Felicity. "He came earlier than expected."

"I forgot his name! How did he treat you? Has he hit anyone yet?"

The girls looked at me with compassion. I knew that too often, I still winced when I stood up or made a sudden movement.

"He's very impressive. His name is Conall McLaughlin. He's homely, ugly really, but has a gorgeous accent!" Felicity added. Her eyes glinted and she spoke too fast.

I rose and went to the kitchen, fed Jack who was hungry after our long walk. I fixed a pot of tea and prepared a tray of simple roast-beef sandwiches and biscuits to share with the other girls. We chatted amongst ourselves, and agreed that it was bad for business, this changing of police detectives, which necessitated closing the house. We could not be interviewed by the police and carry on working. Mrs. O'Hara had been so careful to cultivate a friendly and mutually advantageous relationship with the constabulary. Hopefully Inspector McLaughlin would continue the arrangement.

The keeper joined us, smoothing her skirts. She had flushed cheeks and was panting slightly. "Inspector McLaughlin wants to see you next, Charlotte."

"Why me?" I looked at my freshly poured cup of tea. I was thirsty after my long walk home from the farm and wanted to rest.

"Who discovered the body? Bring your tea with you and offer a cup to the inspector as well. Go now." Her tone was sharp. I moved as quickly as I could, carrying the tea pot and cups on a tray. I walked through the door and stumbled, my heel catching in the red plush carpet. I clutched the tray, steadying myself.

The new policeman was one of the least attractive men I had ever seen. *He's clean and well- groomed though.* His hair was bright red, bristly, and just beginning to go grey. He had a deeply receding hairline, which made the vibrant ginger more startling. His dark blue eyes were deep-set. His nose had been clearly broken, re-broken, and perhaps broken again, and was twisted and at the same time flattened against his face. *How does he breathe?* Deep lines beside his eyes and scored around his mouth betrayed that he was well into his fourth decade. To top off his almost ridiculous face, he had protruding ears.

He reclined in our prized brown velvet chair, and had removed the antimacassars from the arms, folded them neatly, and placed them on a nearby table. He'd moved the chair close to the woodstove, and his cheeks were flushed a light pink. His suit jacket was removed and also folded neatly, placed on a stool. He had rolled up his shirt sleeves. On his muscular forearm, I was gobsmacked to note that he sported a tattoo.

Of course, I was familiar with the tattoos that many sailors had on display. Anchors were tediously popular. But this inking was far removed from the simple anchor. It was beautifully crafted, composed of a heart, surrounded by two hands. It surprised me that a high-ranking policeman would have a tattoo and be so casual about displaying it. I tamped down my curiosity and set the tray down with great care. Jack had followed me; I motioned for him to sit.

"Sit down." His voice was deep, a little husky, with a soft lilt. He seemed not unkind. He kept his eyes strictly on mine. They didn't stray once to my décolletage. His were a vibrant blue, the colour of the sky, of the lake…*Careful Charlotte.*

I set the tea tray down, then took a seat in an uncomfortable wooden chair, crossing my legs primly at the ankle.

"I am Detective Inspector Conall McLaughlin." He inclined his head.

"I'm Charlotte Evans. May I pour you a cup of tea?"

"Yes, thank you."

I reached for the teapot. "You're not Scottish!" I blurted, so accustomed was I to the soft burr which was so common in Galt.

He raised one eyebrow. His nose looked even more crooked. "No, I'm from Ireland."

"Are you Catholic?"

"I don't think that is any of your business, Miss Evans."

"No, of course not. I'm sorry. I'm too impetuous." I felt my cheeks flame and my hand trembled as I took a sip of tea. It was piping hot and scalded the roof of my mouth, but I forced myself to swallow as if it did not hurt at all. Inspector McLaughlin frowned.

"Are you impetuous enough to kill?"

"No! Of course not."

"How well did you know the Reverend Crudden?"

"I did not know him at all. The first time I ever saw him was when he was lying in the hall, dead."

"Can you prove that?"

"How can I be expected to prove that I did not know him? I certainly never attended his church."

"I suppose it is quite impossible to prove. If you are to be believed, that is."

"What do you mean by that? Because I am in this line of work, I have no finer feelings, no honour, no spiritual life? You don't know me at all, Sir, and I'll thank you to remember that. It may surprise you that it was a member of your police force who beat me and gave me cracked ribs. You have no reason to act superior to me." I motioned for Jack to move closer to me, and he obliged. I fondled his soft, silky ears. He nuzzled my hand, his cold wet nose comforting.

"What happened?" His eyes crinkled a little, and his mouth set in a hard line.

I noted how he had fine laughter lines embracing either side of his mouth. *He really is homely, but strangely appealing…be careful.*

I told Inspector McLaughlin about Detective Craig's interrogation techniques. His face tightened and his eyes narrowed.

"Were you attended by a doctor? How can I be sure this is true?"

"Yes. Mrs. O'Hara called Doctor Forsythe to care for my injuries. When I came to, he was tending to me."

"What do you mean, 'came to?' He beat you unconscious?" His voice was neutral, but his eyebrow twitched.

"Yes, I was unconscious a few minutes."

"I'll speak to Mrs. O'Hara! I'm warning you. I may very well interview the doctor."

"You do that." I met his eyes without flinching, and he looked away first.

***

He questioned me in great detail about the knife, how it came to be embedded in my bedroom door, and about my discovery of the body. "Why didn't you call immediately for a doctor?" he asked.

"I had knelt down and felt for his pulse. There was none."

"How did you know to do that?" His tone was sharp.

"My father is an apothecary. I have a fair amount of medical knowledge. I know things which could surprise you."

I was happy that he did not try to turn this into an ugly double entendre. He raised his eyebrows, then gazed at me for a long moment, his blue eyes unwavering.

"If your father owns an apothecary…"

"Why am I working in a brothel?" His gentleness made me ashamed, and I tried to brazen it out. "How could it possibly be any of your business?"

Once again, he looked away.

"Charlotte. Right now, I don't know what information is and is not of importance to this murder, but I need to learn as much of the background of each person concerned, so I can eliminate the innocent parties."

This time, it was I who looked away. Then, to my horror, I listened to myself as the pain of my mother's death, Tony's flight to Italy, and the baby whom I so desperately did not want, but could not help myself loving, tumbled from my lips. For good measure, I also told him about my father's alcoholism and re-marriage to the still unknown Lavinia.

He listened quietly, only asking for the odd clarification or explanation. When I finished, I felt drained, and mortified that I had so bared my soul to a man, and to a policeman at that. *I should know better, especially after the beating I suffered at Detective Craig's hands.* What was it about Inspector McLaughlin that caused me to throw caution to the wind? *Prostitution is a criminal, moral sin. It offends all sensibilities. I am foul.*

But Conall McLaughlin did not appear disgusted. He only looked sad. The lines on his face were still more prominent, and his skin seemed to droop.

"What do you really want to do with the rest of your life?" he asked. I sighed and looked down.

"You know, Charlotte, women in your line of work typically do not live very long. They lose their looks, turn to alcohol or to other stimulants such as laudanum or cocaine, and become ever more desperate. I've seen it time and time again. If you want to see Thomas grow up, you will need to leave this house and take up more wholesome employment. What do you really want to do?"

"Become a chemist like Daddy." My answer surprised both of us. He looked at me long and hard.

"How would you accomplish this?"

"I'd have to return to Galt to complete my final year of school. Then I could apply to the University of Toronto."

"Would they accept a woman?"

"Daddy says they might. He still has a few colleagues who teach at the university. Most don't know about his drinking problem."

Inspector McLaughlin checked his pocket watch, and then said more formally,

"I advise you to concentrate on that ambitious goal, Miss Evans, and extricate yourself from the lifestyle you are now caught up in. Now, I need to speak to Damone. Where might I find him?"

I swallowed. I had had so much on my mind lately that I had barely spared a thought for Damone, even though we'd been close. We had not shared a meal together since before the Reverend Crudden's body was discovered, and I had passed him in the hall only a couple of times since I recovered from my beating.

I told Inspector McLaughlin this, and he frowned. "The other ladies have said much the same. No one has seen much of him since the Reverend's murder. I'm afraid it doesn't look good. Do you know of his family?"

My stomach clenched, but I judged truth was the best and only option. I was sure my friend had nothing to hide, and I did not want to appear to be shielding him by withholding information. Besides, I was certain the inspector could easily track down Damone's mother.

"Damone's mother is Mrs. Barrett. She escaped from the Confederate States on the Underground Railway when she was a young girl." I was very proud of my adopted town's role in the liberation of Negros fleeing slavery.

Inspector McLaughlin smiled. His homely face transformed.

"Indeed. Where does Mrs. Barrett live?"

"She has a small flat on 7th Avenue East, close to the Little Zion Church. Damone took me there one day to visit, and Mrs. Barrett fed me scones. They were delicious."

"I need to speak to him."

"Well, I am perfectly certain that he did not commit murder! He is a pianist. If he were white, he could have had a real career in music. As it is, he is stuck here. He's lucky that Mrs. O'Hara treats him exactly as if he were white. Most keepers wouldn't. Like I said, he's no murderer." My words were lame, and I knew it.

"She's the soul of kindness," he said drily. "Be that as it may, if and when you see Damone, send him to the police station immediately. I expect to be notified."

His soft Irish lilt no longer seemed so appealing.

"Fine. May I leave now?"

"You are a suspect in this inquiry. You can go about your affairs, but you need my permission to leave Owen Sound," he said.

Did I detect a sneer? I looked carefully into his eyes, but they were merely bland and blue.

I rose to my feet and winced slightly, clutching my still aching ribs.

"I will speak to Detective Craig about his violence towards you. How much do you weigh?"

"I beg your pardon?" I asked.

"I want to make an official report, to put on his police record of employment," he said patiently. "It would help if I could note your height and weight to make it clear that you were in no way a physical threat to him." He took out his notebook.

"If you talk to him, he'll know that I squealed. He'll come back for me!"

"I'll make certain he never touches you again, Miss Evans. You have my word." I had no choice but to accept it. I mumbled my height and weight.

He marked this down in his notebook.

"Good day Miss Evans."

"Good day Inspector."

He bent down and fondled Jack's ears. Jack gave a satisfied little grunt, and wagged his tail happily.

He departed, and I sank down on the couch. The image of the marbled white body flashed back to me. I could swear I smelled the sweet, cloying, rotting flesh. I batted away an imaginary fly. The air felt cold and clammy, and I huddled into my shawl, and Jack.

***

After what seemed like a long time, I retreated to my room. Although I worked for part of the evening, my mind was not on the men. I thought over and over about Inspector McLaughlin's warning that women in my line of work did not live long. I knew in my heart he was right. I could almost feel Mamma's sorrowful presence at my shoulder, her grief and shame at what I had become.

I did not know if Daddy was aware of my shame. *Come home,* I heard his voice in my head, and knew that even if he did find out about my descent to prostitution, he would welcome me back. He'd be angry, and disappointed, but I was his beloved, only child. But Lavinia! And what about Thomas? How could I leave him and live a day's journey away?

Wrestling with my problems made me extremely pre-occupied, and the men paying for my services received only rote attention. Normally, I liked to establish a connection beyond the purely physical and listened patiently and asked questions as they told me about life at sea, their mothers, sweethearts, and too often, their wives. I believed it was my patience and listening skills, as much or more than my physical charms, that made me much sought after in Mrs. O'Hara's establishment. But tonight, I did not pay them much heed at all.

Certainly, I earned a very steady, gratifying income. But at what cost? I could no longer bear to look at myself in the mirror. I couldn't look into my own eyes. I spent long minutes scrubbing myself in my washbasin, but I could never seem to expunge the smell and taste of the men I'd been with.

Mrs. O'Hara had provided me with crude contraceptives when I first entered her establishment. But I knew they were far from fail-proof, and each month, I dreaded pregnancy. I had been careful, and very fortunate so far, but I knew it was only a matter of time before I would fall pregnant or become ill with disease. I had been so lucky to this point! After my last sailor finally left, for once I forced myself to meet my own eyes in the mirror. They were completely the same and yet utterly different since those carefree Galt days. I looked haunted.

I missed Daddy. I lay down on my bed, first liberating my old Teddy Bear from its box under the bed, and I was awake, dry eyed for much of the night, with Jack curled into my legs. Finally, I slept.

It was late the following morning when I awoke to Jack's soft whining. I needed to take him outside. I dragged myself out of bed, quickly washed my face, and left my bedroom. Mrs. O'Hara was in the kitchen, and she looked at me inquiringly as I moved to pull on my boots and don my cloak. *She is greedy, but she also is truly kind, and cares about her girls.* People never ceased to amaze me with their complexity.

"I'm going to take Jack for a walk," I told her. "Inspector McLaughlin wants to speak to Damone. I'll see if he's at his mother's home."

"Yes, the inspector told me that too," she replied. "Have you seen Damone?"

"No, not for a few days. Have you?" I asked rather boldly.

Mrs. O'Hara frowned, the lines on her forehead deeply scored.

"No, and I blame myself. I worked so hard at keeping the establishment up and running following that wretched man's death. I didn't speak properly to Damone. Of course, you were injured, and I was preoccupied with you. Damone took care of walking Jack when you were recuperating, you know."

I didn't know and hadn't thought to ask.

Jack whined softly once more, and I hustled out the door. I walked to the harbour as usual, and again I immersed myself in the hurly burly of ships loading and unloading cargo and passengers. The sun danced on the water, the sparkling, undulating waves bringing forth a swelling of pure joy in me.

I said a quick prayer, as I always did, for Thomas' continued health and well-being, then continued my walk to Mrs. Barrett's rooming house. It was built of a rough-hewn pine board. It had not been painted. I knew from Damone that the roof leaked, and Mrs. Barrett was forced to scurry around with buckets when it rained. The walkway was littered with rotting leaves and twigs.

I picked my way up the rickety, slippery stairs. The porch was cluttered with an ancient sofa and a couple of chairs from previous tenants that were suitable only for the garbage dump.

Mrs. Barrett's ne'er-do-well husband was in Nova Scotia. She could not afford better accommodation than this. *Her poverty is most likely the reason that Damone began working for Mrs. O'Hara in the first place.* He carefully divided his not inconsiderable earnings each month in two, bringing one-half to his mother to help provide for his younger sister. Mrs. Barrett worked doing laundry and as a general charlady for the wealthy folks who lived in the gracious neighbourhood close to Harrison Park. I picked my way past a cracked toboggan, a rusting bicycle, and a decayed and chipped garden gnome, missing an arm and half a leg.

I tapped on the door and waited several long moments, then it opened a crack. One big brown eye peered out.

"Oh, it's you." Mrs. Barrett opened the door wider, but did not invite me in.

"I need to speak to you about Damone. May I please come in?"

"Suppose so. Does that dog bite?" Jack wagged his tail at her, and I sensed that her gruffness hid a soft heart, at least where dogs were concerned.

"No, of course not. He's very gentle with children and loves ladies. He's not so keen on men though."

"No men here. Well, come in and don't let anymore cold air in! My rooms are freezing enough as it is," she said. Her voice was deep and full-bodied. I stepped in and removed my boots and cloak. She was right, the temperature inside the house was bitter, barely warmer than the air outside. I could see my breath. On second thought, I put my cloak back on, grateful for its warmth.

Mrs. Barrett looked at me a bit contemptuously. She wore a simple brown flannel dress, no shawl or sweater to keep her warm. *She's big and a bit chubby and has lots of insulation from the cold.*

"There is a new policeman in charge of the investigation into Reverend Crudden's death. His name is Inspector McLaughlin, and he needs to speak to Damone."

"Why you telling me this?" Her eyes narrowed.

"Because I'm worried about Damone, and I didn't want the inspector to surprise you or him. Besides, I told Inspector McLaughlin I would pass along the message. I do care about Damone, you know. Did the police come here?"

She nodded. "I didn't answer the door."

She looked down, giving nothing away. Just then, Damone's little sister walked into the room. Her shoulders were hunched, and she looked at the floor. She was small, looked no more than five years old, although I knew from Damone that she was in fact six and would begin school next year. She was dressed in a thin shift, which was covered by a beige, misshapen wool cardigan several sizes too big for her. She sucked her thumb solemnly and carried a grubby cloth doll that smiled up at me with red painted lips. The doll had braided hair made of yellow yarn.

Jack's tail wagged so fast it was a blur at the sight of the little girl. He strained on his leash, and I had to hold him tightly. Her eyes widened.

"She's welcome to pat him. He's very good with children." Thomas had pulled his tail too often, and Jack never even growled. Mrs. Barrett nodded.

"What's your name?" I asked the child gently. Her eyes were huge and soulful looking. She had thick, long eyelashes which curved delicately at the tips. She was beautiful.

"Trinity."

"What a lovely name." I climbed off the chair and plumped myself down on the plain pine floor. Jack rolled over for a belly rub, wriggling in ecstasy at the attention. Trinity squealed and clambered to sit beside us. She patted Jack and played with him for a long while, then, without asking, scooted closer and sat on my knee. We did not speak, but I held her. I felt her warmth, a grace.

Mrs. Barrett watched us. Finally, she said, "Trinity, you need to let Miss Evans up off the floor. Go now."

I was disconcerted by the no-nonsense tone, but when I looked at her, her eyes were crinkling, and she was beaming.

Trinity was not intimidated by her mother. She gave her a cheeky grin, then skipped to the other room, without argument.

Mrs. Barrett offered me tea. I accepted, and she bustled about stoking the woodstove with fresh firewood, filled the kettle, and prepared our tea. At last, she sat down opposite me at the worn pine table. One of the legs was shorter than the other, and the tea splashed in the cup when I bumped my foot against the table leg. I moved my chair back as discreetly as I could. I was wearing a dark grey frock and did not want to have a tea stain down its silk front.

I looked up and was surprised to see that Mrs. Barrett's hands were trembling. I took them in mine.

"What's wrong?" I asked her. I kept my voice soft and reached to squeeze her hand. She snatched it away, but then relented, and entwined her fingers in mine. Brown and white interlaced, hers calloused, stubby, and work worn, mine slender and soft.

"I think the police are going to charge Damone," said Mrs. Barrett.

"I beg your pardon?" I knew she realized full well that Mrs. O'Hara's establishment was in fact a brothel. Was she worried about Damone being charged with indecency? Sodomy?

"I think they're gonna try and pin the murder on him."

I pulled my hands away and clutched my throat. Jack sensed my upset, rose, and nudged my leg. I scooped him onto my lap and held him.

"You're squeezin' your dog. You're hurting him. Let him go," said Mrs. Barrett

I relaxed my grip but didn't put him down. Jack was the only living being in my life who had never disappointed me. I needed him always, and now.

"Why do you suspect that Damone will be charged with the Reverend's murder?" I asked. This was my fear as well, but I didn't want to add to her worry.

"Did you never wonder why a healthy, good looking young man with his life ahead of him would end up working in a brothel? My son's a talented piano player." Her voice was raspy.

"I assumed he needed to make a decent amount of money. I thought he helped you."

"He could have worked at the ship yard or felling trees. There are almost as many opportunities for us black folk here in Owen Sound as for you white people. Come on, Charlotte, think, girl."

"I can't think. I have no idea what you're talking about."

"He was *used*." She hissed at me now, and flecks of spittle splashed against my face.

"Used? In what way?"

But she had begun to cry.

"Hush, you'll upset Trinity." I rose and retrieved my handkerchief from my bag. I handed it to her, pulled a chair up close, and held her for a long time. Her body shook as she tried to muffle her sorrow.

"What were you trying to tell me about Damone?" I asked when her grief had abated somewhat.

"I've said too much. Go home now and try to find out who the real murderer is before they pin it on my Damone. He's the only boy there, and black to boot. For sure they're gonna accuse him. Take your smelly dog with you."

She was panting now, and her brick-like bosom heaved.

***

I walked home deep in thought. The murder of Reverend Crudden was like a festering carbuncle, its poison spreading in Mrs. O'Hara's house and beyond. I could not leave Owen Sound until the police arrested the villain. More and more, I wanted to do just that.

I felt a bitter self-disgust at the life I had fallen into, almost as a lark. As I trudged home I realized that I'd wanted adventure, to make easy money, to be independent of Daddy and Lavinia, yet still support my baby. Most of all, I thought, I had wanted to belong, and to be accepted by a group of women. How I missed Mamma. *Her death led to the mess I've made of my life*. But then I shook my head. *I made the mess all by myself.*

I kicked an unoffending rock with a vicious swipe, and pain jolted through my foot. The sailors I serviced would have been proud of my curses.

I no longer felt at home in Galt, with Daddy and Lavinia. I certainly didn't belong on the farm with Thomas. Could I take Thomas away from Bart and Jane and start a fresh life, perhaps in Toronto? It was possible. I would need to find a way to support us both financially. There was not much employment to be had for young ladies, especially young mothers. But I could not even begin to contemplate my options until the murder of the inconvenient Reverend was solved. I wished he had never existed. *What kind of minister gets himself murdered in a brothel?*

The Owen Sound newspapers, *The Owen Sound Advertiser,* and *The Owen Sound Evening Times,* as well as small presses in the surrounding areas, had had a field day with salacious speculation about the Reverend's murder. *Owen Sound Reverend Stabbed in Compromising Circumstances* thundered one. *Unnatural Reverend Slashed* screamed another. Innuendo, conjecture, and downright untruths were being gleefully bandied about, much to Mrs. O'Hara's dismay. That he'd been a devotee of unnatural practices was hinted at in more ways and more delicately than I would ever have thought possible. I thought about the agony the Reverend's family must be experiencing. I wondered if Reverend Crudden had been married? I pitied his wife. What kind of woman was she? Stout, firm bosomed, sure of her overweening self-righteousness, a pillar of the community? How could she stay with him? How could she leave? And what about his children, if he had any?

I quickened my pace as the evening gloom began to fall. My thoughts quickened too. I had asked my fellow girls, separately and together, if they had had any dealings with the Reverend. They all answered in the negative. They all seemed sincere. *I'll go to Calvin Presbyterian Church and see what I can find out for myself,* I resolved. It felt good to have a plan, however tenuous. It felt especially good to be secure in the knowledge that I no longer had to fear Detective Craig. My body was young and had healed, and now my spirit was beginning to heal too.

My gloomy thoughts caught up with me when I was back at Mrs. O'Hara's house. Jack curled up with me on the sofa, and I drank tea, thinking of my lot in life and what a muddle I had made in my short seventeen years. *I have to continue to work, as I need to support myself and*

Thomas. My mind mulled my situation over and over until I felt bored with my own despair. Jack licked my face, but for once, he brought me little comfort.

A few days following my visit to Mrs. Barrett, I was surprised at Damone's appearance before lunch. He looked like he had lost some weight that he could ill-afford to spare. He was seated beside Mrs. O'Hara, and they were deep in conversation. None of the other girls had come down yet. When Mrs. O'Hara saw me, she raised an admonitory finger, and said, "Could you give us another five minutes, Charlotte, please? Shut the door on the way out."

I closed the French doors as quietly as I could. Jack whined softly, sensing my agitation, and I stroked his ears. Why did Mrs. O'Hara need to speak to Damone privately? Did she suspect him, or one of us girls? Was she keen to blame the murder on the most vulnerable of her employees? Perhaps they were discussing something of an entirely different nature?

I shook my head in frustration and waited for Mrs. O'Hara to signal that we could enter the dining room. The other girls trickled down, eager to eat. They looked at the closed doors, and I said,

"Mrs. O'Hara is speaking to Damone. In private."

Felicity sat down on a rather uncomfortable straight-backed chair and pulled out her needles and wool from a crocheted bag she was carrying. She very placidly carried on with her knitting. I saw with dismay that it was a white baby bonnet.

"For my cousin's baby in Collingwood," she answered my unspoken question. "Don't worry so much Charlotte."

I felt a little limp with relief. Unwanted pregnancy was always a real threat. If Felicity were to fall pregnant, I knew her family would show her no mercy, nor come to her aid in any way. What then for my friend? I shuddered.

"I've been wracking my brain trying to think of who killed Reverend Crudden," I said.

Felicity looked up from her work. She was nearsighted, and refused to wear her spectacles, even when the house was empty of men. Her brown eyes looked small.

"I'm sure the police will catch the culprit," she said as her needles clicked.

"Felicity, think! The sooner the murderer is caught, the sooner we can get back to normal here. Your earnings must have gone down."

"Yes, I noticed that business has been slower than usual."

At first, the men flocked to our house, taking perverse pleasure in the novelty of a brothel where someone, a minister at that, had been brutally murdered. But the novelty had worn off over a couple of weeks, and the constant police presence, and the chance of having the police drop in soon tamped down the titillation. We suspected that the other brothels in Owen Sound were benefiting from our troubles. *Mag Matthews, the keeper at Branningham Grove, must be laughing her way to the bank.*

"Felicity, I think we girls should put our heads together and find the murderer."

Now she looked truly alarmed. "Us? We are only women, stupid, silly, women. We have no hope of succeeding if the police can't!" She took a stray wisp of her mousey brown hair and tucked it behind her ear. Her face looked naked and plain without her usual cosmetics.

I swallowed down the contempt I felt for her. *Little wonder women occupy such an inferior position in society. Meek girls like Felicity don't even deserve the vote. Suffragettes like Dr. Emily Howard Stowe are wasting their time as far as girls like her are concerned.* I had a bitter taste in my mouth. Was Felicity really that meek and accepting of her status as a mere woman, or was she playing a clever game? Was she concealing some sort of untoward knowledge about Reverend Crudden's life or perhaps even his death? I looked into her myopic eyes, then looked away. I forced myself to smile at her, a phony rictus. She sighed in relief, patted my hand, then returned to her knitting.

Mrs. O'Hara eventually opened the French doors, and we enjoyed a delicious meal of soup, roasted goose, freshly baked bread smeared with thick butter, and roasted turnips. Dessert was a rhubarb pudding. I looked at her closely. She had a real maternal streak in caring for us girls and Damone, but she also turned that to her advantage. Well-fed and well paid, we were less likely to leave in a snit, or challenge her authority in any way. *She rules with the proverbial iron fist cloaked in a velvet glove*, I realized with a mixture of resentment and admiration. I yearned to leave the house once the murder had been solved, but Mrs. O'Hara made it very easy to stay. I resolved to go to a bank the next day and open a new savings account, a freedom account.

Next, my gaze moved to Matilda. She was examining Felicity's knitting, sharing tips perhaps? I myself had never taken to knitting, although I had tried doggedly during those long months at the farm waiting for Thomas' arrival. I thought of the many dropped stitches and tangled skeins of wool when I had struggled to fashion a simple white cap for Baby, and Jane's amused, scornful patience as she corrected each mistake I made.

"Really, Charlotte, you're useless!" she had finally pronounced after carefully untangling my wool yet again. "You're far more adept at needlework. Why don't you complete the frock you started last week? I'll finish the cap." I'd been surprised to learn that both baby girls and boys were dressed almost identically, in white, until they reached nine months.

I agreed, sullenly, and relinquished knitting for good. My needlework was superb. Mamma had seen to that. *Perhaps I can support myself and Thomas by my needlework while finishing school? But it pays so little, an entire day's work for what I earn in an hour at the brothel.* I felt overwhelmed and my head was beginning to ache. *Enough! Concentrate. Could Matilda have had a prior connection to the unfortunate Reverend? What did I really know about her? And it was she who had held the knife…*

I gazed at her as discreetly as I could while eating the hearty vegetable soup and newly baked bread. Our housekeeper, Mrs. Davidson, cooked two meals for us daily, at noon, and in the evening. She took great care that our diet, while simple, was nutritious and delicious. She was a superb cook and I worried that my frock was growing too tight.

As I slurped, I reviewed what I knew about Matilda. Her father was Ojibway and had been crushed to death in a logging accident on the Bruce Peninsula, close to the Cape Croker Reserve where he was born and raised. Matilda was raised by her white mother in Owen Sound. I knew that she was bitter and angry with the way the two of them were ostracized by her grandparents for the marriage with a "no-good Indian." Her Ojibway grandparents felt equally disgusted at their white blood and had been just as unwelcoming.

"My mother never had a chance," Matilda confided one evening after she had enjoyed too much surreptitious wine. "My grandparents would have nothing to do with her, said she was dirt, for marrying an Indian. She had to provide for me, so she married another logger, a white one this time. But he was scum." She hissed the word. "He beat us…I left as soon as I was 17. Mrs. O'Hara took me in. This is the only real home I've ever known."

She rubbed her nose. "My stepfather beat up my mother for years, until one day I walked in on him backhanding her. I grabbed a stick of firewood and hit him hard over the back of his head. Knocked him out. When he came to, I told him that if he ever laid a hand on my mother again, I'd kill him." Her eyes gleamed at the thought.

I slurped my soup again, then said quietly,

"Matilda, had you ever met Reverend Crudden before we found him in the basement?"

She flushed beet red, a very unflattering look on her dark skin. I saw tiny beads of perspiration on her forehead, which was pitted with old acne scars.

"What do you mean?"

"My question is straightforward. Did you ever meet Reverend Crudden while he was alive?"

"How dare you?" she flushed darker crimson, shoved back her chair, and pushed herself up from the table. Before she left, she slammed her chair back into the table with such vigour that the soup splashed and spilled on the navy linen tablecloth that had belonged to Mrs. O'Hara's mother in Dublin, Ireland. In fact, Mrs. O'Hara's mother had painstakingly crafted the tablecloth for her daughter before she left for the new country, and its careful stitches and delicate lace borders spoke of her love.

There was a shocked silence. Mrs. O'Hara rose, her back ramrod straight. Her wrath was evident, but under control. Just.

"Girls, you know I do not tolerate fighting amongst ourselves in this house. Charlotte! What did you say to Matilda to upset her so?"

I looked at Matilda's scared, pleading face. We had each lost a beloved mother. Her childhood had been indescribably harder than my pampered upbringing. And besides, she could very well be innocent of the murder. But if she were guilty, I would do my best to find proof, and turn her in.

"I made an ill-judged remark about Indians, Ma'am. I forgot about Matilda's father. I'm sorry Matilda. Sorry, Mrs. O'Hara. If everyone could gather their dishes, I'll take the tablecloth and soak it in a mixture of grated potato and ammonia. My Mamma taught me that it cleans linen perfectly."

The tension dribbled away. Mrs. O'Hara took Matilda's hand and squeezed it.

"Yes, thank you Charlotte. You are young, but you need to keep better control of your tongue in the future."

I lowered my eyes. "Yes, Ma'am."

My mind whirled. It appeared very likely that Matilda had known Reverend Crudden before. She certainly seemed to have strong feelings about the wretched man. *She is in my debt now for rescuing her from Mrs. O'Hara's fury. I'll confront her again, in private.*

I bided my time, then shortly before the house opened for business that evening, I tapped softly on her door. She opened it, expecting a gentleman caller, but tried to slam it shut when she saw me. I was quick and wedged my slippered foot between the door and the door jam.

"You can speak to me quietly in your room, or I'll shout my questions through the door," I said.

She cursed, but she let me in.

I sat down on her bed without asking and gazed at the photograph of her mother on pride of place on her wardrobe. *How could she stand to have her mother watch over what takes place in this room?*

I cleared my throat. Matilda sat, seething.

"Matilda. I had the distinct impression that you had a prior acquaintance with Reverend Crudden while he was alive. You can tell me, or I'll go and tell Inspector McLaughlin my suspicions."

"You wouldn't dare!"

"Oh, yes I would. Our lives are all suspended until this murder can be solved."

"So, what? Nothing has changed," she said.

"Maybe I want things to change. I want more than this life. Way more." I hadn't intended to let that slip. Best never to make oneself vulnerable, especially to a whore.

Her eyes narrowed, and I knew she was tucking away that piece of information for future use. Too late now to do anything about it. I pressed on.

"Did you know the Reverend? Did you attend Calvin Presbyterian Church?"

"Why do you want to leave here? I'll tell Mrs. O'Hara," she said.

"You do that." I did my best to hide my vexation. "Why did you become so angry when I asked you about the Reverend at lunch?"

All of a sudden, her belligerence melted away, and she sank beside me onto the bed, our silk dresses touching. She reached for my hand. I flinched and forced my hand to relax in hers. Her hand was a little scaly, and her skin was peeling. It felt dry and hot. Why was she holding my hand? With an effort, I did not withdraw my own.

"I did know him. He married my parents in secret, when my mother was expecting me. She was a member of his choir. He saw her expanding figure, wormed the truth out of her, and forced my father to marry her. The original plan was for her to go to the nuns in Toronto, have the baby in secret, give me up for adoption, then she could begin her life again."

I blinked. Her story hit close to home.

"He told her that because I was half-Indian, no respectable couple would ever adopt me. Who knows, maybe he was right. Maybe he did have some compassion for my mother, but I will never forgive him for what he did after my father was killed."

I sat in silence, our hands still entwined, willing her to continue. She took a ragged breath, then said,

"He seemed hell-bent on *saving* my mother. My mother was a very pretty lady. She had a flawless complexion, and her hair was a soft brown. She maintained a trim figure, and swayed when she walked. I don't think she realized her appeal to men.

"He brought her clothes and food baskets that were donated by the parish, all throughout my childhood. We were always so poor, you see. She had to accept, for my sake. But she never liked him. His hair was greasy, and he didn't brush his teeth. She said his personality was as greasy and unwholesome as his hair."

I sighed and listened to the sound of wagons groan and squeak as they passed slowly by on the stony road outside the house. Jack whined softly; I patted his silky ears.

"Was he interested in her romantically?" I asked.

"I think deep down, but he would never admit it, even to himself. He saw her as a fallen woman, ruined by a shotgun marriage to an Indian, raising a half-breed, and a girl at that. He told her once that he had found a family who were so desperate for a child that they would raise me as their own, despite my mixed blood. They even offered her $100 – to buy me!

"My mother was furious. I think I was seven years old by then, and she loved me. I worshipped her. We were all each other had. But he wouldn't stop pestering her. He said if she were to give me up, she could be reunited with her family, return to school, and marry well. She finally told him to leave us be, to never return.

"Even then, he didn't completely leave us alone. Somehow, he found out every year how well or how poorly I was doing at school.

He was on the Board of Governors, due to his position as a clergyman, so I suppose it was not that difficult for him. He'd come to our little rooms, bringing food and clothing, which we needed badly, as I kept on growing. You can see how tall I am! Footwear was especially hard for my mother to afford for me. Each gift was an opportunity for him to lecture me or praise me, as he felt I deserved.

"He had such piercing blue eyes. He'd stare at me as though he could read me to the bottom of my soul. He would quote verses from the Bible, *thou shalt love thy neighbour, vengeance is mine said the Lord,*" Matilda practically spat, "and even the most beautiful of Jesus' words sounded nasty coming out of that man's mouth.

"My mother and I felt unclean after each visit, but we had no choice but to eat the food. I hated the clothes, but I wore them until they wore out, or until they didn't fit any longer. He was a miserable misfit of a man, and I'm glad he is dead. But I did not kill him."

I looked at her, searching deep into her dark eyes, trying to determine if she was telling me the truth. I couldn't be certain. Was she sincere, or in admitting her rage, was she trying to befuddle me with honesty? Jack whined softly at my feet. He had heard a knock at the door. Our gentlemen callers had begun to arrive. It was time to return to business.

I squeezed Matilda's hand and said mendaciously, "I believe you. Thank you for your honesty."

The tension drained from her shoulders and she sighed. I felt an instant's regret at my own falseness. But I could not go to Inspector McLaughlin until I was certain I had discovered the true villain.

***

I dressed reluctantly for my working hours, rubbing a slight tinge of pomade rouge into my cheeks and then prettied my mouth with a touch of rose lip-salve to polish my look. I fluffed my hair, told Jack to stay in his bed tucked away near the stairs, and went to the parlour to greet the men.

As I descended the stairs, the same tired thoughts swirled in my head. I stopped, gripped the rail, and shook myself as Jack did when wet; no point in ruminating. I had to work for the time being, no matter how unpleasant that work might be to me now. Jane, Bart and Thomas would appreciate the money. I continued doggedly down the stairs, put on my brightest smile, and entered the parlour.

My first gentleman that evening looked to be in his forties. I had never seen him before. He sported a rough sort of beard and a number of tattoos on his muscled arm. His arm muscles looked like ropes. He caught me staring, and I looked away. He was clearly a sailor. I knew that the wooden hull ferry, the *S.S. Caribou*, had just come into port from its once a week "turkey trail." The ship's meandering route encompassed the many ports scattered along Georgian Bay, Manitoulin Island, the North Channel, Sault Ste. Marie, and up to Garantua Harbour, Michipicoten Island and as far as Pukaskwa Depot. The ship was often overcrowded with food, livestock, vehicles, fish and too many passengers.

The man nodded at me, signaling his choice. "My name's Carl," he said, when I moved to sit beside him. His voice was deep and pleasant. We chatted easily. He smelled like Pears soap, a pleasing sign. When he indicated that he was ready to go upstairs, I acquiesced. As we walked hand-in-hand past Jack lying obediently on his bed, Jack growled.

"Quiet, Jack," I said.

Carl reached with his booted foot towards my dog.

"No," I said sharply. "The dog means no harm."

Mrs. O'Hara looked at me, eyebrows raised. She put her finger to her lips and frowned.

"Please, Carl. The dog's mine." My tone was now under control. I wished myself a million miles away from the accursed house.

Carl scowled but turned away from my Jack. We climbed the stairs, and I reluctantly invited him into my bedroom. Once inside, Carl began to kiss me, more roughly than necessary. I tried to break away, but he tightened his grip.

"Let go of me!" I said, but he clamped his big, muscular, calloused hand over my mouth. I could barely breathe. I wriggled frantically and tried to kick him in the shins and higher. My feet were clothed in house slippers and my efforts were useless.

He threw me onto the bed, finally releasing his grip on my mouth. Mrs. O'Hara had insisted that all of her girls keep a bell on the night table to ring in case of such an emergency. I thrashed around and managed to grab it as he began to unbutton his clothing. I rang it frantically.

"You little harlot," he shouted and grabbed me by the hair. He pulled so hard that a handful of my yellow curls came free in his hand. It hurt so much I saw stars and blacked out for a few seconds. When I opened my eyes, I saw him standing there, looking bemused at the long strands of my hair in his hand. I felt my head. There was a bald spot about three fingers wide on top. It felt smooth and entirely unnatural. My head pounded.

He began to laugh when Mrs. O'Hara, followed by Damone carrying a large hammer burst into the room. Jack's sharp barking added to the frenzy. He jumped on the bed, stood on my chest and continued to bark. Carl backed away, leering at Damone, in whose skinny arms the hammer looked outsized.

"Everything's fine in here. Easy, black boy."

"Fine?" shouted Mrs. O'Hara. "You're holding a handful of the girl's hair."

She ran to the big sailor and tried to push him out the door. Damone swung the hammer. I could tell from the look in his eyes that he meant business. I felt my head once more. The bald patch was throbbing. I felt for blood but it was dry, soft and utterly hairless. Jack continued to wriggle and kiss me. I grabbed hold of his collar, and he relaxed into my arms.

"Damone. Put the hammer down," I said.

But it was too late. Carl grabbed it, and began to swing it in large arcs. Everyone cleared out of my bedroom. He stood over my bed, hammer in hand. His eyes were bloodshot, and his short hair stood up in spikes.

"You bitch!" I felt the flecks of spittle as he leaned over me. "I should brain you for causing this commotion. I paid good money for you."

I was too afraid to scream. I was too afraid to breathe.

But my intrepid Jack leapt off the bed and bit the brute on the ankles. He screamed and lunged, but was not quick enough for Jack who leapt away.

"Run Jack," I screamed, "go to your bed!" Jack heard the desperation in my voice and obeyed.

Just then, two big, burly men, regulars in Mrs. O'Hara's house, burst into my bedroom. They seized Carl's arms, took away the hammer, and handed it to me. They dragged him out of the room, down the stairs. Mrs. O'Hara was still incensed and screamed abuse at his retreating figure. For once, Jack disobeyed my command, and he returned to jump back on the bed, barking his high-pitched signature yelps that were ear-splitting.

I didn't have the heart to order him to stop. He'd saved me from a beating, or worse. Carl had intended serious damage. I read it in his mean little eyes. I held my dog, stroked him, and thanked him, over and over. Mrs. O'Hara, now downstairs, continued her volley of curses, but more softly now.

Finally, all was quiet for ten minutes or so, while I lay on my bed, dazed.

"Charlotte. Come down here," Mrs. O'Hara commanded from the foot of the stairs. Reluctantly, I stepped out of my room and walked toward her, Jack right beside me. I knew the girls were peeking at me and I wished for oblivion.

"Where's Carl?" I asked.

"The men locked him in the storage shed out back. Don't fret," she interpreted my look of concern, "it has a good, sturdy padlock. I have the only key right here." She pulled a shiny key from her skirt pocket.

"Felicity has gone to fetch the police."

"The police?" I was amazed. "The police won't care about an attack on a whore."

She walked over and took me in her arms.

"But the police won't do anything about an attack on a whore," I repeated.

She let go of me and taking my hand, led me into the kitchen. She sat me down at the well-used pine table, and said, "What you need is tea with a shot of whiskey."

"No whiskey."

She had a pretty good idea about my Daddy and nodded. How could a keeper be so kind? "That's fine. No whiskey," she said.

***

It took a long time for her to prepare the tea. She stoked the woodstove with fresh firewood. Wood was cheap and plentiful in Owen Sound. She held my hand and we sat in silence waiting for the kettle to boil. After a time, she stood up and looked carefully at my poor denuded head. I couldn't bear to think about it. At the same time, it was all I could think about. After she prepared the hot tea which she sweetened with a generous dollop of maple syrup, we sipped for a long time in silence. Finally, Mrs. O'Hara said, "I'm very sorry for what you've been through tonight, Charlotte. If you need a few days to recuperate..."

Just then, there was a soft knock at the kitchen door. Matilda peered in.

"Inspector McLaughlin is here."

Mrs. O'Hara motioned for him to join us. She poured him some tea and arranged some biscuits on a china plate, then sat down beside me. He sat down across from us. The chair looked undersized with him in it. I had forgotten how big he was. He frowned at me, then his eyes travelled to the top of my head. I kicked myself for not having put on a bonnet, but it was too late. He drew in his breath sharply, realized his mistake and turned it into a phony cough.

"What happened here tonight, Charlotte?"

I told him, and he took careful notes.

"Why didn't you send Sergeant Craig for a minor problem like this?" I asked.

"The last person you need to deal with is Sergeant Craig." He smiled, and I noted the crow's feet at the side of his crinkled eyes. He was so homely that he was attractive, at least to me.

"Have you a prior acquaintance with this Carl? Was he a regular customer here? Do you know what made him so angry?"

"It wasn't my fault!" I was outraged.

"No, I didn't mean that." He touched my hand.

I calmed down somewhat. "I've never set eyes on him before. Are you going to arrest him?" It was too much to hope he'd be hanged.

"Yes, as soon as I finish speaking with you. I'm going to charge him with assault. I'll make sure he never bothers you again. I wanted to make sure for myself that you'll recover, and to see if you had any other pertinent information for me. Can you see any connection between this man and Reverend Crudden?"

"No. None at all. All I know is that Carl is very strong. And angry. Look what he did to my hair." I couldn't stifle a whimper.

"Yes, I noticed." His voice was gentle, and his eyes crinkled again, this time with concern. His soft Irish brogue became thicker.

"Charlotte, you're still a most attractive young lady. Your hair will grow back. Surely you see that you must leave this life! You deserve better…." This time it was he who blushed, and I looked away. My humiliation was complete. Mrs. O'Hara cleared her throat.

The policeman turned to Mrs. O'Hara. "How was it possible that Damone was here to confront Carl? I thought you didn't know where he had gone." His voice was stern.

She blushed, then said stiffly, "He no longer works for me. He came to collect the last of the money I owed him."

"I need to speak to him. Could you please fetch him?" he asked politely.

She shook her head. "He's gone again. As soon as Carl was restrained, he took the money and left. I told him you would want to speak to him, but he just ran out the door."

Inspector McLaughlin frowned, and his crooked nose looked even more squashed than usual. He ran his fingers through his hair, then took my hand and squeezed it, then let go as if my skin had burned him. "Think about what I said. I'll deal with Carl now."

I couldn't meet his eye. "Thank you." I got up and walked him to the front door. No tradesmen entrances for him.

"Goodnight then. Mrs. O'Hara." He bowed briefly to the keeper as he donned his hat and walked swiftly down the front steps.

Mrs. O'Hara returned and poured me more tea. It was lukewarm now, but I was thirsty.

"You will need time to recuperate before returning to work…" she said.

"What do you mean, *returning to work?* What man would want to touch me, looking as I do?" I patted my bald spot, then banged my head on the table.

Mrs. O'Hara wrapped her arms around me in physical restraint, and said sharply, "Charlotte. Stop. Stop this moment."

Matilda and Eliza peered into the kitchen.

"We heard banging…" Eliza said, her eyes darting back and forth between us.

"It's fine, girls, go back to work. Are there no men in the parlour?" asked Mrs. O'Hara.

They retreated, Eliza casting an inquiring look at me. I looked away.

"Charlotte, listen to me. You have beautiful hair."

"Had beautiful hair. It's gone." I stroked Jack, whose hair was intact and constantly shedding. He had no concern whatsoever about my mutilated locks.

"Take ten deep breaths," she ordered.

I obeyed, shaky at first, but then deeper, calmer.

"You are a very pretty girl. Your face is your chief attraction, not your hair."

"But everyone knows me for my hair. Because it's blonde and curly." My voice wasn't entirely in my control.

"Listen to me. You're much more than your hair. I have a little ability at hair dressing, and I'm certain we can style it so no one notices."

"You're wrong! How can they not notice this?" And I banged my head once more.

She held me. Her arms were surprisingly strong. She had a sweet, clean smell. I had never been that close to her before.

"Everyone will not notice. Tomorrow, you and I will go to town, and we'll shop for hats, bonnets, and the most fashionable caps available. I'll buy you scarves too. My treat."

I was amazed that Mrs. O'Hara would be so caring, especially as in my mutilated state, men would certainly not flock to spend time with me. But I was in no frame of mind to inquire about Mrs. O'Hara's life when mine was in such upheaval.

"Thank you. But are you not going to send me away? Men will not…"

"Nonsense! Your hair will grow back quicker than you think. I'll keep you busy. I've noticed that you're a fine cook. Perhaps you can take over the cooking for a time. Mrs. Davidson's mother is ill. She's asked me for a couple weeks now for leave to go to Toronto, to tend to her. So we need a temporary replacement. Besides," and here she shot me a look, "it's my impression that you lost interest in working here in your original capacity some time ago."

"What did Matilda say to you?" I struggled to tamp down my outrage.

"Matilda said nothing to me. I do have eyes and some intelligence. I've noticed your unhappiness. Why did you stay as long as you did?"

As if from a distance, I heard myself telling her about my continuing relationship with Thomas and my cousins.

She listened impassively, without interruption. How could I trust her? She was a madam, a keeper. She earned a lot of money exploiting vulnerable girls. But she was also genuinely kind and caring, and I had missed my Mamma for a long, long time.

When I had finished my long story, I felt humiliated, but also emptied, and a little free. I had been keeping Thomas' role in my life hidden ever since his conception, and the secrecy was a dreadful burden. Mrs. O'Hara may be disgusted with me, she might throw me out, tell all of the other girls, ridicule me…but the very core of me was inviolate. Even partially bald, living the life of a whore, and an unwed mother, I was still Charlotte Evans. I still had a life ahead of me. My path forward was no longer smooth and easy to discern, but I was determined that I would move forward. It was a life, and it was mine.

Mrs. O'Hara must have seen something of this defiance, because she pulled back from me, and released my hand. She cleared her throat.

"You have been carrying a heavy burden. Would you like to stay here and cook for us? I can afford to pay you a small amount. I think your time with the men is over, and I don't suppose you will remain in Owen Sound for long, but why not stay, let your hair grow back, and make your plans here? There is no haste for you to move on."

"And Thomas? Will you keep that confidential?"

"It will remain between us. But I think you will need to tell Inspector McLaughlin the truth."

"I already did," I said in a low voice. "Everything is police business in a murder inquiry. I want him to catch the killer, so I can move on with my life! I'm only 17. Your life is half over. Mine's just begun."

She flinched as if I'd struck her, the lines on her face deeper than usual. Her face was white.

"I'm sorry," I apologized. "That was inexcusable. I'm not myself. My poor hair." I was weary to death.

"I'll take Jack for a quick walk, and you go to bed. I'll bring him up to you. Things will look more hopeful in the morning," she said.

She pushed her chair from the table and stood up slowly. I heard her knees creak. She left the kitchen and returned shortly with a leather-bound copy of *The Adventures of Sherlock Holmes*. She gave it to me.

"Read this until you are sleepy." She had one of her own silk scarves in her hand, which she tied quickly and deftly around my denuded head. "Go now. You can talk to Inspector McLaughlin in the morning. I'll make certain you are not disturbed tonight."

I obeyed, marveling yet again at her kindness. The girls and fellows in the parlour looked at me with open curiosity, but I stared at the floor as I climbed the stairs and shut my door tight.

I lit the lamp but avoided the mirror. I quickly washed my face, put on my nightclothes, and fell into bed. When Jack appeared half an hour later, he leaped enthusiastically on my bed and began to lick his paws in utter oblivion to the fact that my life had shattered once again.

"Thank you," I said softly as Mrs. O'Hara closed the door.

***

I slept an exhausted, dreamless sleep, awakening the next morning to aggressive sunshine peeking in through my brown damask curtain. I stretched lazily, then felt the darkness encroach.

Perhaps I had dreamed it, maybe I had had a nightmare. I felt my head with tentative fingers. No, it was not a dream. The bald spot, the size of a small tea saucer, was there. The skin felt as soft and fuzzy as Thomas'. We were unmistakable as mother and son now. I started to laugh a trifle hysterically, but Jack whined softly, and I was saved once again from immobilizing self-pity by my pet's urgent and basic needs.

I quickly pulled on an old frock and tied a bonnet under my chin. Normally I went bareheaded as much as possible, cherishing the freedom. For the foreseeable future, my head would be covered.

I walked downstairs softly with Jack, hoping the clicking of his toenails on the gumwood stairs would not awaken the girls. I did not want their pity. It might lead me to drown in my own. Jack certainly spared me no sympathy as he jumped with excitement as I pulled on my cloak and boots and fastened his lead. I could never let him run due to his wandering beagle ancestry.

As always, I headed to the bay. I took us to a private spot on a deserted dock, and Jack and I stood for a long time. The water was healing to me; the closest I ever felt to God. The waves lapped gently underneath us, and a few fishermen in small craft sat patiently, casting, waiting. There was a steamboat further out, chugging towards Georgian Bay. The capricious wind ruffled my skirt, and tried to niggle at my bonnet as well, but I tied it even more firmly in a double bow. No one was going to see my razed head.

I made some decisions standing there, accepting the chill breeze, the love of my dog, and the cleansing motion of the little waves. I would never sell my body again. I would have to provide for Thomas some other way. I had to wait until the murder was resolved. Then, I'd go home to Galt, at least for a time, and make my peace with Daddy and even Lavinia. Perhaps accept Daddy's help. He could afford to help me, and his heavy drinking had led to many of the sins I had committed. I shuddered, but my path was clear.

I walked slowly back to the house on 3rd Avenue East. It was a prison now and I rued the day that I ran willingly into its walls, and locked myself in. Thankfully, as far as I knew, I was not with child; nor did I have a disease. I cringed as the full realization of my criminal stupidity hit home. The brute Carl, who had torn away my hair, had also torn away the last of my denial. Thomas deserved a mother so much better. I knew that although Bart and Jane would raise him, I could never entirely let go. I would be his doting Auntie Charlotte who would spoil, indulge, and guide him. I'd see him as often as I could, despite Jane's disapproval.

I continued to trudge towards the brothel. One foot in front of the other. Today was Wednesday; it had been only a short time since Reverend Crudden's death had shattered my life. If I ever got out of this mess, I might even be grateful for this crisis.

I resolved to attend Sunday's service at Calvin Presbyterian Church…no, I realized, I didn't have to wait until Sunday. I could go sooner, and start nosing about, under the pretext of volunteering at the Thursday soup kitchen.

Mrs. O'Hara greeted me at the back door. "Inspector McLaughlin is here again. He wants to speak to you."

I did not hurry to the parlour. Instead, I said quietly,

"I'm going to accept your offer. I'm a good cook. I had to be, after my Mamma died. When do you want me to start? And why are you being so nice to me?" This burst out of me, I couldn't help myself.

"Next Monday will be fine. Mrs. Davidson can finish out her week. If I have to eat boiled chicken one more time however…. Mrs. Davidson's mind has not been on her work."

She looked at me, twisting the ruby ring on her rather stubby finger with real anxiety. She was comfortably plump; she enjoyed good food. Still, she had avoided my question.

"I've never cooked boiled chicken in my life. I do know some very fine recipes from *The Galt Cookbook*. I'm particularly good with rabbit."

"You mustn't keep Inspector McLaughlin waiting any longer. And Charlotte," she squeezed my hand, "I'm happy you've accepted my offer. The girls will thank you too, if your cooking is as good as I think it is. My motivations are frankly none of your business." She lifted her chin and swept out of the room. I watched her depart with admiration.

Inspector McLaughlin frowned when I entered the parlour. "Were you going to keep me waiting all day?"

I winced. "I'm sorry. I've had many sorrows of late."

"Too many to obey a police command? I need to speak to you."

I yanked off my bonnet and he flinched at my bald spot, which I was sure was glistening in all its glory. I imagined the sun reflecting off my pate, blinding him.

He looked at me. He was still homely. *His eyes are the colour of the bay on a sunny day*. My insides somersaulted, and I looked away. He patted Jack, scratching behind his ears. Jack gave a little grunt of pleasure. My insides lurched again.

"I know you have questions for me," I said quickly, before I could lose my nerve, "but there's something I need to tell you. If I don't say it now, I might lose my nerve."

"Sit down," he said, and motioned that I should take the chair opposite his.

I obeyed. He turned from Jack and gave me his full attention. I told him what I learned of Matilda's history, and the bad blood between her and Reverend Crudden. When I finished, I felt greasy, disgusted at my perfidy. He remained impassive, steepling his fingers. Why did I care so much about one man's opinion of me, a policeman at that?

When I finished, he said,

"Thank you for your honesty. Best to tell the police everything and let us determine what is important and not."

"Do you need to tell your colleagues? I don't want Detective Craig to hurt her as he hurt me. I don't want him to try to beat a confession from her." My bruises were gone now but the memory still fresh.

"Detective Craig has moved to Hamilton."

"Hamilton? Was he promoted?" I couldn't keep the outrage out of my voice.

"I think you'll find it was a demotion." He smiled. "I made life very uncomfortable for him. I doubt he will be hitting a woman any time soon. His arm was accidentally broken in the police cell. An unfortunate fall." His eyes hardened. *Did he break Detective Craig's arm himself?* I rather thought he had.

"I can't abide men who hit women. My father..." He looked at me, shook his head and stopped himself.

I was burning to know about his father, but a curtain had come down. In my experience, the more curiosity one shows, the less it is satisfied. I learned this from my hours in the apothecary, straining my ears for the latest Galt gossip. When I melted into the background and kept my face blank and my mouth shut, customers would be freer in their speech.

Inspector McLaughlin's eyes were still hard. He looked at me, and I realized that he had revealed more of himself than he was comfortable with, and I'd be suitably punished, I supposed. I felt a little sick and stared at the ground. But he surprised me. He relaxed, his face softened, and he smiled.

"You're a good listener, Charlotte. But this is a murder inquiry. Are you sure you don't have any more thoughts as to who killed Reverend Crudden?"

I shook my head no.

"Do you remember anything out of the ordinary, no matter how small, before he was killed?"

I cast my mind back but could remember nothing. Again, I shook my head.

"Have you found out if any of the other girls here knew the Reverend before the murder, despite their previous denials?"

"No, not at all. I had never heard him discussed before he was killed. And after the murder, no one other than Matilda has given any indication of a former relationship with him."

He thanked me, stood up and shut the parlour door. He grabbed my hand, kissed it, then opened the door and left. He didn't say goodbye.

My heart pounded. I patted my head. Surely, he could not find me remotely attractive? I was a prostitute, an unwed mother and now partially bald. I grinned at the absurdity and walked with a spring in my step up to my bedroom.

I thought of Thomas. I had not been to visit him since the murder had occurred. I decided that I would make the long walk to the farm in the following days and resolved to buy a few gifts for my son. I was going to reform my life.

***

The next day dawned, rainy, cold and with thunder rumbling over the bay. I still had five days until I began my work as cook. I had done no volunteering since my days in the Temperance Club at Galt Grammar School and I was quite looking forward to it. I decided to wear a dark maroon silk dating from my school days. I ate carefully and had regained my trim figure after Thomas' birth, so it still fit. It was sober and respectable but was still a welcome change from the unrelieved black I had worn in the months since joining Mrs. O'Hara's establishment. I pinned my hair up and disguised my bald spot as best I could, and set a large, fashionable hat firmly on top, pinning it rigidly into place. Jack watched me intently, with an imploring look in his beautiful brown eyes, anxious to accompany me.

"Not today Jack. It's rainy, and I doubt you'd be welcome in a church."

He looked downcast, his ears limp and tail limper. I patted him and gave him a kiss on the top of his head, then slipped him a crust of bread I had saved from breakfast.

"Go to your bed." He obeyed and turned around in circles a few times before laying down with a tortured sigh. *He should be in the theatre.* I was still grinning as I walked downstairs. Mrs. O'Hara was doing accounts at her desk, and I told her quickly where I was going.

"I certainly hope you can help find the villain. The police have made no headway that I've seen, and business is down, way down." She tapped her pencil on her account book, her lips pursed.

"I don't want to have to let any of the girls go, but this is not a charity. The police presence makes many men stay away entirely. Especially local men, who have families and don't want them to know what they get up to at night."

I felt a churning in my gut. The poor girls, most of whom, unlike me, had nowhere else to go, no other choices to make.

"I'll do everything I can. Still, Inspector McLaughlin seems competent and a good policeman. Not like Craig..."

"All police are corrupt. Especially to us working women." She sighed heavily and pressed her fingers to her temple. She was good to us girls, but at heart she was a businesswoman. The brothel provided Mrs. O'Hara with a very decent living, and I had seen her often at the Dominion Bank in downtown Owen Sound. I was certain her purpose was deposits, not withdrawals. Would she sell up and relocate to another town?

What would come of meek Felicity, sparky Matilda, and the other girls? Damone? Who on earth would hire him? What career could he possibly carve for himself in Owen Sound? Certainly, he could move farther afield, but I knew that his ties to his mother and Trinity ran deep, and much of his earnings went to support them. Most important: where was Damone? His disappearance surely would make the police very suspicious. I myself had a worm of doubt about my friend.

I walked briskly towards Calvin Presbyterian Church downtown. It was made of limestone with granite corners, in the Gothic Revival style, similar to our own Knox Presbyterian in Galt. It had a very impressive six storey central tower, along with pointed arched windows containing tracery, limestone buttresses, and a slate roof. The house of God seemed to loom over me as I approached the side door, obliterating the weak sunlight that was trying to poke through the rainclouds.

A big-bosomed lady in tweed greeted me when I entered. "I'm Mrs. Morton," she introduced herself in a booming voice, "and who are you?"

"Miss Charlotte Evans. I'd like to volunteer in the soup kitchen."

"I haven't seen you before. Do you live in Owen Sound?"

I had prepared myself. "Yes, I live with my cousins on a farm on the outskirts of town."

She still regarded me suspiciously. *I hope her husband isn't one of my regulars….* I struggled not to smirk at the thought. After a moment, she motioned for me to follow her and I obeyed meekly. We walked through a long hall, then down a steep set of stone stairs to a large basement, whitewashed, cheery and obviously well-used.

To one side, was a large, well-appointed kitchen, with a huge cook-stove taking pride of place. I could hear the crackle of a roaring fire, and I felt a bead of sweat drip down my neck. I wished I could remove my hat. I felt a sour amusement at the thought of how the well-heeled ladies working busily chopping potatoes and vegetables would react to my baldness. The sharp tang of onion made my mouth and eyes water. Beef was sizzling on the range, and the ladies were chatting and laughing as they prepared a hearty stew for the poor.

I was very familiar with soup kitchens as I had helped Mamma before she became too ill at Trinity, and the doctor's wife, Mrs. Gordon, had gently coerced me into chopping vegetables after school and before Easter and Christmas. I felt right at home.

"I brought an apron. Would you like me to peel or chop?"

I pulled the apron from my handbag. The ladies became quiet at the sight of me. I heard a cough, a little titter of laughter, and some whispering. *Some of them must know what I am.* A wave of sadness nearly bowled me down.

I yanked my chin up high and marched into the kitchen, my haughty demeanour daring anyone to stop me or question my right to be there. *I have just as might right to respect and dignity as they do.* My feelings did not match my bold attitude. I stopped at the counter beside one sweet-faced young matron. She had a thin, plain gold band on her left-hand ring finger.

"I'm Miss Charlotte Evans."

"Mary Eliot. Mrs. Eliot," she clarified proudly.

"Do you volunteer here often?" I asked her.

"Yes, every Thursday. It helps to pass the time. I have not been blessed with children. Yet." Her voice was wistful.

"How can I help? I'm a good cook."

She looked surprised. Most genteel ladies were able to employ a cook, and only affluent ladies had the leisure time to volunteer at a soup kitchen. Working-class wives and mothers were kept busy with the incessant, mundane and entirely necessary tasks I had experienced first-hand on Bart and Jane's farm.

Mrs. Eliot smiled, and looked down. I wondered why she was so timid.

"Would you mind awfully helping me to peel the potatoes, and grate these carrots? Boring tasks…"

Actually, I did mind. I'd rather cook than peel. However, I pasted a cheerful smile on my face, and set to work.

"Tell me about your husband," I prompted, as she seemed content to work in silence.

"Oh, he's a senior clerk at the Dominion Bank on 2nd Street. You know, the big grey building with the columns…He has such an important position." Her pride was nearly tangible. She continued chattering about her domestic bliss, and I allowed my mind to roam when she touched on how much the estimable Mr. Eliot perspired in the evenings while they read in front of the fire.

I was daydreaming about pushing Thomas' pram proudly down the tree-lined streets in Galt when I noticed Mrs. Eliot looking at me, waiting for a reply. I must have missed a question.

"Pardon me?"

"I asked, what made you come here today to help? It's a long way from the farm where you live. Don't you have enough to do at home?"

I hadn't prepared for this question. Not at all.

"Mmm, I used to volunteer with my mother at the soup kitchen in Galt, where I grew up. I miss her, and this makes me feel close to her."

She seemed to accept my explanation, probably because a good part of it was true. She lost interest and continued to chop and peel dutifully. Her skin looked paper thin, almost translucent, and I looked at her bony wrist and realized how thin she was. She set down her knife and leaned on the counter.

"Do you need to sit down?" I asked.

She stepped back from the counter. "No. Why do you ask?"

"You look a little tired, that's all."

She shifted her body away from me, closing herself off. *This isn't good. I need her to talk to me.* I began to babble about Jane's son Thomas, telling her about his first tooth, his thatch of spiky brown hair, and his utter sweetness. Her body seemed to tighten even further, and I realized that Thomas was the worst possible subject to talk of to a woman who desperately wanted a child of her own.

"Is it true that the Reverend at this church was murdered?"

Her body relaxed, and she straightened, resumed chopping. "Yes. And I've heard gossip that he was found in a house of ill-repute." She pursed her rather thin lips. I tried to look shocked.

"Oh, my goodness. I had no idea. Why ever…" I stopped as though too overcome by feminine delicacy to continue. My simpering disgusted me.

"No one knows," she spoke in a quiet tone, so none of the older ladies would hear. "He was married, surely he did not need the services of a brothel." I smiled inwardly at her naiveté as at least half of my gentlemen callers were married. I was very curious about his wife.

"Is Mrs. Crudden here today?" I asked.

"Oh, no. She's prostrated with grief and has taken to her bed. She's not receiving callers." A pout spoiled her pretty features, and she face became flushed. "I called on her, and her maid turned me away. She was most saucy!"

"Did he have children?" I kept my voice quiet.

"Yes, one daughter who is a missionary in China. She went off on her own against her parents' wishes. She isn't even married." Her scorn was evident. Again, I marveled at Mrs. Eliot's conventionality, and crossed the daughter off my list as potential murderers.

"Her parents wouldn't speak to her after she left against their wishes. I don't know if Mrs. Crudden has even written to her daughter to tell her of her father's death."

I was amazed that Mrs. Eliot would know so much about the Reverend's intimate family affairs. I raised an eyebrow, and she rushed to explain.

"I know this because my husband is a church warden, and he overheard Mrs. Crudden discussing what to do about her daughter with one of her closest friends, Mrs. Irene Able…"

She looked down at the vegetables and chopped more quickly.

What mean-spirited people. A man of the cloth to sever ties with his own flesh and blood simply because she disobeyed him…. Daddy would never cut me off, and I had brought real shame to our little family. *Even if he knew my sins, he'd still forgive me. And he would always welcome me back home.* I thought of the gracious, tree lined streets in Galt, and my eyes felt dry and gritty.

I cleared my throat. "Did you yourself know the Reverend well? Was he a dynamic church leader?"

"Oh yes. Goodness, the sermons he would preach. Sometimes I'd be upset for days. He made Hell seem so real, I almost felt the fire on my cheek. Hellfire is such a motivator. Such a preacher he was. We'll miss him terribly."

I thought of dear Reverend Cahill at Trinity Church in Galt, who preached earnestly and patiently about God's love and mercy. I sighed.

"It seems he had a real gift. Too bad I never had the chance to hear him." I put my hand in my pocket and crossed my fingers. My shoes were too tight, to cross my toes.

"Oh, he was marvelous. He could reduce grown men to blubbering puddles. Repent! Repent!" Her voice thundered and the other ladies in the kitchen looked our way, curious. She blushed. It did not suit her.

"What was he like when he wasn't preaching?"

"Oh, he was so caring, so giving of himself. He worked with young mothers who…" here she lowered her voice, put her finger to her lip theatrically, "were never married."

My contempt for this bourgeoisie housewife solidified like a brick in my throat. She was so complacent, so sure of her place in the world as one of the chosen, that she would never be capable of seeing an unwed mother as a human being, rather than a social pariah. She'd never think about why women could end up in less than ideal circumstances. The gold band on her ring finger was like a judge's wig. *In her small mind, she is the arbitrator of social norms.* I had met many women like her at Trinity Church. When I was a member of the Temperance Club at Galt Grammar School, I had been just like her.

"My, what a wonderful pastor." My mouth tasted sour. "What other Christian duties did he perform?" For the life of me, I couldn't see an impoverished, unwed mother chasing the Reverend into a brothel, unnoticed, and stabbing him to death in the basement.

"He organized a Young Christian group."

My ears perked up. "Oh?"

"Yes, it was for young men between ages 13 to 21. He tried to keep them away from the taverns and licentious living. When the weather was fine, he'd take them fishing, and they'd sleep in tents. They'd travel by ferry, usually to Tobermory. I don't know if you've been there, but it is splendid. Rocky, and the water so blue and clear, you could sit and stare at it all day and count the fish. Once they took the ferry to Manitoulin Island. It's the largest freshwater lake island in the world. My husband was lucky enough to accompany them on that trip. Imagine swimming in Lake Manitou - a lake on an island in the middle of another lake…My husband said Manitoulin Island has a hushed, almost reverent feel to it." Her eyes looked starry at her husband's poetic prowess. I cared not one iota about her husband or Manitoulin Island, but I matched my voice to hers, and said,

"Tell me more."

"There's not much more to tell. The youth performed acts of Christian charity when the weather was poor, such as stacking firewood for the elderly, hunting rabbits and even deer and donating the meat to the needy…why our Reverend was so selfless that he even included a Negro youth in his group." I couldn't stop myself from gasping. I tried to cover myself by coughing. It sounded fake to me.

She stared at me. "Are you overly warm? It is toasty in here with the woodstove going. Why don't you remove your hat? I can take it for you." She stretched out her hand.

My face flushed hotter than ever as she took me by surprise by the sudden turn in our conversation. I gawped at her. Could she somehow have seen my gaping bald spot under my head gear? I licked my very dry lips.

"No, thank you. I'm perfectly comfortable."

"But your cheeks are quite pink. Truly, you'd be more comfortable. It's a lovely hat; I'll take care not to crush it."

I clutched the offending article in both hands, hoping against hope that they were not smeared in flour or even worse, egg.

"No. I am most comfortable, and besides, it will have squished my hair.... will you excuse me for a moment?" I bolted from the overly warm kitchen and ran outside, taking big, gulping breaths, relishing in the cold, clean air.

There was a gust of wind, my hands flew to my hat, and accidentally ripped the feather, which floated away in a capricious fashion. I ran after it, but each time I approached, it darted in another direction. I knew I should return to the soup kitchen, but I couldn't face the phony atmosphere and the phonier Mrs. Eliot. I was almost certain the Negro youth she had mentioned was Damone – but what did it signify?

***

I gave up on the feather and walked back to 3rd Avenue with heavy steps. I tiptoed up to my bedroom, not wanting to speak to the other girls. Hair-dressing sessions were out of the question for the time being, and the other girls were constrained with me now that the terms my employment had so dramatically altered. They needed to know sooner than later, and Mrs. O'Hara had told them without fuss at breakfast the day after I accepted her offer.

"I suppose you weren't really that popular with the gentlemen," Vicky said after Mrs. O'Hara left the room, her voice thick with toast smothered with maple syrup. "Shame about your hair, really." Her smile was as sweet as the food in her mouth, and I resisted the urge to punch her and knock out her teeth. She swallowed, then grabbed a toffee from an ornate crystal bowl that was perched on the hutch and plopped it into her small mouth.

"Charlotte is very popular; she has just changed directions. She is a wonderful cook." I shot Eliza a grateful look. "You best be careful not to eat too many toffees, Vicky," Eliza continued, "they belong to Mrs. O'Hara and they are her particular favourites." I enjoyed the look of dismay on Vicky's face for the rest of the evening, and Eliza and I had a good giggle about it before her evening began.

After the house had begun its work for the evening, Jack and I descended as quietly as possible. We took a short walk, then returned and made a quiet meal of beans on toast, and a few pieces of fried liver for Jack in the kitchen, my new domain. It got late; I let Jack out and began to think of going to bed. I relished the thought of my bedroom being wholly mine. The gentlemen callers had no idea at how we girls laughed at them once they left, cheerfully gossiping about their lives, their shortcomings and their insecurities.

"Samuel Findlay was drunk tonight, as usual. He just wanted me to hold him and tell him what a big strong man he is, and so unappreciated by his wife," Matilda confided one cold December afternoon as we sat cozily around the fire.

"I have a better story than that. The sailor kid, Billy, I think his name is, gets seasick! He has to hide his illness from his Captain to keep his job. He's happy now the ships are in port, content to clean and repair for the winter. He's dreading the ice breaking up in March," said Eliza. We all had our stories, and few of them were complimentary to the gentlemen involved. Now it was nearly bed time, and I luxuriated in the thought of sinking into my own clean sheets, alone.

There was a light tapping on the back door. I opened it a crack, and was flabbergasted to see Inspector McLaughlin, accompanied by Bart, cradling a sleeping Thomas.

"C-come in," I said, opening the door wide. Bart stepped through, stepping carefully so not to jolt the baby awake. In the weak candlelight, I could see that he had tears running down his face.

"What's wrong? Would you like me to hold Thomas?" I searched for a clean handkerchief for Bart to wipe his face. Bart nodded no, and maintained his tender hold on Thomas, while wiping his eyes with one hand.

Inspector McLaughlin looked at me. My stomach lurched. I realized that I was bareheaded, and quickly retrieved my bonnet from its hook by the door. I fumbled as I tied it up. He smiled, and a flush of warmth spread through me. Then, all of a sudden, I was furious. *I don't need your pity*. But I held my tongue.

"Bart, you should sit down. This chair looks nice and sturdy," the policeman said. His voice was kind. "Charlotte, I think you should make us tea. This may take a while," he said.

I did as I was told, sneaking looks at Bart, who sat down heavily, huge shoulders quivering.

"What's wrong?" I whispered to Inspector McLaughlin. He touched my arm, and shook his head, no. My skin tingled at his touch. *Charlotte, don't be so stupid. You're bald. No decent man would ever want you.* But still, my body betrayed.

I assembled the tea as efficiently as I could, prepared a tray, and brought it to the rough pine table. Bart continued to hold the sleeping Thomas.

"May I take him now?" I held out my arms. I was almost free of my old life now; I no longer cared about the other girls finding out about my son.

"Not just yet Charlotte," said the inspector. "I'll take him; you and Bart need to talk." And he took my baby.

"Bart, you have to tell me what's happened." Bart was pale, his large round cheeks dotted with day old stubble. His hands were dirty, and I noticed a black rim of grime under his fingernails. *Jane could never accept that at her dinner table. She's so picky."* I felt sick.

"Where's Jane? What happened to Jane?"

Finally, Bart met my eyes. His were bloodshot. "She's dead." His voice was thick, as though his mouth were full of sand. He swallowed.

I pulled out a chair and slid into its hard embrace. "What do you mean – she can't be dead. She's a young, healthy woman. She has everything to live for."

"Well, she is dead. She took sick with influenza. At first it seemed like a mild case, but last night, her fever got worse and worse. She was burning up. She became delirious, thought she was a young girl. She didn't even remember who I was...." His voice faded. He looked exhausted, his sink pale, his eyes bloodshot and underlined with dark circles.

"I have to go back to the farm." His voice was hoarse.

"Yes, of course." Then I realized the significance of what he had just told me. "What about Thomas? Who'll look after my baby?"

"You'll have to take him. God help me, there's no way I can raise a baby on my own. I don't know how I'll manage without Jane as it is." His voice was shaky, and he fought for control. "Thomas' clothes and toys are in the cart outside."

A jolt of sheer joy shot through me. Thomas was mine, and I'd never, never let him go again. I stood up, and walked, nearly floated over to Inspector McLaughlin and took my sleeping baby in my arms. I looked at his sweet, rosebud lips, his closed eyes, and the tiny crust around his nose. *He's mine. If I have to go back and live with Daddy and Lavinia, so be it.*

I realized that my joy was in exact proportion to Bart's despair, and sat down beside him, quelling my exuberance. He had always been good to me, in his own quiet, undemonstrative way. He was a simple, poorly educated, hard-working farmer who rarely complained, and who had been unflinchingly loyal to Jane, and her unquenchable desire for a child.

"Bart. I'm truly so sorry." He looked at me. His eyes were still red-rimmed, and when he spoke, his voice croaked, as though from long disuse. "You are a good girl Charlotte. For God's sake, take Thomas away from this place. You and him deserve better."

"I will. I promise to bring Thomas to the farm as often as I can to see you."

"I want that very much. He's a good little chap."

"How will you go on?" I asked.

He looked at me. His face was lined, as he was exposed to the weather day in and day out. He was plump and round and his hair still resembled the tonsure of a monk. His eyes were brown, surrounded by tiny crinkles. It made his face look so kind, *how had I ever thought him homely?* I don't recall ever seeing a man display such a simple dignity.

"What choice do I have? The livestock need me. My parents are still alive. They live in town now, but they've said they'll stay with me at the farm until I get back on my feet. I loved Jane so much. She was everything to me.

"Will you be able to cope with Thomas?" he asked. He looked around him, and I knew that he knew exactly what kind of a house this was.

"I think Charlotte will manage just fine." Inspector McLaughlin touched my hand, and I felt a tingle. "I don't see her remaining in this house for long."

Just then, I heard quiet footsteps, and Mrs. O'Hara walked into the kitchen. She looked sleepy, her hair, usually so tightly scraped into its bun, disheveled. She took no notice of her appearance, still carrying herself with her usual poise and confidence.

"What on earth?" She looked at the sleeping Thomas in my arms.

"Mrs. O'Hara, come with me into the parlour and I'll explain." Inspector McLaughlin took her elbow and guided her out of the kitchen.

Bart remained quiet until the pair had left, but then began to speak, the words now spilling from him in a torrent.

"Jane was fine on Sunday. We went to church as usual. Thomas was as good as gold, slept in her arms throughout the service. I thought that Jane's cheeks looked a little bright, and her eyes looked a bit watery, but she insisted she was just tired, and cooked us a nice dinner when we got back from church. She made roast pork, roast potatoes, and yams. But she hardly ate a thing, just picked at her food, and you know how she always had such a healthy appetite.... When the dinner was over, she cleaned up and washed the dishes. She was cleaning Thomas' bottle when she got sick all over the place." I reached for his big, calloused hand and squeezed.

"She insisted on cleaning up, handing Thomas to me. I felt her head, and it was burning. She was sweating through her dress, although the fire was banked, and it was damned cold inside."

"You don't have to tell me this Bart. I mean, if you don't feel like talking about it. If it's too painful..." I really didn't want to hear the details of Jane's death. I was in my own happy bubble, still cradling Thomas.

"I have to talk about it, God damn it." Even in his distress, he kept his voice low, so not to scare Thomas.

"Sorry," I mumbled, angry with myself at my insensitivity. "What happened next?" Never had I wanted to know less.

"I put her to bed. She kept throwing the covers off then she'd start shaking with cold. I had to look after Thomas, plus the livestock. I wrapped Thomas up warmly and buttoned him inside my coat while I did my chores. Every time I came in, she seemed sicker."

"Did you go for the doctor?" I was staring at Thomas' face, marveling at the way his eyelashes fluttered ever so slightly as he dreamed.

"I did. Of course, I brought Thomas with me," he said defensively. "But the doctor was out on a call, delivering a baby. Some lucky soul was born while my Janie lay dying." He choked up, but continued, "I went to town, and picked up my parents. They came back with me, and Mum tended to Jane while my father helped me with the chores and with Thomas.

"I think Mum knew that Jane was going to die, because at some point during the evening, she told me to go into the sick-room and talk to Jane, to tell her how much I loved her...I would have done anything,

anything at all to save her, but I couldn't." His big head drooped, and his shoulders shook.

So, this is it. This is the face of true love. Comical looking Bart has the secret, while for all my advantages, I had no idea. At least until now.

Still holding the baby, I moved awkwardly closer to Bart. I took his hand once more, and we sat there for several long minutes.

Mrs. O'Hara walked into the room. The deep lines on her face were unsmiling. "You had promised me that the complication of your child was taken care of." Her voice was hard.

"I did take care of it. But my cousin Bart's wife…"

"Yes, the inspector has explained. I don't like it. I don't like it one bit. I have tried to be understanding towards you Charlotte, but you have tried my patience."

"Now, Mrs. O'Hara." Inspector McLaughlin looked at her, turning on all of his not inconsiderable charm. I was amazed that she didn't run and throw herself into his arms, given his crooked smile and mesmeric blue eyes. But she remained stern.

"Yes, I know my business only continues due to police sufferance. I know you can shut me down at any time. But if you do shut me down, you tell me where the men will go to get their needs met? I keep the house and the girls clean, well behaved, and discreet. Do you want *ladies* soliciting on street corners?"

Bart looked down at his hands and squirmed. He cracked his knuckles, then mumbled an excuse, and went outside to retrieve Thomas' possessions from the wagon.

"Do you know how many women in our society are prostitutes?" Mrs. O'Hara continued. "The latest, most informed guess is one prostitute for every twelve males. There very well may be a higher ratio in Owen Sound, given the number of ships that are berthed in the harbour." The woman was magnificent. She barely paused for breath.

"Actually, that wasn't my point, Mrs. O'Hara. I have looked the other way time and time again, and I agree with you that this house does provide a distasteful, but necessary service. I'm going to continue to look the other way. But we must solve Reverend Crudden's murder, and Charlotte can't return to Galt until it is solved. She is still a suspect, as are all of the girls here. The fact that her cousin sadly passed away isn't her fault, and I'm certain that Charlotte is such a resourceful young lady that she'll be able to manage the kitchen as well as look after Thomas."

Mrs. O'Hara closed her mouth, pursed her lips, but held her peace. Inspector McLaughlin winked ever so subtly at me, and again, I felt that hot betraying lurch, and again, I pushed it down. "So, it's settled," he said.

"Not so fast, young man," said Mrs. O'Hara. "What progress have you made into the Reverend's death?"

The twinkle in his eyes dimmed. "Not as much as I'd like. I need to speak to Damone. Have you had any word from him?"

She looked away. "None whatsoever, since the incident with Carl," she said. Was this a lie? I wasn't sure.

He looked at me. My heart sank. I had been so happy about having my baby back that for some brief, sweet moments, I'd forgotten about the murder. "No, I've had no contact," I said. This was the truth, but not for lack of trying. I had misgivings where Damone was concerned, and I felt sad.

Bart had finished unloading the wagon and sat back down. "Charlotte, this is no place for a baby. Especially with the murder. Can't you take him to Galt straightaway?" He looked at Thomas with such tenderness.

"I'll take him away as soon as I can." I closed my eyes, ashamed of the sullen tone in my voice.

"I am sure that Charlotte will take very good care of Thomas. He's too young to understand what kind of a house this is," said Inspector McLaughlin. "Now, I'll accompany you home. You must be exhausted."

"No, I can get myself home." Bart turned to me. "The funeral will be on Thursday, at St. Paul's..."

"I'll be there," I said.

"Will you bring Thomas?" His eyes were pleading.

"Yes, of course. You're the only father he has ever known."

His shoulders heaved. I looked away, pretending not to notice. After a moment, I hugged Bart goodbye, and Inspector McLaughlin bade us good evening. He pressed my hand a second longer than necessary as they left, and I felt my face flame. I turned quickly away and looked at Mrs. O'Hara.

She appeared exhausted, the skin under her eyes paper thin and bruised looking. She looked back at me steadily for a few long moments, then said, "Your cousin is right. This is no place for a baby. But for the time being, we'll make do."

"Where should I put his belongings?" Bart had left the baby's cradle, clothes, and mostly handmade toys in the kitchen.

"We'll have to move you and Thomas to the tiny back room. We can't have the gentlemen callers seeing or hearing a baby. Babies are the very last thing they want to think of when they come here!" She displayed a ghost of a smile, and I felt reassured.

"Yes, Ma'am." I tried to sound meek, but my heart was singing. Jack looked at me pleadingly, and I realized he needed to go outside. Mrs. O'Hara helped me set up the cradle and we carried my mattress downstairs to my makeshift room. Thomas had not awakened once, little realizing that his life had just been turned upside down. When I laid his sweet head down in his cradle, I kissed him on his forehead, and still he slept. I quickly hooked Jack on his lead and walked him out the door.

"No long walk for you tonight," I told my energetic dog. He seemed to understand, took care of his needs, trotted back inside, and curled himself into a tight little ball under the cradle, let out a big sigh, and set himself to sleep.

I slept more peacefully that night on my mattress on the floor, than I could remember since before my Mamma had died.

***

When morning came, Thomas blinked at me with sleepy eyes, then began to howl. "Mamamamamamama!" he screamed. I picked him up, tenderly, but I knew that to him, I was not his Mamma. He was screaming for Jane. I changed his napkin, gave him a bottle of warm milk, dressed him in soft, snug clothes that Jane had painstakingly sewn, and we took Jack outside. He stopped crying when he saw Jack running around the yard, chasing his tail, rolling on his back, and being his usual exuberant self. He even shrieked with laughter when Jack ran to him and gave him a sloppy kiss, and I sighed with relief.

I had a very busy day, getting used to Thomas, whose needs had changed significantly from when I had lived at the farm six months ago. Thomas was wary of me, and cried intermittently for "Mamma," but he was enchanted by Jack. When my housemates came downstairs around noon, their reactions were amusing.

Felicity cooed, "Who's this little angel?" and picked him up and twirled him about, much to Thomas' alarm. He began shrieking, and I scooped him from her arms. Eliza looked at me, her dark eyes beaming, rejoicing in my happiness.

"Oh," said Vicky, holding her nose, "I had no idea that you had a child. How inconvenient for you, dear Charlotte. What's that dreadful stink? Did you forget to change him, my dear girl?" I bit my lip and tasted blood.

"He has a funny face," Vicky continued. "He looks like a monkey."

The slap was loud and the reverberation bounced off the pots and pans hanging from the kitchen ceiling. I looked down at my hand. It was shaking, but not stinging. I looked up through a red haze, and saw Eliza standing at Vicky's side, holding her own hand, a look of astonishment on her face. Vicky clutched at her right cheek, screaming cuss words that would make my sailors proud.

"What on earth?" Mrs. O'Hara threw open the door.

"Eliza hit me. Hard." Vicky whined, holding her cheek. I noted with satisfaction that she had real tears in her eyes. By the loudness of that slap, her cheek must have stung like the devil. This thought did not make me feel any compassion for her at all.

Mrs. O'Hara turned to Eliza. "Is this true?"

Thankfully, Thomas had stopped crying, and seemed as mesmerized as the rest of us at the drama unfolding in the dark, damp kitchen. Laundry was hung to dry from the ceiling. I hoped my undergarments were not on display. I shook my head, trying to clear away this inconsequential thought, and listened closely as Eliza spoke. Somehow, I felt like I was distant from the drama, but of course I was right at its heart.

"Yes, I'm afraid it is true." Eliza met Mrs. O'Hara's gaze with respect, but she stood her ground, and her voice was steady.

Mrs. O'Hara stared at Eliza for several long moments, then turned to Vicky. "Vicky, will you come with me." She did not say please.

Vicky looked at the keeper. Her face was expressionless, but her tone, when she spoke, was insolent.

"I don't want to come with you. That cow Eliza hit me. My face is probably marked for life. I demand that you call the police. I want that nice inspector who dealt so effectively with Charlotte. What was his name? I don't remember his name. I liked him, even though he's so ugly."

I gasped, and the other girls let out their breath, almost as one.

"Your voice sounds slurred, Vicky." Mrs. O'Hara's own words were clipped. Her fist was clenched, and her face was white. By some continued miracle, Thomas remained silent in my arms, although I had to restrain him from pulling my hair. I was bald enough already.

"Have you been drinking?" asked the keeper. Vicky touched her skirt pocket, an involuntary motion. I knew that was where she carried the small flask she kept full of red wine. She drank it as if it were juice. She made no secret of it in front of us girls but was careful to keep her drinking hidden from Mrs. O'Hara and sucked hard candies continually, to hide the smell.

"Of course, I haven't been drinking." Her fleshy lips trembled, and I could see a fine sheen of perspiration on her face although the kitchen was cool.

"Open your mouth and let me smell your breath. I don't believe you." Mrs. O'Hara took a step closer to Vicky, and the girl lashed out, pushing her away with a hard jab at her chest. She then stomped up the stairs and slammed her bedroom door. It banged so loudly that the crockery rattled. This did not escape Mrs. O'Hara.

"Ladies. Have you observed Vicky drinking?"

We all stood silent, staring intently at the floor, the wall, or in my case, at Thomas.

"Your loyalty is commendable, ladies, although it is misplaced. Vicky has come to me repeatedly with complaints about each of you." Still, none of us spoke. "Very well, your silence condemns her," said Mrs. O'Hara with a crisp finality in her voice. "If she did not drink habitually, one of you would have spoken up for her. You all know I will not tolerate drunkenness in my house. Vicky will have to leave."

She turned to Eliza. "I don't condone violence either, but in this case, I am going to overlook it." Eliza opened her mouth.

"No, I don't want explanations or gratitude. I only want a smooth-running house. Has anyone seen Damone?" We shook our heads, no.

"Hmmm. Well, keep your eyes and ears peeled, and go about your day. Charlotte, perhaps you can prepare lunch for us today? How about the beefsteak and kidney pudding that you made last week?"

"Do we have a rump steak, kidney and suet?" I enquired. The beef pudding was a lot of work, and I wanted to spend my day admiring Thomas.

"Yes, you can go to the butcher, and push Thomas in his pram."

"I'll have it ready," I promised.

"Thank you." She flashed me one of her rare smiles that lit up her face. She walked over to me and took Thomas in her arms. Her nose wrinkled, and she handed him right back.

"He is a little malodorous, Charlotte. I'll leave him to you and deal with Vicky now."

She smiled at me, and again her face lit up. I took Thomas in my arms. The smell was beautiful to me. I hummed as I got to work, cleaning then bathing him. Jack barked a couple of times and cocked his head, and I grinned at him. "We're a family of three now." Jack sighed, turned himself around a few times, and plumped himself down on the wooden floor where he would be most underfoot. I grinned again.

***

I had finished bathing the baby and was singing him a little ditty Mamma had sung to me, when Jack let out a low growl. I heard a shriek, and a thud, then multiple thuds. Eliza screamed, then Matilda yelled,

"Someone send for the doctor!"

I grabbed Thomas and ran to the front of the house. Jack was barking frantically by now.

"Quiet Jack," I hissed, but he paid no heed.

Mrs. O'Hara lay in a heap at the bottom of the very steep wooden stairs that led to the bedrooms. She was not moving, and her head was twisted at an unnatural angle. Vicky was leaning against the wall at the top of the stairs. Her hair was undone, and her plump figure was shaking. She kept moaning, over and over "It's not my fault. She fell. It's not my fault." Matilda, our dear, large, practical Matilda, carefully stepped over our employer, and climbed the stairs deliberately, each step making an articulated sharp clack, as she ascended. Once she reached the landing, she slapped Vicky with all her might, once on each cheek. Vicky was effectively silenced, and she sank her plump frame into a seated position on the top stair, her skirts disarranged around her thick, white ankles. *She has bare legs.*

The rest of us girls stood, transfixed, while Thomas, sensing the poisonous atmosphere, began to whimper softly. Jack ran over to Mrs. O'Hara, and I was frightened he'd start to lick her. I quickly handed Thomas to Eliza, then ran and restrained my dog. I knelt down by the keeper and felt her wrist for a pulse. It was rapid but seemed strong. I leaned over and put my ear to her mouth; her breathing was shallow, but constant. I gently straightened her head, after first ensuring she had no broken bones.

"Matilda, run and fetch the doctor. Please. Eliza, can you hand Thomas to Felicity, then come here and help me?" I spoke slowly and calmly, focusing on keeping my breathing steady and even. In. Out. The girls obeyed me, happy to have someone take charge.

Eliza knelt down beside me, and I said loudly, "You must fetch blankets and a pillow. Clean water as well." She nodded and gathered her skirts, about to rise, but I grabbed her hand as tightly as I could. She looked startled, then relaxed a little as I looked deep in her eyes and breathed, "Ignore what I just said. Slip out the back door and fetch Inspector McLaughlin. As fast as you can. But leave this room slowly; we don't want Vicky running away or getting violent again." I spoke so softly my lips barely moved, and I hoped against hope that she had understood.

Eliza's eyes widened, and she looked towards Vicky, still sitting at the top of the stairs. She gave me the barest of nods, then slid gracefully away. Vicky didn't seem to notice. *Was she inebriated to the point where she no longer was aware of her surroundings?* Speculation was useless, and I made Mrs. O'Hara as comfortable as I could, then took Thomas from Felicity, and held him close.

The time passed so slowly that every beat of my heart felt like it pulsed in slow motion. Felicity slowly walked out of the room to prepare tea. Vicky didn't challenge her departure. Matilda took care of Thomas, who played solemnly with his wooden blocks, wide-eyed and self-contained. *Is he missing Bart and Jane? He has been through so much upheaval this week.* If he was upset, he gave no indication, other than to suck his thumb. I sat in silence on the pine floor, holding Mrs. O'Hara's hand, waiting for help to arrive.

There was a quiet knock on the front door, and Jack barked. We all started, and looked at Vicky, who continued to sit as if unaware at the top of the stairs, alternating between humming and singing songs I had never heard before. I released Mrs. O'Hara's hand, and walked as quietly and calmly as I could manage to see who was calling. I didn't want Vicky disturbed. *Surely the police wouldn't come to the front door and knock...* I opened the door, silently cursing its rusty, squeaking hinges. A burly sailor was waiting, looking scrubbed and bashful, cap in hand.

I had forgotten to close the curtains, our sign that the house was closed to business. I quickly stepped on the porch, shutting the door quietly behind me.

"I'm sorry, there's been an accident," I told the sailor. "Please spread the word that the house will be closed for at least a couple of days. Sorry to disappoint you," I said quickly, as I saw his large hands clench. "You'd better leave quickly; the police are on their way." He looked up and down the street, then slouched off.

I returned to the foot of the stairs. The tableau remained the same, but Mrs. O'Hara was moaning softly now. Vicky remained motionless at the top of the stairs, still humming in a strange, guttural tone that only added to my anxiety. Thomas sucked this thumb as we waited and waited.

***

I felt a hand on my shoulder and started. It was all I could do not to cry out. I turned around, and Inspector McLaughlin had a finger to his lips, shushing me. He was dressed completely in black and he had his hair slicked back. From the coconut fragrance, it seemed he had used copious amounts of Macassar oil. I remembered Mamma covering the back of Daddy's chair with a lacy "anti-macassar" cloth she had made specially to protect the fabric from the oil from his hair. The inspector smelled fresh, like Pears soap, which was a small luxury I refused to do without. I shook my head. These pleasant thoughts were no help to me today.

"Mrs. O'Hara requires medical attention," I muttered as quietly as I could.

"I've come to review some paperwork with you Charlotte," said the inspector loudly. "Can you, Matilda and Eliza come with me? Bring Thomas," he said in a false, jovial tone. His jaw was set in a grim line, however, as he ushered us down the hall and into the kitchen.

"Does that girl…" he looked at me, and I responded, "Vicky."

"Does Vicky carry a knife?" he whispered. Most girls who sold their bodies hid one in their skirts, to protect themselves from drunken, vicious men. *What a brutal profession.*

"I think she does," said Matilda, and I remembered Vicky showing the knife to us one afternoon. "It's a real tortoise shell handle, my beloved bought it for me on a business trip he took to New York City." Another opportunity to boast.

"Is there a set of stairs on the outside of the house, a fire escape?" asked Inspector McLaughlin. "I'm hoping we can surprise her and avoid more bloodshed."

"What about Mrs. O'Hara?" I demanded.

"Doctor Forsythe won't come in until I have Vicky in custody. He says it's too dangerous."

"He's afraid of a girl?" Eliza asked.

"He's afraid of a villain with a knife." The inspector frowned. There was no twinkle in his blue eyes.

"There's a rickety old staircase out back. I think it stops at Mrs. O'Hara's bedroom. But her window will be locked at this time of year," I said. My stomach knotted. I noticed I was panting a little, and despite the coolness in the house as no one had stoked the woodstove, I was perspiring freely.

"Take Thomas and lock yourself in the kitchen. In exactly ten minutes, create a big distraction. You can get Jack to bark, bang pots, kick the door…I want as much noise as possible so that Vicky won't hear me when I break the window. Is there a neighbour you can leave Thomas with?"

I had no hesitation. "No. They all despise our line of work."

"Fine. I'll leave one man with you girls. Are you clear about what I need you to do?"

"Yes. It won't be hard to get Jack into a frenzy of barking," I promised. "Be careful when you sneak up on her." I had forgotten the baldness of my head, but now I felt it, stroked the soft fuzz that was beginning to grow in ever so slowly.

He looked at me. His gaze was kind, soft, tender, and the lines around his eyes crinkled ever so slightly. He took my hand, and brought it to his lips, and kissed it ever so lightly, then released it and marched away. I shook my head. *Did he really do that?* I rubbed my skin where he had kissed it, then turned my attention to the task at hand. Eliza, Matilda and Rose were looking at me, mouths gaping. I looked at Thomas and rubbed Jack's ears. My face was hot.

I checked my pocket watch, which was pinned to my black frock. It was a blue enamel fob, hanging from a fleur-de-lis. An ardent gentleman had pressed it upon me. "This belonged to my sister, who was a nurse," he said as he tenderly pinned it on my night robe. "I don't think I can accept it," I said, but he replied, "I've already asked Mrs. O'Hara, and she said as long as you don't make a habit of accepting gifts from gentlemen, she'd allow it this once." He left the following day for Collingwood, to be married to a rather fat lady with protruding eyes, who was heiress to a prosperous shipping business.

Tick. Tick. Time passed inexorably but so very slowly. Thomas remained quiet, sucking his thumb, clutching Matilda. Eight minutes. Nine minutes. I got up slowly. Jack followed me with his big brown eyes, intelligent, alert, trusting me.

There. Ten minutes had passed. I rushed to the screen door; rapped sharply on it. Jack erupted into a gale of sharp barks. I banged the door, hard. Jack's barking became more and more frenzied. Bang. Bang. Bark. Bark. The barking became even more shrill. I heard a loud scream from upstairs, then the house fell silent, except for Jack's whimpering and excited pants.

Time once again stood still, heavy. Thomas made a soft moaning noise, then fell asleep on Matilda's shoulder, nestled into her neck. I felt a sudden, fierce rush of jealousy. *Will I never come first with my own son?* But then I felt an equally sharp flash of joy. I had years ahead of me to make up for lost time. "Lie down," I whispered to Jack, and to my surprise, he obeyed.

More time passed and passed. Finally, a police constable I didn't recognize tapped lightly on the kitchen door. Jack growled, low in his throat, and I shushed him.

"It's safe to come out now, Miss. The suspect is under arrest, and Doctor Forsythe is tending to Mrs. O'Hara."

"Was anyone hurt?" Eliza's usually soft voice sounded harsh.

"No. We were able to apprehend her without any fuss."

We walked slowly to the foot of the stairs. As we got there, I heard the front door slam shut. I walked to the window, and saw another constable lead a handcuffed Vicky into a covered wagon. I winced as she delivered a swift kick to his shin. I knew she was wearing her boots with a very pointed and unforgiving toe, "I bought them on Yonge Street in Toronto, darling, in the cutest little store…." The wagon was black and had "POLICE" written on the side in large yellow, block letters. *The neighbours will enjoy this spectacle.*

"Can you watch Thomas for a few more minutes, Matilda? I want to check on how Mrs. O'Hara is faring." I had decided days ago that Matilda had most probably told me the truth about the murder.

"Of course." I smiled at my friend, and kissed Thomas lightly on the top of his head. His dark hair was getting longer; he would need a haircut soon. I stifled another pang and ran once more to the foot of the stairs.

"Can I help, Doctor Forsythe? My father is an apothecary, and I've tended to a fair number of emergencies."

He looked down his nose. "How did you end up in a house like this?" He sniffed. "Not much can be done, young lady, and certainly not by you."

"Will you at least tell me; does she have a broken neck?" I had been worried about this, because of the odd and twisted angle of her head.

"No, I don't believe she does." He sighed heavily, and a little of the stiffness seemed to drain from his body. He said more gently, "She is badly concussed, and will require around-the-clock attention for the next few days, perhaps longer, much longer."

"We can take care of that," I promised.

"With a severe concussion, she will require utter peace and quiet, no stimulation whatsoever. She'll have to stay in a dark room, for the most part alone…" He looked at me intently under his large, shaggy eyebrows, which were liberally sprinkled with grey.

"You seem awfully young, and if you'll excuse me for pointing out the obvious, you girls are all…" he swallowed, unable to speak the word.

"Whores. Yes, I know what we are, Doctor. Mrs. O'Hara has been a very fair and gracious employer towards us, and we will close the house for however long is necessary and we will nurse her, and make sure all of her needs are looked after." I kept my voice even, although I knew my face was flushed, and I could feel perspiration trickle and tickle my eyebrows.

His eyes rested on my still prominent bald spot, and his lip curled. I could see a large vein in his temple throb, and his jaw was tightly clenched. However, he had little choice but to accept me at my word. "Very well, I will return tomorrow and check on her progress. To whom shall I submit my bill?"

I disliked this man more with every minute that passed, but I smiled sweetly, and said,

"Mrs. O'Hara has ample funds to pay you. This is a very well-run business, you know. You need not concern yourself."

He flinched, not even trying this time to hide his disgust. My disdain towards him was equal if not more, but I hid it better. He gathered his medical equipment, clicked shut his black medical bag, and marched out the front door with a curt, "Good day."

"What about moving her to her room? You don't want us to leave her on the floor, surely."

"The police can help you. I cannot strain my back. Good day to you."

***

I slammed the door after him so hard that the windows rattled. *Apparently, the Hippocratic oath does not extend to whores in the good doctor's estimation.* I cursed silently, then smiled the thought of how regally Mrs. O'Hara would have put him in his place had she been well. I held my head as high as she would have, and sailed back to the foot of the stairs, where Inspector McLaughlin and one constable remained, keeping an eye on the still prone Mrs. O'Hara.

The inspector stood up and dismissed his constable. "Charlotte, I'm concerned that you won't be able to manage both Thomas and Mrs. O'Hara." He pushed a stray lock of hair out of my eye with his big hand, then cupped my head for a brief moment, so the bald spot was embraced by his palm. I flushed and panted slightly. I was that warm.

"We'll manage. We don't have any choice, and I am used to dealing with medical concerns."

"Yes, I know. I'll speak to the other girls, to make sure they give you plenty of assistance."

"They will, Inspector. Mrs. O'Hara is a kind and fair employer. They'll want her back on her feet as speedily as possible for her sake, and for their own."

"Please, call me Conall."

I blushed even more furiously, lowered my eyes, and said nothing. I could hear Thomas fretting in the kitchen, and Matilda's answering, soothing tones.

"We should carry Mrs. O'Hara upstairs," I said.

"I sent the Constable for the stretcher we keep at the police station for emergencies such as these. He'll be back in ten minutes or so."

He took my hand, and I let him. We walked to the couch and sat a chaste distance apart, holding hands, until the Constable returned. In some ways, he returned far too soon; in others, not soon enough. When I heard the door open, I sprang to my feet, face still warm. Inspector McLaughlin, *Conall,* stood more sedately, releasing my hand slowly. He winked at me, and I touched my bald spot. Thomas stopped fretting; Matilda must have soothed him to sleep.

The two men positioned the stretcher beside Mrs. O'Hara, who seemed to be dozing now, and I held her head steady and straight in my hands while they carefully and slowly moved her. I had to release my hold on her head while they carried her up the narrow wooden stairs, but I followed them closely up to her bedroom, and we repeated the process in reverse, laying her in bed.

"Best to let her sleep now," I told the men in a low voice. "The body best heals itself when in deep slumber." We left the room and walked quietly downstairs, where the ladies were clustered still in the kitchen. The police bade us goodbye and departed.

Thomas was asleep in his crib, and I was annoyed that Matilda hadn't thought to remove his shoes. *She has no experience with babies, but mine is painfully limited too, and whose fault is that?* I had some challenging days ahead of me. Suddenly, I felt a swell of fury towards my mother, my sainted mother. *Why didn't she take better care of her health? How dare she leave me alone, motherless, with a useless, alcoholic father?* The waves of emotion washed over me and I cried silently, in the rocking chair Daddy had bought for me in Owen Sound before Thomas was born. Back and forth I rocked, trying to comfort myself, soaked in rage and grief. *If Mamma had lived, I never would have become pregnant. I would have finished my high school education, and perhaps even been accepted to the University of Toronto, for pharmacy. Even though I'm only a girl.* I blew my nose in a most unladylike way. *I'm no lady.*

I thought and thought, then finally I had a moment's peace, as I realized that had Mamma not died, I wouldn't have my beautiful baby boy, who was snoring now ever so softly in his crib, his thumb resting gently in his open mouth. Daddy used to say that life was a circle, and as I watched Thomas, lulled by his lusty breaths, I realized that the only way forward was one step at a time. The other girls were chatting quietly now in the parlour. I made my way there.

"Are you hungry?" I asked.

An affirmative chorus was my reply, so I returned to the kitchen, donned my apron, and prepared a simple, hearty lamb stew. I didn't have time to prepare dessert. *Mrs. O'Hara certainly enjoys pears,* I realized as I peered into the pantry and saw row upon row of the jars. *Good for the digestion.* My stomach rumbled, and I realized that I too was hungry. Very hungry. As if in response, Thomas began to wail, and I heard Matilda begin to croon. My stomach clenched. *I can't wait to have him to myself.* I quickly got some meat and vegetables from the icebox, cooked and pureed them as best I could, and handed the bowl to Matilda. She set about feeding Thomas, while I continued my work in the kitchen.

While the stew was simmering, I took Thomas from Matilda, cuddling him in my arms. He began to fuss immediately. "I think he wants to be let down, so he can explore," said Matilda. I scowled at her, but obeyed, and he immediately began to crawl towards the woodstove. I grabbed him by his frock and hastened him back to my lap. Immediately, he demanded in no uncertain terms to be put down. I acquiesced, and he crawled right back towards the woodstove. This game was repeated numerous times until I was frustrated, and handed him back to Matilda, who clambered down on the floor with him and they played with his blocks contentedly. I tried to smooth the frown from my face and went to the kitchen to finish the meal preparation.

My mind wandered as I set the table and bustled about, and I wondered, *Did the police finally have the killer? Did Vicky murder the Reverend Crudden? But why would she kill him? Surely it would be too much of a coincidence to presume that there were two homicidal maniacs attached to the brothel?* But the image of Vicky stabbing the Reverend then shoving the knife into my bedroom door just didn't sit well. Like me, she was an outsider to Owen Sound; when and where would she have encountered the Reverend? Whores did not frequent churches. *Did she even know him?*

Vicky had always seemed to feel some sort of odd kinship with me, priding herself that we both belonged to a higher social status than those from Owen Sound. Of course, she felt herself comfortably in the ascendant as a former resident of Toronto, rather than tiny Galt. But in her eyes, Galt was a huge step up from the rough and tumble nature of Owen Sound.

"Charlotte, did you know that in the 1850's, Owen Sound's roaring seaport made it so rowdy that it was known as 'Corkscrew City'? I bet boring Galt wasn't so lewd."

Eliza rolled her eyes and said, "Vicky, you've told us this before."

"That's why the 'Bucket of Blood' tavern got its name, at the intersection of Damnation Corners," I said.

Vicky looked miffed, that I knew something she didn't. I smiled a little at the memory. She was sullen, pompous, a dipsomaniac, irritating beyond belief, and obviously prone to violence. But I couldn't see her cunning enough to cover up a crime that had been committed three weeks ago. She would have burst with pride and excitement and told one of us. *But had she told Mrs. O'Hara and silenced her when the keeper threatened to expose her to the police?* If only I knew.

***

I set the table carefully, using Mrs. O'Hara's second-best china. We girls sat together for to eat the meal I prepared. Once my own hunger had been satisfied, I wiped Thomas' face, settled him comfortably on my knee, then asked, "Is Vicky the killer?"

The room fell silent. "Of course, she is," said Felicity, whom Vicky had taunted about her very slight overbite, and called her "Bucky" as often as she could. "It's beyond belief that we have two killers at work in our house."

"What was her connection to Reverend Crudden? Does anyone know?" asked Matilda.

We shook our heads, no. I fed Thomas a mouthful of mashed up beef (it looked disgusting but he chomped away enthusiastically with his few sweet teeth), then I asked, "Was he one of her gentlemen?"

The girls looked doubtful, and Eliza said, "I've never seen him here before the night he was killed. Has anyone else seen him here? Mrs. O'Hara said he wasn't a customer, but Vicky might have gone to his house?"

"No one has seen him here. You really think Vicky might have paid him a visit? At a Reverend's home? He was married." I tried to keep any trace of scorn from my voice, because as ludicrous as it seemed, it was not as ludicrous as the Reverend being found fatally stabbed in our cellar.

"Yes, he was married, but he was also stabbed to death in our basement." Felicity's voice sounded thin and scared. We were all scared. Would I have to return to Galt with Thomas to live with Daddy and Lavinia? How could I bear Lavinia overseeing my relationship with Thomas? And how could I afford to take him elsewhere? Further education seemed out of the question now that I had Thomas full-time.

I felt a tear slide down my cheek and brushed it away. Not such an awful fate compared to what my friends faced if Mrs. O'Hara did not recover sufficiently to ensure that the business would continue. Where would they go? What would become of them? I hoped they wouldn't migrate to Toronto. Small-town girls did not thrive in bigger cities, and I knew that there were many unsavoury men only too willing to take advantage of vulnerable women. We needed to resolve the murder of Reverend Crudden, whom I loathed now with such an almost murderous passion myself. I pictured his white belly, the subcutaneous fat underneath the flabby skin, the few hairs, brown and grey, sprouting around his navel, and shuddered. Try as I might to put it from my mind, I saw that image every night before going to bed. He had been violated in the most profound way possible, but had he himself violated innocents in life? A man of the cloth? I remembered our kindly Reverend Cahill at Galt's Trinity Church. He was upright, scholarly, and always kind and respectful, and I tried to imagine him stabbed to death in a brothel. It was unthinkable. But I couldn't rid myself of the image of Reverend Crudden. He was part of the brothel now, seared into its very walls, his noxious, rotting vapours emanating from the basement, permeating every room….

I shook my head vigorously. I was being fanciful and I needed to be strong for Thomas. He had fallen asleep, and I went to his crib and checked on him. He looked so peaceful, rosebud lips twitching, clutching the tiny teddy bear Bart had impressed upon me when he left, "Charlotte, he can't sleep without this. Jane made it for him…." His voice had choked and he thrust it in my hands and left.

"Where is Damone?" I asked the question we all had been thinking.

"We need to find him," said Eliza. She covered her face with her hands. "Do you think he is the murderer?"

"It seems suspicious that he keeps disappearing." I finally spoke the words. I didn't want to scapegoat the most vulnerable among us, but it was a relief to have my worst fears out in the open.

"I'll go speak to Mrs. Barrett again," I said. My stomach clenched at the thought, but this murder was destroying all of us, Vicky and Mrs. O'Hara included.

"Yes, that's best," said Eliza. "You know them better than we do. Perhaps she will trust you more."

"Will you look after Thomas?" I asked Matilda.

Eliza took my arm. "Perhaps you should bring Thomas with you. She might be more inclined to trust you when she sees you with a bairn of your own. Mother to mother."

I shook my head no, but I knew she was right. I needed to use any and all advantages at hand. We needed to find Damone. I kissed the top of Thomas' sleeping head, and mentally apologized to him for the thought of using him for any purpose at all.

The next day, bright and early, I put Thomas into his pram, folded him into the quilt that Mamma had so painstakingly made for me, and fastened Jack to his lead. I had debated whether or not to bring Jack, but I remembered the happiness he'd brought to Damone's little sister, Trinity, and hoped this too would help soften Mrs. Barrett in my favour.

It was a crisp morning with a gentle breeze, the leaves twinkling on the trees. Thomas burbled in the pram, struggled to sit up, looking at me with his huge brown eyes, Tony's eyes. *I should write to Tony in Italy,* I thought, *and let him know that I'm going to raise his son, and never let him go. Perhaps I can take him to a photographer and have his picture taken.* I knew there was one in Owen Sound; I'd seen samples of his work in the store window. They were quite good, if stiffly posed, but somehow still capturing the essence of the subject. I still had a soft spot for Tony, despite his lack of backbone. Compared to most of the men I'd met in my erstwhile occupation, he was a gentleman, although I still felt an incredulous contempt at his complete refusal to accept any responsibility for his son. *His loss.*

Jack scampered ahead of me on his leash, sniffing the myriad of smells discernable only to the sensitive canine nose. I enjoyed the walk so much that I was almost sad when arrived at the Barrett's door. I swallowed, patted Jack's silky head, and kissed Thomas's sweet, chubby cheek for moral courage, then tapped gently at the door.

I heard footsteps padding heavy on the wood floor and smacked my forehead. Today was Jane's funeral. The Anglican church was just around the corner. I had promised to attend, yet here I was at the Barrett's tiny house. I thought of how hurt Bart would be at my absence, and nearly ran away. Too late; the door opened, and Mrs. Barrett squinted at me. She frowned, then looked at the pram. A smile lit her lined face and transformed her entirely. Jack greeted her with enthusiasm, jumping up, and she stoked his silken ears, frowning once more.

"Why are you here?"

"I want to talk to you. I need to find Damone. May we come in?"

"What, so you can blame him for the murder, the only black boy in a whore house?" Regardless of her fierce words, she opened the door, and motioned us in.

Once I had hung my cloak on the hook by the door, and sat down, I continued, "No, Mrs. Barrett. That's exactly what I want more than anything to avoid."

She looked sideways at Jack, who had laid down at my feet. "He's a very clean dog," I reassured her. "There will be no messes, I promise. Thomas is the one likely to mess...."

My attempt at humour brought a weak smile to her face. She bent over Thomas' pram, and he sat still, staring at her with Tony's dark huge eyes, framed by his long, black eyelashes that no cosmetic enhancements could replicate.

"He don't have your colouring honey," said Mrs. Barrett.

"No, his father is Italian." She flinched little at my matter-of-fact acceptance of my past immorality, then smiled sadly, seeming to understand how an upper-class white girl like me came to work for Mrs. O'Hara.

She offered me refreshments, but I declined. I put Thomas down on a blanket on the floor to play with his toys, and then Damone's little sister, Trinity, slowly walked into the room, her shoulders hunched, looking down at the floor.

"Would you like to play with the baby?" I asked her, and she shrugged, then smiled at me. *Her brown eyes are almost as beautiful as Thomas',* I mused, as I showed her how to assemble and disassemble the wooden train Daddy had mailed me to pass along to Bart and Jane. *Thank heavens he's all mine now,* I caught myself thinking, then remembered with a flush of shame that I was even now missing Jane's funeral. Attached to the train was a small card, in which Daddy had written simply, *Please come home.*

I need to tell Daddy that I have Thomas permanently now, I realized. *Perhaps he is at Jane's funeral?* I didn't know if Bart had informed him in time for him to make the arrangements to attend. I swallowed a lump in my throat the size of Georgian Bay, and left Thomas playing with Trinity, and turned to Mrs. Barrett.

"I don't believe for a moment that Damone attacked the Reverend. Why would he do that?" I asked her. I was surprised to observe Mrs.

Barrett clench her large hands into tight fists, and was even more shocked when she pounded one fist, hard, on the pine table. The children started, and Thomas looked frightened. Trinity approached her mother, took her hand gently, unfolding the fingers, and said, "It's ok Mamma, take a deep breath. Calm down," in a voice as soft as butter.

Mrs. Barrett's eyes turned red and welled up. She put her arm around Trinity, patted her head, then pushed her away. "You go play, honey," she said. Her tone was gruff, but the love in her voice was evident, and the little girl went back to Thomas and the train.

"Are you really that ignorant girl?" Her voice was harsh now, and I realized she was addressing me. I said, "Ignorant of what?" My voice was as hollow as the pit in my stomach.

"You are. You're totally in the dark. Aren't you?" Mrs. Barrett smiled, a rictus that revealed her white teeth, but did not reach her eyes. "White people think they're so smart, but they can't see what's in front of their noses."

"There's no reason to insult me, Mrs. Barrett," I said. My face felt stiff. "I really can't help the colour of my skin, any more than you can. I counted Damone as my friend, my dear friend, and I want to help him. Plus, to be honest, I want my life back. I'm trying to put my mistakes behind me, but I literally can't move forward until this murder has been solved. The police have forbidden me from leaving Owen Sound."

"Damone will hang," said his mother in a harsh whisper.

"Only if he's guilty. Inspector McLaughlin," I felt my face grow hot and I cursed myself for blushing. Mrs. Barrett looked at me with eyes that missed nothing. "Inspector McLaughlin is a fair and decent man."

"McLaughlin is white."

"Yes, he is white, but we aren't all monsters. Some of us are, I know, but please, there are decent white people, and the inspector is one of them."

I had raised my voice, and of course I felt the heat in my cheeks. Again. Thomas looked at me with his big brown eyes, and to hide my embarrassment, I rose from the table and sat down beside him on the clean pine floor, giving him a kiss and playing with the train. Mrs. Barrett approached, took my hand, and pulled me up.

"You're not so bad, for a white whore. But can't you see how scared I am for my son? I only have your word that the inspector is a decent man. It would be so easy for him to pin the blame on Damone, and who'd care if a black boy hanged for the murder of a white man of the cloth?"

"I would care." My throat felt dry and constricted, and my eyes prickled, as though I had grit in them. "And McLaughlin cares too. He comes from Ireland and is no stranger to violence, and hating people just because they look different, sound different, worship differently."

Mrs. Barrett looked at me, eye to eye, for a long moment while the children played, oblivious to the tension between us. "Damone, is here," she said, so softly that I barely registered what she said. "He's in the woodshed."

It took a few long seconds for me to grasp what she had just said. I shut my eyes to try to quell the red mist that was rising in waves from my chest to behind my eyes. All this time, I had suffered, and suffered, the girls at the brothel had suffered, and what about Mrs. O'Hara? Would she ever recover? I'd been beaten to a pulp by Detective Craig, and I was not allowed to leave a situation I now loathed. Vicky was in jail, and the one person who could possibly shed some light on what had happened that fateful night of the Reverend's murder was here, hiding in his mother's woodshed?

I stuffed my fist into my mouth, to try to forcibly hold back the bitter tirade that was on the tip of my tongue, ready to hail down on the sturdy woman standing before me. Mrs. Barrett seemed to have physically deflated. She stood slumped before me. Her large shoulders were no longer held proudly, and her rather large belly stuck out almost as though she were with child, as though she did not have the energy to suck it in and put her best self forward. Her feet were splayed like a duck; *she's braced herself for what's to come.* Her very vulnerability enraged me. I took my fist out of my mouth, the tirade just trembling on the tip of my tongue, when Damone's sister shrieked, "The baby stuck a wheel in his mouth!"

I heard a gurgling, choking noise, and Mrs. Barrett pushed me aside and sprinted to Thomas. I ran after her. I tried to reach my baby, but Mrs. Barrett shoved me away like a bear swatting a fly. She threw herself down on the floor, grabbed Thomas, and angled him so he was facing the floor with his legs and torso elevated. With the heel of her big hand, she delivered five firm and distinct blows between his shoulder blades. Even in my horror, I saw how she kept his head supported by holding his chin between her thumb and forefinger.

Thomas coughed, spat, coughed, then shrieked with terror. He threw his head back, then vomited all over his clothes and Mrs. Barrett. I quickly picked through the vomit and then went weak in the knees with gratitude when I felt the tiny wooden part between my fingers. Mrs. Barrett motioned to Trinity to fetch her a clean rag, which she took and calmly cleaned the now sobbing Thomas who was clinging frantically to his saviour, his arms practically in a chokehold around her neck.

She rose heavily to her feet, and gently disentangled herself from Thomas. "You need to go to your Mamma now, Son. Sit down, Charlotte," and she pushed me gently towards the threadbare sofa. I obeyed, and she handed my baby to me. She was matter-of-fact, as though she had not just saved his life. I looked at her and did not say anything. The lump in my throat was too large. I could barely breathe. I tried to convey the depth of my gratitude as I gazed at Mrs. Barrett, and I must have succeeded, as she nodded at me, looked a bit stern, then with surprising grace moved swiftly to my side and kissed the top of my head. Thomas grew heavy in my arms as his breathing steadied and he relaxed into sleep, overwhelmed from his trauma. I would not recover as quickly as he.

"I'll fetch Damone," said Mrs. Barrett. Due to the drama with Thomas, I'd nearly forgotten about Damone and my other difficulties. When she left, I felt an overwhelming desire to flee with Thomas and Jack. I didn't want to have to cope with Damone, even though I had come here expressly to seek him out. Most of all, I wanted to go home, to Galt, to Daddy. *Maybe Lavinia isn't so bad after all. I can tell everyone that I married in Owen Sound, and my husband died, or I can say I adopted my cousin's baby….*

My thoughts were wild and disorganized, as I was engulfed with homesickness, missing our house on stately Aberdeen Road, missing the Grand River, the blue herons, and Daddy most of all. I thought of my cozy bedroom that Daddy had painted soft grey. My quilt made the room cheery and welcoming. I had a small woodstove in the corner to keep me warm during the bitter winter nights. My quilt always smelled a bit smoky. I wanted to visit Mamma's grave in the leafy Trinity cemetery on Blenheim Road, lay flowers, and apologize over and over to her for the mess I had made of my life. I wanted to promise her that I'd mend my ways, become a good girl, and raise Thomas the way she'd raised me. I wanted home. I wanted to go home and I wanted to be home.

***

The door creaked a little, and I lowered Thomas back into his pram. I took a deep breath, turned around, and looked into Damone's eyes. They were bloodshot and darted back and forth. They protruded more than I remembered, and I realized that he had lost a great deal of weight, weight that he could ill afford to lose. His skull was clearly visible under the dry parchment skin. He smelled earthy, pungent; he clearly had not bathed in a very long time. His breath was sour. His clothes hung from his thin frame. Damone had always been a natty, careful and particular dresser. Now the clothes that he had brushed, hand washed, and ironed so carefully every afternoon at the brothel were dirty and worn, although the original quality was still evident when I looked more closely.

Oddly enough, he still sported his signature red polka-dotted bow-tie. When he worked for Mrs. O'Hara, it used to look jaunty, but now it looked worn, droopy, defeated. There was a dark stain on it, and I refused to think of what it might be.

Thomas was sleeping heavily, emitting the occasional sweet, soft snore. I moved to give Damone a hug.

"Don't," he said. His voice sounded dry, as though he had gravel or dust in his throat, and was long unaccustomed to speech. "I'm not clean."

"I want to hug you anyways. We're friends."

"Don't you understand Charlotte. I'm unclean." His thin arm held me at bay. As skinny as he was, he was strong, and I stood rebuffed. I swallowed and tried to ignore the prickling in my eyes.

"We need to talk," I said.

"My mother can mind the children, and you can come with me to the woodshed." I must have looked alarmed, because he laughed without any trace of humour whatsoever. "Not so fond of me now, are you, *Friend?* I'm not going to hurt you. Or doesn't a nice white girl like you want to spend time with a filthy black boy?"

He'd never spoken to me so harshly before, and in my mind, we had truly been friends. My heart thumped.

"Damone, you know I've never thought like that. I'm sorry…"

But am I truly sorry? It isn't my fault that he's black and I'm white. I've done my best to be his friend, I've stood up for him with Inspector McLaughlin and even now, I'm here behind McLaughlin's back. I looked into Damone's eyes, and I saw that they were full of tears. He wiped them away roughly. *He's embarrassed that I've seen him cry,* It seemed to me that I did not know my friend very well at all.

Mrs. Barrett said, "I'll mind Thomas. I think you two need to talk privately. It's best that you don't return to the shed Damone, because if anyone saw you with a white girl.... You know people always put the most wicked interpretation on the most innocent actions. Take Charlotte to my bedroom and close the door so the children don't hear. Little pitchers have big ears," and she looked meaningfully at Trinity. Damone took my hand in his. I willed myself not to flinch. *Am I holding the hand of a murderer?* I wonder if he read my mind, because he let go as though my flesh burned him and motioned me to follow him down the dark and dingy hall to the back of the tiny house.

Mrs. Barrett's bedroom was unpainted. The rough pine floor and walls had shrunk with age, and she had stuffed rags into the gaps, to plug the cold draughts. Her bed was tiny, just a mattress raised on wooden crates. I was fascinated with the quilt on her bed. The room was surprisingly bright, and I could examine it clearly. I knew that secret messages were embedded in quilt patterns. Damone himself had told me this over hot chocolate one leisurely morning.

"Slaves weren't allowed to read or write; it was illegal in the Confederate states for the slave owners to teach them any literacy skills." I had flinched at his matter-of-fact tone describing such ruthless inequality. He continued as though he had not noticed my discomfort, "Codes were part and parcel of the slaves' existence, and a way to passively and sometimes actively resist their complete ownership. Some forms of dance, spirituals, code words and phrases and symbols were memorized so we could communicate with each other so the owners wouldn't understand." Here he grinned, a delicious glee evident on his face. But he must have noticed me squirm, so he said, "Some whites created codes to help the slaves. You're not all bad." He smiled lopsidedly at me. "Even the youngest Negro child was taught to keep those codes and symbols secret."

Mrs. Barrett's quilt was simple, in muted colours of mostly black and blue, obviously put together from scraps of old clothing. In the top left corner, there was a brown flying goose stitched carefully into some material that looked like an old shirt. It looked mostly like triangles to my untrained eye, but Damone assured me it was indeed a goose. "A Canada goose," he said, a bit impatiently, but then he relented and said, "The flying geese symbol is so that escaped slaves would follow the actual geese as they migrated north. Along the way, the birds stop for food, water, and find themselves safe places to rest, and the slaves took advantage of these too."

"Will you tell me about the pattern on the bottom of the quilt? It looks like a square with diamond edges."

"It's the North Star symbol. It carried two meanings: for folks to prepare to escape, and the other to follow the North Star to Canada, where they would be free. The slaves also sang a song, *Follow the Drinking Gourd,* as two of the Big Dipper's stars point directly to the North Star. This quilt is almost in rags now, but my Ma will never let go of it. It's the symbol of her freedom. From the Barretts and all the whites who used us and owned us. Owen Sound has been good to us, or it has until now. My Ma's free, but I'm not."

I squeezed his hand gently, let go, and said, "Now, you need to tell me what happened to that dreadful Reverend Crudden. It's time."

He stared at me for a moment. His face appeared stronger somehow, the thin cheeks and bony chin held high. "You have no idea how evil that man truly was Charlotte. *Dreadful* is far too kind."

I was full of dread myself. I didn't want to hear what was to come but listen I must. "What do you mean? Did you know him before he ended up dead in Mrs. O'Hara's basement?" I was pretty sure I knew the answer, and my heart sank again.

"Ma is a very religious lady. Most slaves were, they had to believe in freedom in the next life, because they sure didn't have it in this life."

"Yes, I know. I understand." I tried to conceal my impatience.

"You know nothing! You're a spoiled white girl who made a mistake and turned to a life of sin on a whim. You can be free any time you like, you have a baby, a nice home and a rich Daddy to go back to."

I remained silent.

He took a deep breath, then continued, "So, Ma has always attended church. She used to attend a Methodist Church on the other side of town that was closer to where we lived, but Reverend Crudden persuaded her…."

"How did she know the Reverend?" I interrupted.

He shrugged his thin shoulders. "She took in his laundry."

I sighed.

"That's how she supported my sister and me all these years, you know that," he said.

"I just feel bad..."

"Well, don't feel bad. She's so happy to be free, here in Canada, and she loves Owen Sound. She loves the water, she enjoys watching the hustle and bustle of the ships, and she has a passion for ice-skating, of all things!" He grinned, and I smiled back at him. "Fancy a slave from the cotton plantations of South Carolina ice-skating."

The smile faded from his face and he stared at me with huge eyes. "I'm going to be hanged Charlotte." He grabbed my hand and held it in a vice-like grip.

"Let go, Damone. You're hurting me." I kept my voice low as I tried to pull my hand away.

"Sorry," he mumbled. He let go and looked away.

"Why do you think you'll be hanged? My dear friend..." Our words hung between us, suspended, almost tangible.

"Because I killed him. I stabbed him through the heart. I'm not sorry I murdered him, but I'm sorry that I'm going to die. I want to live more than anything. I'm only 19. And I'm so scared."

He grabbed my hand once more, and this time, although his grip was still painful, I did not pull away. But I couldn't speak.

"Didn't you hear me, Charlotte? I killed Reverend Crudden."

"Shhh, the children will hear," I said. My voice had a quaver that I couldn't steady. I was breathing quickly and shallowly, and my throat felt constricted. My face was burning, I could feel the heat on the top of my head, although it was very cool in the cottage.

He took me by the shoulders this time and shook. "Stop it Damone. You're hurting me. Really hurting me."

"You stupid bitch, say something." His voice was quiet now, a hiss.

"Just give me a moment, and stop hurting me, for God's sake, stop hurting me." I was wheezing, unable to control my breath.

Finally, he let go of me, threw himself on his mother's bed, bunched her quilt in his arms and huddled into himself, curled up like a ball. His shoulders shook. I knew I should move to comfort him, but at that moment, I had nothing to give. I moved to the battered wooden chair beside the bed and hugged my arms tight to my chest while Damone remained curled up, like a baby. I felt like I had been swallowed into a nightmare. *Will I wake up to find this is a bad dream?* I pinched myself on the arm, hard, and let out a tiny groan. No, I wasn't dreaming. Damone had killed the Reverend and had caused untold destruction to all of our lives.

We remained in silence for a long time, the only sound that of our breath, which for both of us was jagged and uneven. I could hear the children's laughter at the front of the tiny house and I smelled sausages cooking. My mouth watered. I was hungry but felt sick to my stomach. Jack lay sprawled at my feet, his nose twitching at the smell of the food. He remained still, however, perhaps having absorbed the charged atmosphere.

Finally, I touched Damone's shoulder. "I guess you'd better tell me why you killed that poor man."

"That poor man?" He stared at me, then laughed, a grating, mockery of humour. "There was nothing *poor* about that man. He was a foul, hideous excuse for a human being and the fact that he was a preacher made it even worse."

"What did he do to you? Why do you still hate him so much?"

"Can't you guess, Charlotte? Educated, smart, intelligent girl? Given what you are? What you were?"

I closed my mouth and shook my head. "I honestly don't understand."

"He raped me."

The word was as ugly as the action it conjured up. Had I heard him correctly?

"What happened? How old were you?" My voice was barely audible, even to myself.

"Six when he started."

"Started? You mean it went on for a period of time? It happened more than once?" I shut my mouth firmly once more.

"It went on for fucking years, Charlotte. Until I turned 11."

I tried not to wince at his profanity. I still had a patina of my good girl respectability despite my fall. I guess it was easier to focus on bad language than the enormity of the Reverend's exploitation of my friend when he was so young.

"Did he hurt others?" My throat felt dry and scratchy.

"I think so. He insisted on private meetings with other children too, to *discuss our growing faith in the Lord Jesus Christ.* Girls as well as boys."

"But you never discussed it with them?"

"For Christ's sake, it's something that's impossible to talk about. You're the first person I've ever told. I wish I'd kept my mouth shut. You're such a prissy white bitch. You make me sick." He pushed me, hard, so my thigh slammed against the chair. Then he threw himself on the bed again, his back to me, panting.

What an unholy mess. Why did he have to tell me? I closed my eyes, thinking of how I'd feel if I found out that Thomas had been thus abused. I'd be capable of murder, I knew full well. I was glad the Reverend was dead, but I didn't want to be part of the ongoing struggle and repercussions of it all. I opened my eyes and looked at my hands. They were shaking. Anger, fear, shock? I wasn't sure. Damone seemed calmer, while my emotions were so churned up that I could barely breathe.

"You didn't tell your Ma? Why Damone? She would have stopped it."

I regretted my words as soon as they escaped my lips. Damone sprang to his feet, fists clenched. He leaned over me, and I was afraid that he would hurt me. But he regained control and hissed, "How could I? Do you have any idea of how ashamed and dirty, filthy and disgusting I felt about myself? I wanted to kill myself after every session with the Reverend. One time I even threw myself into the Potawatomi River, but it was too shallow, and I had to walk home in the freezing cold, dripping wet, and got a scolding from Ma to boot. I just kept silent, let it happen, and I'd clean myself up as best I could after.

"It hurt, he ripped my flesh, and I bled every time. Ma was so proud of me for the special interest the minister took in me. My reward was to sing in the choir, and he taught me how to play the piano. That was my payment after every encounter, he'd give me a private piano lesson…I promised him I'd keep quiet if he stayed away from Trinity, and he did leave her alone. I think he liked boys more than girls…

"Finally, when I was 13, I told him, *no more*. 'No more what?' he asked me. He didn't care, he'd lost interest anyways. He liked his children young. The worst part was that sometimes I enjoyed it. It hurt but felt pleasurable too. That only made me hate myself more." He dropped back onto the bed, and this time I had no hesitation at all as I turned to him and hugged him tightly to me for what seemed ages, for what seemed no time at all.

He cried silently, but his whole body shook. I couldn't hear the children playing any more. *Thomas must have fallen asleep. Thank God Mrs. Barrett is leaving us alone.* I felt dirty, smeared by Damone's revelations, and I didn't want to return to my son until I had cleansed myself emotionally. I let Damone cry, holding him uncomfortably, while my thoughts spun. Was I obligated to tell Inspector McLaughlin the truth? I felt torn, as I genuinely liked and respected the man, plus I felt a real spark between us. I wanted to tell him, to further our friendship, but I felt a fierce loyalty to Damone especially given what he'd been through. *He does not deserve to hang but hang he will if the law catches up with him.* My decision was made.

Jack, my sweet Jack, leaped onto the bed and began licking Damone's ear. *Why can't people be as kind and colour-blind as dogs are?* I wondered, as I let go of my awkward hold of Damone's shoulders, and grabbed onto his hand, waiting patiently for him to calm down. He reached for Jack and began to stroke the dog's velvety soft ears, and his shoulders slowly seemed to relax, the tension slowly draining away. Jack grunted, licked him again, then turned around a few times on the bed, before plopping down in the crook of Damone's leg, with his head resting on his knee.

"What a sweet little dog you have, Charlotte. My family's always been afraid of dogs. Dogs were used to hunt escaped slaves, sniffing out their path." He gulped, and wiped his eyes with his sleeve, then continued. "Slaves ran through rivers, sometimes drowning, as the only way to hide their scent. But Jack is very sweet."

I squeezed his hand again, then said, "We need to decide what to do. We need to get you to safety."

He looked at me. There was not a spark of hope in his eyes and his bleak resignation blanketed the room. The air was stale and sour, and I wanted to go home. Not to the brothel, but back to Galt, to Daddy, and even Lavinia.

"Didn't you hear what I said, Charlotte? That man forced himself on me for years. I murdered him. End of story. His life is over, and so is mine." He squeezed my hand so hard it hurt, and his stale body odour seemed even more pungent and pervasive.

"How did you end up at Mrs. O'Hara's?" I asked. Surely work of that nature was the last thing he'd seek out after such a tormented past.

"What else am I good for?" Spittle caked his lips, which were pink and cracked. "It was all I knew, and I made good money at it.

Gentlemen pay more to lie with a boy, even a coloured boy. I think my being a Negro was really an added attraction. It makes me more a forbidden fruit, exotic. I've saved most of my money for Ma. We're going to move to Halifax where there's a big Negro settlement and buy a house. Or at least we were…I guess she'll need the money just to survive and get Trinity some education, to find her a position of some sort." His voice trailed off.

"You will still get to Halifax if I have anything to do with it." The promise was out of my mouth before I could regret its rashness. How could I help Damone? I had no doubt that I was on his side, and that he did not deserve to hang. In my opinion, Reverend Crudden was a hypocritical piece of scum, richly deserving of his violent fate. But hang he would if Inspector McLaughlin were to discover his guilt. I shuddered at the image of his thin body twisting, the noose around his scrawny neck. *Would he turn blue?* I gave my head a shake at the hideous turn my thoughts had taken. I couldn't let this fate happen to my friend, Inspector McLaughlin or no Inspector McLaughlin. *Think of the anguish Mrs. Barrett and Trinity would experience. They'd never recover, after trying so hard to start a new life in Canada.* I had to do something. But what?

"I need to leave now. My cousin Jane is being buried. I'll probably be late as it is. I must get there because her husband Bart will never forgive me.... After the funeral, I'm going to go back to Mrs. O'Hara's, and think really hard about what to do. You stay here with your Ma and lie low. Don't draw any attention to yourself whatsoever, do you hear me?" I winced at my nagging, motherly tone, and took his hand. "Sorry, but I'm afraid for you. I'm going to write to my Daddy and ask his advice. I have a plan, but I'll need help."

I actually had no plan whatsoever, but I wanted to give Damone some hope. It seemed to work, as his eyes sparked for a moment, before he lowered them once more. I noted how long and luscious his eyelashes were, and then I did have a glimmer of an idea. It was audacious and it was unexpected, but perhaps for those reasons, it would work.

I gathered my skirts, and hugged Damone goodbye, and left the tiny, cold, rank, claustrophobic bedroom. Thomas was just stirring in his pram, and I was thankful I'd thought ahead, packing a bottle of milk in my reticule, along with an oatmeal cake I'd made yesterday, following the recipe of Mrs. W.B. Wood, from St. George, from my *Galt Ladies' Cookbook*. Two cupfuls flour, two cupfuls of oatmeal, one cupful of sugar, one cupful of lard, half cupful of hot water, two teaspoonfuls of baking powder. Roll them, cut in small squares and bake. Simple to make and Thomas loved them, munching happily, with crumbs scattered all around his adorable mouth.

***

I repeated the recipe to myself, reciting it over and over under my breath after mumbled good-byes to Mrs. Barrett and Trinity, as I walked as quickly as I could to Bart's farm. The cozy banality of Mrs. Wood's recipe helped to distract me a little from the horror of Damone's revelations. I glanced at my dress and realized that I was wearing a plain grey poplin work dress that I'd taken to wearing while preforming my domestic chores at Mrs. O'Hara's. I hadn't thought to put on my bombazine mourning attire I had so long ago sewed for myself in Galt. I carefully cut and sewed the frock as soon as I turned 16, to be prepared for any sudden death, a requirement that every well-bred woman had hanging in her wardrobe. *Well, I'm no longer a well-bred lady. I'm not a lady at all any more. Bart will just have to accept me and my dress.* I dreaded the look of disappointment he'd show when I turned up late, although I knew Bart would never reprimand me openly.

I quickened my pace even more, puffing a bit as I pushed Thomas in his pram. I tried to respond to his burbling and occasional yelps with as much intelligence and patience as I could muster. Jack trotted happily beside the pram, oblivious to my raging emotions, ever happy, ever loyal. Sometimes in my heart of hearts, I wondered if I'd ever be able to love my son as much as I loved my dog.

Despite the brisk, cool temperature and stiff wind off the lake, I was panting and perspiring when I finally reached Bart's farm. I knew I had missed the funeral, but I also knew the well-lubricated wake would continue until the wee hours of the morning. Bart had one fault only that I could think of, and that was that he had a still hidden in his barn, where he made very strong moonshine. Owen Sound had a very complicated relationship with alcohol, and at different times, its bustling port was known as *Corkscrew City*, *Chicago of the North*, and *Little Liverpool.* This unsavoury reputation was embodied by a tavern named *Bucket of Blood*, and of course, by the intersection known as *Damnation Corners*, sporting taverns on all four corners (from whence many of Mrs. O'Hara's customers stumbled). When Bart drank, he drank at home snug by the woodstove, with Jane in her rocking chair by his side. *He'll drink alone now.*

I pushed open the door and Jack wagged and ran in as familiarly as if he were home. He sniffed at the people milling about until he found Bart, and he jumped up on him, demanding his attention. Bart stopped talking to the black-suited gentleman across from him, and scratched Jack's ears with affection, while Jack wriggled and wagged, and made his joy at their reunion plain. Bart rose, turned around, and looked me in the eye.

My stomach churned, and I felt my cheeks flame. Bart's blue eyes looked cold. I had hoped his easy-going nature would lead him to forgive my latest transgression, but he had loved Jane heart and soul and the slight of my missing her funeral service would have been unendurable in his eyes. Nevertheless, he made his way over to me, and took Thomas from my arms. My baby squealed in delight as Bart hugged him to his cheek, then threw him into the air and caught him in his big arms and hugged him some more.

Thomas still feels more comfortable with Bart than with me. I tried to clear the lump from my throat and said, "Bart, I'm so sorry that I missed the service. Thomas was not feeling well." The lie stuck in my throat like a huge chunk of dry bread, harsh, and unyielding.

"He looks fine now," Bart said, and I looked fondly at my son whose cheeks were pink, plump, and whose brown eyes glistened with good health. He was gurgling happily, babbling in an unknown tongue, while holding tightly to Bart's fingers.

"Yes, he did recover quickly," I muttered. Bart put his arm around me. "You came," he said, "That's what's important."

The knot in my stomach loosened, and I realized that I loved this big, gruff farmer of few words but an enormous heart. "Did the funeral go as well as possible?" I asked.

"Yes, the Reverend Dupris did her proud."

"Did you say the eulogy? What did you say?"

"No, I couldn't bear to speak. As a matter of fact, your father delivered the eulogy."

"What? Daddy's here? Where is he?" My stomach churned.

"He took Lavinia out to the barn. She wanted to see the horses and cows…"

"Of course. She's a city girl." I didn't even try to keep the contempt out of my voice.

Bart looked at me, his bushy eyebrows knitted. "She seems like a very nice lady." His gentle reproof stung. *Am I still not willing to give Lavinia a chance? What if Daddy is truly happy with her? Is it time to make my peace with his marriage?*

I sighed. "Do they know about my living arrangements?"

Bart licked his lips. They were cracked, with tiny pieces of flaking skin at the edges. "No, I told them you were living in a boarding house in order to be closer to town. I didn't know what you'd told them." He looked at me and his eyes hardened. "Charlotte, you must take Thomas away from that house." His hand shook slightly as he reached to stroke Thomas' head, and I realized again how much I cared for my cousin. I reached up and kissed his cheek. He blushed beet red.

"I am going to leave as soon as Inspector McLaughlin gives me permission. You are a dear, good man, and I promise to do you proud with Thomas. Now I'm going to take him to meet his Grandad and Lavinia." I couldn't bear to refer to her as Grandmamma.

"Give her a chance. That's all I ask." Bart seemed to have an uncanny knack of reading my mind. "Maybe your father will drink less now that he's not so lonely. Loneliness is hell." He blew his nose roughly into a wrinkled handkerchief. I pretended not to notice, gave him another kiss and squeezed his hand, trying to convey my love, gratitude, respect and sorrow for his loss. He straightened himself and tickled Thomas on the chin. Thomas whooped with delight, and Bart said, "Take care of your Mamma, little fella, and make sure she brings you to see Cousin Bart a bunch of times every year."

"Dadadadadadada!" Thomas shrieked and Bart blushed red. Even his thick neck took on a beet shade above his shiny black suit. He choked up in earnest, and I turned away, carrying Thomas who waved goodbye to Bart as we left the house and walked towards the barn, Jack trotting at my heel. My feet plodded one in front of the other with soft thuds on the still unfrozen ground. Fallen leaves were everywhere. *How can so much decay smell so fresh and sweet?* Thomas continued to burble dadadadada, delighted with himself. *He hasn't even once called me Mamma. But whose fault is that?* I knew full well it was my own fault, but I still hoped in my heart of hearts that he hadn't called Jane "Mamma" before she died. *But for her sake, I hope he did.* My pace slowed even more with that charitable thought. The barn was just ahead now. Its rough-sawn walls were grey, bleached by weather. I could hear murmuring, *no doubt Daddy lecturing Lavinia on the needs and variety of livestock.* As I came even closer, I heard him say,

"Now, as for work horses…" I just knew he was on the verge of a long, pompous lecture. I smiled to myself and pushed open the door, careful to hold Thomas' head so it wouldn't bang on the low beam. They were engrossed in quiet conversation and I was able to watch and listen unnoticed. Daddy's black suit hung on him a trifle limply. *He's lost weight and looks well.* As if on cue, I noticed him suck in his abdomen and stand a bit taller. He gesticulated with his gloved hands. *He's trying to impress her.* My thoughts were half-contemptuous, half-fond. Lavinia, meanwhile, stood looking up at him, listening intently. Her black frock looked to be silk, cut fashionably. *She looks smart, even though she's short, and her figure is a little dumpy.*

I noticed the swell of her bosom, and thought of Mamma's skeletal frame near the end, as her illness consumed her flesh. Bile rose in my throat but I swallowed it down, pasted a big phony smile on my lips. They felt like they might crack and break but I marched grinning up to the happy couple.

"Thomas, there's your Grandad. Say hi to Grandad…" My words sounded tinny and a little false, as Daddy and Lavinia turned as one accord.

"Hello Lavinia," My phony smile became a rictus as Thomas shrieked, "Dadadada!"

Lavinia smiled in response to Thomas, then looked at me. Her smile seemed natural, unforced. Her eyes crinkled, and her laugh lines deepened. I hadn't realized how old she was. Her face was worn looking and she'd clearly known both sorrow and joy, but her hair was pinned in the latest style. I knew that as we girls at the brothel spent long afternoons poring over the latest adverts in *The Toronto Daily Star* which was delivered to Owen Sound once or twice a week, depending on the vagaries of the weather. Daddy forgot all about his new bride and rushed over to Thomas and me and embraced us in a bear hug, squeezing so tightly that Thomas' cries of "Dadada" became a little choked.

I pushed against his chest, and said, "Daddy, you're squeezing too hard." But I was laughing and happy to remain in the warmth of his arms. He smelled of pipe tobacco; he smelled like home. We remained in an embrace for long moments, and I was meanly aware of how excluded Lavinia must feel from our happy reunion. Daddy seemed oblivious, but I peeked at her, and I saw that she was twisting her wedding ring, as she kept a smile pasted on her lips which had become rather white. She stood in an awkward position, legs splayed under her black silk skirt, her head twisted slightly away.

Finally, I broke free from Daddy. I couldn't stand to hurt her any longer. Daddy still remained heedless to the pain he was causing his new wife. I turned to her and kissed her cheeks.

"Lavinia. We met a long time ago, when you taught nursery at Trinity Church. Welcome to Owen Sound." I took a few steps towards her, still carrying Thomas, and presented my cheek for her to kiss. The gratitude in her eyes was an embrace in itself. She kissed me, took a step back, then held out her arms to Thomas. He went to her willingly and did not make shy. I guess by now he was used to being passed around from girl to girl at Mrs. O'Hara's house. He was still mumbling "Dadada."

"He just saw Bart," I said by way of explanation.

"How is my grandson faring? Has he adjusted to living with you? Does he miss Bart and Jane?" Daddy seemed anxious, tentative. We had not parted on the best of terms the last time he'd come to visit. Once again, rage, my old enemy, rose bile-like in my throat. I remembered Daddy passed out on the sofa too many nights to count, the smell of stale booze, sour and skunky, fouling the pretty sitting room Mamma had decorated with such care. I remembered the blue hexagon quilt that Mamma had sewn for Daddy so lovingly before she died, the same quilt I pulled over him night after night as he slept off his latest overindulgence. "The blue matches your eyes, my dear," she told him when he unwrapped it the last Christmas morning we had spent together.

I shook my head, and curled my lip, and scowled at my father. I couldn't help myself and I didn't even try. Pain shadowed his face and deepened the crow's feet around his eyes. The lines embracing his mouth sagged. He turned to Lavinia, cleared his throat and said, "Well…" He put his arm around her and looked at the ground. *You've well and truly botched up this fond reunion,* I scolded myself, and impulsively thrust Thomas back into Daddy's arms, then turned and embraced Lavinia.

"I'm sorry," I said, "I haven't been very welcoming. It's hard to have you take Mamma's place, and I've just been with a very dear friend who is in such a lot of trouble…"

Thomas grunted softly. Daddy frowned. "It would be best to let her sort out her difficulties for herself," he said.

"Nonsense," said Lavinia, and her eyes narrowed. "If you can aid a friend in need, that's a very high calling."

"Dada..." Thomas was finally running out of steam. He seemed content in my Daddy's arms, but he still kept one sleepy eye on me. I gazed at my stepmother, and she winked, slowly and deliberately. She standing beside Daddy, facing me, and she knew and I knew that her small rebellion of the eyelid would go unnoticed. I had resolved to at least dislike, at most hate my stepmother and now I felt a real warmth and feminine complicity towards her. *I wonder why she has no children of her own?* I knew she was a widow, but until now, had never given her first husband even a glancing thought. In my mind, Lavinia had not been a real person, rather a shadowy intruder intent on barging her way into Daddy's arms and heart and displacing me and Mamma's memory.

I tried to quell any positive emotion towards her. I frowned, but she smiled in return. "Can we help you and your friend?" she asked.

"Lavinia!" Daddy's disapproval was crushing, but she stood her ground. *She's small, dumpy and determined.* I stopped a grin from washing over my face.

"Charlotte may need our help. At least let's listen to what she has to say."

He stepped away from her side, the physical distance making clear his disapproval.

"Why don't we go back in the house and say goodbye to Bart?" I suggested. "Then perhaps we can walk to…Where are you staying?" Were they sleeping at Bart's house? I didn't want to include Bart in any plans to rescue Damone. Bart did not have much sympathy for "darkies," as he called the Negro race. Most people, rural or city, shared his prejudices. Besides, he was raw with grief, and had a farm to run. I also wanted to ensure that Bart did not slip and reveal my living arrangements to Daddy and Lavinia.

"No, we're staying at The Queen's Hotel, along Union Street. It's about a 45-minute walk from here. But Lavinia and I can escort you home," said Daddy.

"Oh no, I'll come with you back to the hotel!" My voice was hoarse, and I cleared my throat. I had to keep them from knowing. "My landlady has been sick, and I have to keep Thomas quiet. It's best for us to stay away from my house for most of the day, and only return when Thomas is ready to sleep for the night." The most effective lie is always a part of the truth.

I squeezed Daddy's arm. We walked back to Bart's house through the crisp air. I was prepared to stay and be sociable, but most of the ladies had already returned home, leaving the hard drinkers to drain every drop of alcohol Bart had left. It would be a long night. Bart had never been a heavy drinker himself, but on occasion he indulged himself. Who could blame him tonight? Heavy drinking and rowdy behaviour were the norm in my adopted town, and I was sure Bart was prepared for the worst at his wife's wake. I looked worriedly at the hardcore drinkers seated at the big pine kitchen table, not communicating with anyone but their booze. *Oh well, he's big enough to throw almost any drunk bodily out the door. Or will he get drunk himself?*

I motioned to Daddy and Lavinia to come back outside with me, and I said, "I think we should feed and bed down the animals before we leave, in case Bart…" Lavinia smiled in agreement, and the four of us returned to the barn and did just that. I'm certain Daddy was relieved to escape the fumes of temptation, and Lavinia and I were just as pleased for him. It was soothing to work with the animals once again, and I compared the simplicity of their care to my subsequent work and felt equal measures shame and relief. *Lavinia probably could care less about barn animals but diverted Daddy to the barn in the first place to help him escape temptation.* My respect for my new stepmother kept growing in spite of my worst intentions. *But she's no-where near the lady Mamma was,* an evil little thought popped into my mind. *Her silk mourning dress is too showy. She didn't even know Jane! Mamma would have worn a simple but dignified crepe dress to the funeral. I hope Daddy didn't give her Mamma's matching jet broach and earrings. They're meant for me.* I looked at her closely but she was wearing no jewelry whatsoever, other than her simple gold wedding band.

I lowered my head and flushed as I remembered that I already had the broach and earrings in my jeweler box that had belonged to Mamma. I had left them back home in Galt, safely locked inside my desk in my old bedroom. *That's why I didn't think to wear them.* I sighed. *Thank God, I didn't hurl accusations…It's not Lavinia's fault that Mamma died.* I didn't know if I liked my more reasonable self, but her voice seemed stronger. *Maybe Thomas has helped me grow up. About time.*

Finally, after we finished giving the animals water, Daddy mucked out the stalls as carefully as he could in his mourning attire, and we returned to the house and said our good-byes. Bart held Thomas tenderly once again in his huge arms. His face drooped, his eyes were bloodshot, and I was certain he wished he could leave with us. "We looked after the animals as best we could," I gestured to my dress, "but you can use them as an excuse to rid yourself of unwanted guests…" His eyes twinkled momentarily but they quickly lost their sparkle as he heaved a sigh. *A wake makes the burden of grief even harder on the bereaved.* I hugged him quickly, only too happy to escape. The alcoholic fumes made my stomach twist, and I looked at Daddy who was practically tripping over his feet in his hurry to escape temptation.

"Does he drink much these days?" I asked Lavinia when Daddy was trapped in a protracted goodbye with a distant cousin whose slurred words seemed to mirror his fuzzy mental state.

"Only occasionally," she replied, "when I go to Hamilton to visit my sister. When I come back, he's usually…" she paused delicately.

"No need to tell me more. I grew up with it." My mouth tasted sour. My sentiments must have been conveyed in my tone of voice, for she squeezed my hand, our gloves entwined for a brief moment. *She's really quite nice. Forgive me, Mamma.* But I knew that Mamma would want Daddy and me to be happy and would be pleased at the stability and reconciliation Lavinia was bringing to our tiny family. Mamma was not petty. I was. I withdrew my hand abruptly. Daddy returned to Lavinia's side, and we slipped out the door, me pushing the pram, Jack trotting along contentedly, after Bart scratched his ears goodbye.

We walked quietly through the crunching leaves to the Queen's Hotel. This was a gracious three storey yellow brick building. "The hotel manager says it was built around 1871," Daddy said. "The rooms are well appointed and very comfortable." *Nothing but the best for Lavinia. But Daddy has always been generous.* Mamma and I had wanted for nothing, ever. We climbed the elegant stairs into the lobby, which boasted plush carpeting and was lit brightly with electrical lights. We went to the dining room and requested tea and scones. It was quiet before the evening rush, so we could speak without fear of being overheard. Thomas was fast asleep.

"What happened to your hair Charlotte?" Daddy's voice was soft, concerned. I thought I'd pinned it up cleverly to disguise my bald spot, which was now growing in with a soft, downy fluff, but clearly not. I felt my face grow hot.

"I had an accident."

"Whatever kind of accident?" His tone was sharper now.

"I can't tell you. Let it be."

"Charlotte, you must tell me. I'm your father."

"Oh, for goodness sake. She's a grown woman and entitled to some privacy. Let's get back to the issue at hand, how we will rescue her friend." Lavinia smiled at me. I felt a rush of gratitude.

"It's best that I don't tell you what my friend is accused of," I began, after devouring a scone which dripped with melted butter and strawberry jam. I wiped my mouth with a linen napkin.

Daddy frowned. "Why ever not? Surely he's not a murderer?"

I cringed inwardly but met his gaze calmly. His eyes were so similar to my own.

"No, of course not. He has been unjustly treated. I need to let you know that he is a Negro."

"A Negro?" Lavinia's dark eyes were huge. "Only, I've never seen one before."

"He's just like everyone else." I tried to keep the contempt I felt out of my voice. "There's no need to be afraid of him. He's very skinny, in fact, much skinnier than I am these days." I looked at Thomas, then at the few crumbs that remained on my plate.

Daddy smiled, but it didn't reach his eyes. "Not everyone is like us, Charlotte." *Thank goodness for that. They don't drink as much as you, and don't fall pregnant at 16.* I tried to keep my face pleasant.

Lavinia said, "Oh, don't be stuffy, Joseph. I'm sure Charlotte chooses her friends with care." *She's trying too hard. If they ever found out that almost all of my friends in Owen Sound are prostitutes...It doesn't bear thinking about.* I wrinkled my nose but smiled at her.

"I'd appreciate any help you can give me."

"Where does he want to go?" Daddy asked.

"Halifax. His father and an aunt live there, as far as he knows."

"What do you mean, 'as far as he knows'?" Daddy's eyebrows climbed high on his forehead.

"His father abandoned the family when they came to Canada, but Mrs. Barrett, Damone's mother, knows that he settled in Halifax. Apparently, there's a very large Negro community there. Damone can lose himself in the crowd and I doubt the Owen Sound police have the time or money to look for him in Nova Scotia."

"Charlotte. Is he guilty of murder?" Daddy's tone brooked no prevarication.

"I don't believe he is. He's worried the police will accuse him falsely, because he's Negro." I had had plenty of practice lying, mostly to cover up the embarrassment caused by Daddy's drinking, but I had rarely lied to Daddy himself. It didn't feel good. Lavinia looked at me, and her sharp gaze seemed to pierce through my obfuscation. But she held her tongue and looked away.

"So how do we transport him to Halifax?" She licked her lips. They were plump and glistened in the shaft of weak light penetrating the overlarge windows. *Not hard to see why Daddy married her. But she is kind, and she's trying to help me.* Daddy's back was ramrod stiff; it barely touched the back of his chair as he glared at me. *He's totally against me giving Damone any help whatsoever.* This hardened my determination and seemed to have the exact same effect on Lavinia.

"I don't think I can smuggle him on the train directly from Owen Sound. The train station is bound to be watched by the police."

"It's hopeless. They will alert the railway officials to keep an eye out for him," said Daddy.

"Yes, I did think of that. I have thought this through, and I think the best way is for us to take a ship to Collingwood, catch the train there to Union Station, and I can put him on another train from Toronto to Montreal. From Montreal, he can take a ship along the St. Lawrence River to Halifax. He'll have to fend for himself once he arrives, but I'll give him a little money to begin with."

"How much money could you have my dear?" Daddy's tone was kind but his eyes had narrowed.

"You've always been so generous to me, I've saved some through the years." *I hate lying to him, but it comes so easily.* Daddy remained still. Lavinia wrinkled her nose. She touched my hair. Tendrils had escaped despite my best efforts to keep it pulled back tightly. "Your hair is very distinctive. Can you find yourself a wig? A dull brown would be best," she said.

I thought of the brothel. Mrs. O'Hara had a supply of wigs on hand. Occasionally, we girls would be called upon to entertain the men in more wholesome ways, such as singing, dancing and performing amateur skits. "Yes, I think I can borrow one quite easily from a friend of mine."

Lavinia didn't bat an eyelash at the idea of me having a friend who would own a wig, but Daddy's frown deepened. Still, he held his peace. He was outnumbered.

"Well then," said Lavinia, "I'll purchase three tickets on the next ship from Owen Sound to Collingwood."

"Three?" asked Daddy. His lips were tight.

"Yes, three. One for Charlotte, one for Thomas, and one for her maid."

"Maid?"

"Yes. Charlotte has told us Damone is slight of build. The police are looking for a young Negro male..."

"And they won't be interested in a white woman travelling with a baby and a maid," I finished her sentence and stared at her in admiration. It had taken her fifteen minutes to size up the situation and to come up with a plan – a very good plan. "Will people believe that Damone is a girl?" But I pictured him in my mind dressed in a maid's unrelieved black attire and head covered in a cap. *His eyelashes are long, like a girl's. It'll work. I might be able to save him.* I reached for Lavinia's gloved hand and squeezed.

Daddy still wasn't finished disapproving. "I'll not have my daughter and grandson put into danger for a criminal." His face was flushed.

"Shh." Lavinia put her finger to her lips as customers at a table some distance away looked over at us curiously. In a low voice, she said, "You don't want us to attract attention."

"Attract attention." His voice was a hiss. "I don't want my daughter ending up in jail." He scowled at his new wife.

"Nonsense Daddy. Lavinia's plan is perfection. I promise, no jail for this daughter." But I wasn't so sure. I knew Inspector McLaughlin had a soft spot for me, but I was forbidden to leave Owen Sound until the inquiry was completed and he had made an arrest. Never mind me helping a murderer escape justice. *But Damone isn't a murderer. Not really. We all make mistakes. That filthy hypocrite Reverend deserved his fate.* Of this, I was sure. I was more than fond of the Irish policeman, but I would not, could not let Damone swing for the murder of a man who interfered with children. I looked at Thomas' innocent face. *Nothing good would come from Damone's death. He did Owen Sound a favour by knifing that man and think of Mrs. Barrett and Trinity.* My mind was made up.

Daddy, who knew me so well, could see my determination. He sighed, reached into his jacket pocket, pulled out his wallet, and counted out five crisp ten-dollar notes. Without a word, he passed them to me.

"Daddy." I tried to convey my profound gratitude through the look I gave him. "Thank you." I deposited the money in my reticule. I felt nervous carrying such a vast sum on my person, and I wondered why Daddy would have the money on hand but dismissed that thought as none of my business. *Perhaps Lavinia has expensive tastes. It looks that way, judging by the cut and quality of her frock.* I excused myself and went to the lavatory. They had an indoor water closet, so swanky was the Queen's Hotel. I took the money out of my reticule and hid it in my undergarments. Just in case.

I returned, said my goodbyes, and thanked them profusely again. I had to hurry; Jack was tied to a post outside, and I knew he'd be pining for me. Lavinia kissed me on both cheeks and I hugged her warmly. She had been magnificent, and I knew that without her support, Daddy never would have helped me in my risky scheme.

Thomas is going to wake up soon. I must be getting home, as he'll be hungry, and when he's hungry, he has a lusty pair of lungs. I finally broke free of their goodbyes with a promise to return to Galt as soon as I helped Damone out of his trouble. Little did they know how much his trouble haunted my life as well, and I was grateful for their ignorance. Daddy slipped me yet more money before I left. I walked quickly back to the brothel.

***

When I entered the house, I found Mrs. O'Hara resting in the parlour. "Resting" may not be the most accurate word; she was directing a massive cleaning operation. It was early afternoon; the men would not arrive for some time yet.

"Rose, run your finger along the mantle. I want to see the result. No, not with your bare hand, your silly girl. Put on an old white glove." Her voice was shrill, but she smiled at Thomas when we entered the room.

"Charlotte. How good of you to pay us a visit. I'll entertain Thomas while you scour the kitchen. Standards have slipped while I was ill."

"I'm glad to find you so much recovered." I gave her a kiss on the top of her head. She tried to frown but I could tell she appreciated the gesture. "I need to clean and feed Thomas. After I'm done, I will certainly attend to the kitchen. But I need to speak to you most urgently."

She frowned again but nodded. I attended to Thomas' needs and in a short period of time returned to the parlour. I put Thomas on a blanket on the floor with a few toys to occupy him. I had to watch him closely now as he was learning to crawl, and he put everything in his mouth.

"My china ballerina!" said Mrs. O'Hara. I leaped to action, barely averting disaster.

"Rose," said Mrs. O'Hara. "I have another job for you. You need to watch Thomas while I speak to Charlotte. Not in here, we need privacy. Take him to a bedroom and watch him carefully. He's not to be trusted." She wagged her finger, but her eyes twinkled, now that her figurine had been rescued.

"I'm so happy to find you in better health," I said.

"No thanks to that demon Vicky." Her voice was bitter. "Did you have no inkling of what she was capable of?"

"Me?" I tried to keep my voice even. I forbore from pointing out that it was she who had hired Vicky. "No. I knew she was vain, petty and self-centered, but she seems now downright deranged. Have you heard if she'll be charged with attempted murder for the violence she committed against you?"

"She will if I have anything to do with it." Mrs. O'Hara's face was still pale, and her voice lacked its usual deep timbre and air of authority.

"She may be sent to the new Asylum for the Insane in Penetanguishene," I said. "It opened just recently at the former site for the Reformatory for Boys."

"As long as she's locked up. I hope they throw away the key." She blew her nose vigorously into her handkerchief, a trumpet of outrage. "The worst thing," she continued in a calmer voice, "she has an alibi for the time of that disgusting man's murder. I did know the Reverend Crudden, you know." I tried to keep the shock I felt from my expression. She had lied to the police.

Mrs. O'Hara continued, "I warned him not to come to this house. I offered to send him a girl or Damone to the privacy of his home, when his wife was away. But he became bored with these tame visits and insisted that he come here to have his choice."

I was unsuccessful at keeping my face neutral. She said, "Oh, don't look so shocked Charlotte. You are no blushing virgin. You know some men like the danger and excitement of a whorehouse. He was one of them."

I felt the heat in my face. I'd never heard her use vulgar language before. It was a measure of how angry and upset this affair had made her.

"How do you know Vicky has an alibi?"

"Inspector McLaughlin told me earlier today. He came to check up on my recovery. At the time of the murder, Vicky accompanied a favourite customer to his rooms, at his request. McLaughlin has verified her whereabouts with the man and with his landlady, who was not happy with the company he was keeping."

"How is the inspector?" I strove to keep my voice casual.

"He's still no closer to solving the murder. He's getting frustrated. He asked where you were, seemed put out that you weren't at home."

My face got hot again. "What did you tell him?" I asked.

"I couldn't say much, could I? I hadn't seen you, and I had no idea where you were."

I lowered my eyes. "I'm sorry. I have something to tell you. You're not going to like it."

She looked at me, her eyes sharp little beads. Her usually immaculately penciled eyebrows looked naked as they knit together in a frown.

"Out with it. I've never backed down from a fight or an unpleasant truth yet, and I'm not about to begin. Go on."

And so, I told her the entire tale of Damone's childhood, how the minister interfered with him, and how my friend snapped when he discovered that so-called man of God at Mrs. O'Hara's establishment, ready to indulge in its seedy pleasures.

Her eyes were dark, hostile beads when I finished. "You have to turn him in," she said.

I gaped at her. "But he'll be hanged."

"So be it. It'll resolve this abominable situation once and for all, and my house will be able to return to normal." She actually smiled.

"But what kind of normal will that be?" I argued. I should have remained silent, but I'd been so certain that Mrs. O'Hara would see Damone as I did, an innocent who must be saved at all costs. I had persuaded Daddy. *No, Lavinia persuaded Daddy.*

A wave of despair washed over me. Jack's soft ears drooped. "Will you at least give me 24 hours' grace before you turn him in?" I asked.

Mrs. O'Hara's eyes were flint. "What's in it for me?"

I felt like I'd been punched.

"Decency." I said exactly the wrong thing. Her nostrils flared and her eyebrows shot up to the top of her forehead, black crescents stark against the whiteness of her skin.

"Decency doesn't put food in the mouths of my girls." Her voice dripped acid.

"If Damone is hanged, I'll make sure to tell Inspector McLaughlin exactly what your business dealings are with Alderman…"

"You wouldn't dare." Specks of spittle flew out of her mouth, and she punched the sofa, hard. Rose poked her head in the door,

"Are you feeling ill Mrs. O'Hara?" She glared at me, and I flinched.

"We're fine," said Mrs. O'Hara. "Mind your own business, Rose. Leave us please."

I was reeling. I had seen and benefited for months from Mrs. O'Hara's maternal side, enjoying her warmth, thoughtfulness, and kindness. But warmth and kindness had not made her a wealthy businesswoman. *She has to be tough to survive.*

"You seemed to really care about us girls and Damone too. What changed?" I spoke quietly, leaning towards her so my lips nearly brushed her cheek.

"How do you think I can provide for the girls with the police here constantly? If the murder remains unsolved, they will probably close me down. Think Charlotte." Her voice was raspy, but her dark eyes remained implacable. "I'm too old to start over. And the girls. How would Felicity survive under a keeper who'd be little better than a roadside pimp? Think of the brothel in Collingwood. The keeper there, Diana Saunders, is without mercy. As soon as one of her girls loses her health, or her looks, Mrs. Saunders throws her out on her ear. She could care less about the girls who slave for her. All that one cares about is money. She hires a strong man, Larry Archer, who used to work on the ships, to keep the girls in line. If they slack off or keep any earnings above her cut, he beats them. Not so it'll show. He makes them take off their hose and whips the bottom of their feet. They can barely walk for days, weeks.

"Don't look so shocked, you stupid, spoiled little girl. And close your mouth. It's the way of the world for those of us who don't have *Daddy* to run back to. For the rest of us who have to earn our living, this isn't an adventure.

"So yes, I do have a real fondness for Damone but I will sacrifice him to keep my house, and my girls, safe." She lay back on the sofa, exhausted.

I swallowed. My mouth tasted bitter, and all I wanted was to brush my teeth, then get into my childhood bed in Galt and cuddle with Thomas and Jack. I understood Mrs. O'Hara's reasoning, but I didn't like it. I didn't like it at all.

"Will you give me 24 hours? For Damone's sake? For my sake?" I despised the pleading tone in my voice.

Her eyes were like little black pebbles. Several long moments passed.

"I don't want to hear your plans," she said. "You're on your own with this. Any repercussions are yours and yours alone."

I let out a sigh of relief. "Yes Ma'am."

"When and if you return to Owen Sound, you are no longer welcome at my house. Your time here is finished. You can have one week after your return to pack up and leave."

My throat was so dry I could barely swallow. For all the sin and degradation, I had enjoyed the sisterly companionship, sharing stories, cosmetics, meals…with the girls, who were also my friends. But Thomas deserved more. I deserved more.

"Yes," I said. "As soon as Inspector McLaughlin gives me permission, I'm going to return to Galt."

"That's a good idea." Her face softened. "You are a good girl Charlotte. Too good to work here. You are beautiful and intelligent. Seize the advantages God has given you and make a success of your life. Now, I'd be grateful if you'd make me a cup of coffee and put a good dollop of brandy in it. I'm still in pain." She passed me her keys, and I unlocked the cabinet where she kept her alcohol out of the girls' temptation and did as she requested. I made the coffee strong and splashed a generous amount of brandy so the cup was full to the brim. Mrs. O'Hara was a lady of enormous self-discipline and I knew there was no danger of her slipping into a drinking habit.

I turned on my heel and began to leave, but Mrs. O'Hara spoke again.

"Pardon me?" I turned back and leaned over the sofa. She had purple circles under her eyes and her skin looked paper thin. Despite her exhaustion, her voice, though soft, was clear.

"Thomas. You'd better leave him here with us. I'll make sure there's always a girl available to watch him, in here, with me."

I could barely speak. "Thank you." I squeezed her hand. "But I'm going to bring him with me. The authorities won't think twice about a mother and baby accompanied by…" I stopped. Best not to be too trusting. Best not to give my plan away entirely.

She turned her head away. I noted that her fists were clenched tight, lips pressed together.

"I'll wait two full days before I co-operate with the police," she said. "In the meantime, this house will carry on as usual."

She sighed, then reached for my hand. "God bless you Charlotte and good luck. Take care of that little boy of yours."

"I will," I said. I bent down and kissed her forehead. She pushed me away with her hands but her eyes were a little teary. This time, I walked out of the room. She did not call me back.

***

I didn't have a minute to spare. I looked in on a sleeping Thomas and approached Rose.

"Can you take care of Thomas for a few hours? I need to make some arrangements for a project. Mrs. O'Hara has given me her blessing and she will give you time off as you need."

Rose's face fell. I knew she needed her wages. She had never confided in me, but I long suspected that she paid for the care of an illegitimate child. I didn't know any details, nor did I want to know. I reached in my reticule and pulled out two dollars. "This should cover your lost wages and I'll give you another two dollars when I come to pick Thomas up. Take good care of him, mind."

She nodded yes. Her eyes lit up and she took the money, folded it neatly and tucked it inside her bodice. "I'll watch him like he's my own," she said. I had to believe her; the other girls were still asleep. I gave her instructions as to his care, brought her changes of clothing and nappies and rushed upstairs to the attic where I knew there was a treasure trove of old clothing. Jack waited at the foot of the attic stairs, unable to follow me.

I tore about, rummaging through trunk after trunk. The smell was musty and dank. *Where did all these clothes come from?* Finally, at the bottom of the fifth trunk I pawed through, I found a maid's uniform.

It was rather old fashioned, about 20 years out-of-date, but it would have to do. *Men will never notice the finer details of a servant's clothing.* I was quite confident of that. *Thank goodness women will never be allowed into the constabulary.* I shook my head at the thought. The discarded uniform, black cotton with grey trim, smelled rank, and was dusty. *It's probably filthy, but the black hides the dirt.* I sneezed.

I searched with increasing desperation for a wig to cover my distinctive hair and my even more distinctive bald patch (although it was now more accurately a short and fuzzy patch). I had no luck. The only girl I knew who owned a wig was Matilda. I'd have to ask to borrow it. But what excuse could I use? I had to hurry; the men would arrive any time now.

I threw the clothing back into the trunks, fastened the lids, then scrambled down the narrow staircase, much to Jack's relief. I stopped by the kitchen, where Rose was happily entertaining Thomas, who was sitting on a blanket on the pine floor, playing with his wooden train. My heart melted and I felt a chill of terror. Was I exposing my baby to unnecessary danger? When he caught sight of me, he dropped his train and screamed, "Mamamama!" then promptly tumbled over. The look of surprise on his face made Rose and me laugh, and Jack rushed over to lick him. Thomas decided not to cry but to join in the fun. I delighted in his peals of mirth as I picked him up and hugged him, then handed him his toy and gave him a kiss goodbye, leaving him in Rose's hands.

His joy quickly evaporated and he began to cry as I waved goodbye. "Mamamama," he shrieked, tears running down his chubby cheeks, nose streaming. I had to leave. I couldn't leave. I scooped him up and gave him another hug.

"Mamma will be back very soon," I promised. He cried harder.

Rose intervened. "Leave, Charlotte. Just go. Prolonging the goodbye only makes it worse." She scowled at me. The knot in my stomach twisted but I knew she was right. I kissed the top of his head and left. Jack looked at me from his perch in front of the door, all tensed and ready to go but for once I was firm.

"No Jack. I'll be back soon." And I fled.

Later that day, my preparations were as complete as I could make them. I spent the night at the Barrett house, sleeping in Damone's narrow and hard little bed.

"It's the least he can do," said Mrs. Barrett when I protested. "Damone can sleep with me one last night." She looked at her son with such naked love in her eyes that I felt guilty, like I had trespassed into her soul. I knew she wouldn't see Damone for a very, very long time. He could never return to Owen Sound and if she left too abruptly for Halifax, the police would surely take note. Besides, I doubted she'd have the money on hand to pay for the voyage for her and Trinity. She'd have to scrimp and save for a long time.

I was relieved not to return to the brothel that evening. It was the last place in the world I wanted to be and I could not face the emotional intensity of Thomas' and Jack's needs right yet. Jack! I'd have to leave him behind. My heart cracked but the trip would take at most a few days. Once I had escorted Damone safely to Union Station, and put him on the train to Montreal, I would return to Owen Sound with Thomas, hoping Inspector McLaughlin would remain unaware of my absence. If not, I'd have to face the music. But not tonight.

I slept surprisingly well in Damone's bed. The house was bitterly cold and Damone insisted that I use three blankets. They were old, but clean and smelled like lemons. I wore Mrs. Barrett's old flannel nightgown and added my shawl to the pile of bedding on top of me. When I awoke, the water in the wash basin had a thin layer of ice on top. I threw on my clothes, shivering. It was still dark when Mrs. Barrett called that breakfast was ready. The *Lady MacDonald* left at 10 AM promptly.

"It's a 140-foot passenger and freight steamer from Detroit," Damone told us over a breakfast of porridge and strong coffee. "It usually makes runs to Manitoulin Island, but for a month or so every autumn, travels to Collingwood to load up with supplies for Owen Sound in the winter." I nodded, genuinely interested. I knew it was a supply ship, and didn't expect a luxurious voyage, but the ticket agent had assured me of a basic lounge inside, which would be warmed by a woodstove. I didn't want Thomas to suffer in the chilly November weather.

"Steamships are an amazingly efficient method to carry cargo long distances." His enthusiasm was palpable. We looked at each other and smiled wryly. No need to ask where our knowledge of shipping came from. Both of us had consorted with sailors for a long time.

Mrs. Barrett offered me a rasher of bacon. "No thank you. I'll stick to plain oatmeal." I loved bacon, but no use tempting fate, or my stomach. As a landlocked Galt girl, I had no idea if I would be able to handle being on a ship. Damone ate my share, and I hoped he was not prone to seasickness.

"Do you think you'll get seasick?" I asked him.

"Of course not!" He looked offended. I bit back a smile.

"Charlotte," said Damone, as we finished eating, "did you know that steamers are mostly built in Clydeside, Scotland, sailed across the Atlantic to the St. Lawrence River...."

"Where they're cut in half, taken through the small canals and put back together in Buffalo, above the Welland Canal." It was my turn to interrupt. "Yes, I did know that." The busy maritime life in Owen Sound was one of its chief attractions for me, and I knew I'd miss it sorely when I returned to inland Galt. "Finish up, and get ready," I said.

After breakfast, Damone emerged from his mother's bedroom dressed as a very reluctant maid. He batted at the bonnet strings tied under his chin. "How can anyone bear to wear this frilly thing? And it's about 20 years out-of-date."

"Stop whining," said Mrs. Barrett, and gave him a playful box on his ear, which was covered by the offending bonnet. "No complaining. You need to show some gratitude towards Charlotte. She's going to great lengths to save your sorry life." Her tone was light, but her eyes were red.

"And the shoes pinch my feet. Why do they make maids wear shoes with any heels at all? And what's the point of pointy toes? Especially when you're on your feet running after other people all day." He sounded outraged.

"You're lucky that I found the costume in the attic, and that the shoes fit at all," I said. "The shoes actually belong to Matilda. She has the biggest feet."

"I'm wearing Matilda's shoes?" He looked revolted.

"Yes, and I'll catch it when I return them to her. She doesn't know I took them."

"You can give them back this morning. I don't want them." He sounded sullen.

"I hope you aren't going to complain for the entire trip," I said. I wasn't truly annoyed, as I knew that his bravado hid the pain of leaving his mother and Trinity behind. And he had not seen his father for more than half his life. Would his father help him get established in Halifax?

Would they even recognize each other? He had no idea what was waiting for him in Halifax. *Better than swinging at the end of a rope.*

The wind howled off the water. I felt grateful that at least the beginning of our voyage would be in the shelter of Owen Sound, which was in fact a 13-nautical mile long inlet, which emerged into the rocky and wide-open expanse of Georgian Bay. It was November, and I knew the water could get rough, but I hoped my stomach would be acclimated to the rolling of the ship before having to endure swells of six feet or more on the open bay.

I already felt a little queasy, in anticipation. It had seemed such an adventure, hatching this plot to save my friend. Even now, the constabulary could appear at Mrs. Barrett's door, and arrest him. I wondered why they hadn't paid more attention to his mother's house. For one mad moment, I wondered if Inspector McLaughlin had guessed my plot to rescue Damone. Was he giving me breathing space to do so? Did the inspector believe that Damone was guilty? Perhaps he didn't like the idea of sending a young man to his death at the end of a rope any better than I did? But the inspector was a seasoned officer of the law and of course he was under enormous pressure to make an arrest following the scandalous circumstances of the Reverend's death. Had he discovered the truth about what kind of a man the Reverend was? I shook my head. Speculation would not save Damone. It was up to me to do that. I checked the pocket watch that had been Mamma's.

"Damone. We must go. I'll run to your room and get ready. We have to pick up Thomas, then get to the harbour for 9:30 AM. The ship leaves at 10 AM, prompt."

I hurried to Damone's bedroom, gathered my things then stood at the front door, looking away as Damone said good-bye to his mother and Trinity. They were all crying, Trinity bawling, and Mrs. Barrett unable to speak.

"I'll take care of him," I promised her and gave her a hug. I slipped Trinity a stick of candy. She nodded her thanks, and for once, Mrs. Barrett didn't correct her.

Damone curtsied to me, hamming it up to lighten the tension. I gave him a cuff on his bonneted ear and said, "see that you obey me, young lady." He kicked my shin, hard, with his pointed boot and we walked out the door, him two steps behind me as a proper maid should, muttering curses as a proper maid should not.

***

We walked swiftly to Mrs. O'Hara's house and entered the back door, into the kitchen. Jack leapt and wriggled with joy at my return, and I quickly kissed his silky ear. For once, I couldn't lavish attention on my dog. Where was Rose? Where was Thomas?

I ran upstairs while Damone sulked in the kitchen, foraging for any food left from the night before. Mrs. O'Hara's bedroom door was ajar. I peeked in, and she was wide awake. She was pale and drawn, her hair stringy and greasy. Was no one looking after her?

"It's good that you've come for Thomas," she said. "Rose was not the best choice for a babysitter."

"Where is he? Is he ill?" I asked.

"He's in with Matilda. Rose got drunk, very drunk on the money you left her. I had to enlist Matilda."

I swore. Mrs. O'Hara pretended not to hear.

"Did you have any suspicion that Rose drinks to excess?" she asked.

"No. If I knew, I'd never have left Thomas with her. If only Eliza were here!"

Eliza's aunt had taken ill with pneumonia, and Inspector McLaughlin gave her permission to take a few days with her family in Guelph.

"I found Rose passed out around midnight and Thomas crying at the top of his lungs. Don't worry, I sorted it out before any serious damage was done," said Mrs. O'Hara in a soothing voice which served only to enrage me further. "A brothel is definitely not a fit place for a baby." She looked rueful. I thought it would be impolite to express the depth of my agreement, so I nodded and gave her a kiss.

"Good luck, Charlotte. Is Damone here?"

"Best that I not tell you Ma'am."

She frowned, then nodded agreement. "When you see him, give him my best wishes. I'm really not a monster...." Her voice trailed off.

I smiled at her with as much warmth as I could convey, trying to tell her wordlessly that I had not and would not tell Damone that she had considered turning him in to the constabulary.

"You are the furthest thing to a monster and the closest I've had to a mother since my Mamma died," I said.

"Go now, before any of the girls wake up and ask questions." Her voice was brusque, her eyes full.

I gave her another quick kiss and rushed into Matilda's room to collect Thomas. He was delighted to see me and shouted "Mamamama." He had a bruise the size of a robin's egg below his eye. The familiar red mist swam before my eyes.

"Mamma will be right back, sweetheart." I gave him a kiss and ran out of the room, down the hall and pushed open Rose's door. The room reeked of stale alcohol and other intimate odours. I was shaking. She laid in bed, legs akimbo. She had not changed into night clothes and her dress was soiled and stained, her hair matted with sweat and Lord knows what else.

I slapped her cheek so hard that my hand ached. I grabbed her hair and shook her head as hard as I could. Her head was heavy and her breath reeked of stale booze.

"How dare you get drunk and let my son come to harm, you slut." I hissed.

She looked at me, eyes unfocused, so drunk that the pain of my actions barely registered. In disgust, I let go of her hair and her head bounced back on the bed. I rushed out of the room, back to Thomas, my only regret that she'd been protected by her alcoholic stupor from the pain I'd inflicted. With Thomas in my arms, I stomped back into Rose's room and I spat on her. The spittle landed on her cheek, and I watched, satisfied, as it slowly ran down by her ear and dripped onto the pillow. I was done.

I felt a huge relief as I carried Thomas down the stairs to the kitchen door where Damone sat, legs wide in a very non-maid like pose. "Damone. You need to sit like a girl. Cross your legs or put your knees together."

He scowled but tightened his legs and transformed himself so he looked like a very young, thin woman.

"How did you do that?" I asked.

"Never mind. We can't miss the ship."

"Right." I had prepared a bag with a change of clothes for me, a few changes for Thomas, and some nutritious food for all of us. By this time, Thomas ate solid food and had the healthy appetite of a growing boy. He drank cow's milk so we were as prepared as we could be. I placed him, bundled warmly, in the pram and we hurried to the harbour.

We made it to *The Lady Macdonald* on time, and the ship employees, busy loading cargo and directing passengers to the gangway and taking their tickets, barely spared us a glance. Nothing uncommon about a well-dressed young matron with her baby and maid travelling by ship. No sign of the constabulary. I wondered once more at the trust Inspector McLaughlin placed in me. I felt dirty and desperately sad at how I was crushing it beneath the heels of my dainty, booted feet.

I raised my chin in the air and summoned up my haughtiest look when I recognized a fellow passenger as one of my regulars. His wife seemed to be scolding him as she hung onto his arm, and his head drooped. I needn't have feared; I was wearing a very grey bonnet, and my hair was covered by Matilda's wig. I had no cosmetic enhancements, and his eyes slid by me with no hint of recognition. *One does not associate a young lady with a baby with a brothel.* I was inwardly amused. The image of the man naked, his hairy belly and slight paunch made me smile to myself all the more.

Damone helped me maneuver the pram to the sitting area. I knew the trip could last from four to eight hours, depending on the weather conditions and the weight of the ship. We arrived early enough that we had our choice of seats. Damone insisted on sitting by the window so he could watch the ship being loaded.

"Put your legs together," I reminded him. I elbowed him in the ribs. He moaned.

"Stop whining and try to sound like a girl. Or better yet, keep quiet! What should I call you? We didn't choose a name." I frowned.

A muscle in his cheek twitched. I assumed his pride was bruised at how feminine he appeared and at his role as my maid. I felt no sympathy whatsoever.

"How about Laura?" he asked.

I wasn't sure how many Negros were called "Laura," but why not? I nodded, smiled at him, and he made a funny face at Thomas, who giggled.

"May I take him? I want to walk with him to the window so we can see better," Damone asked.

I knew Thomas would enjoy the activity and it would be a long voyage, so I nodded agreement. "But keep him away from the railing."

Damone took charge of Thomas who went with him happily, without a backwards glance. I sighed, then noted with amusement that Damone had adopted a mincing, "feminine" gait. I hoped he wouldn't overdo it and draw too much attention to himself. Still he appeared happier, and he was not in jail on a capital charge.

After ten minutes or so, Thomas and Damone reappeared.

"Mamma, cows, cows, cows!" Thomas shouted.

"Yes, but shhh," I put my finger to my lips, hoping not to draw attention to our little party.

"Moo! Moo!" Thomas shrieked. Damone laughed.

"Why is Thomas talking about cows?" I asked.

"They loaded about twenty head of cattle to the bow of the ship," said Damone.

I knew that livestock was often transported on steamers. But this late in the season? The ship seemed pretty loaded down, but I supposed they knew what they were doing. I knew it was the final run, so the last chance for cargo to be shipped.

"Isn't that an awful lot? Are they securely penned in?" I asked.

"Moo!" screamed Thomas. I gave him a stick of candy.

"They're tied up, and there's a wooden fence of sorts. It seems safe enough," said Damone. But he sounded a little doubtful, and I hoped they wouldn't fly off if we hit a big wave. The wind was howling, and November weather was unpredictable at best. I sighed, then said a brief prayer to my long-ignored God.

"Mamma, cows, moo!"

"Yes, Thomas, moo." I joined in the fun. But my stomach was unsettled. And we hadn't left yet.

The loading of *The Lady Macdonald* seemed interminable. *How could they possibly fit so much cargo on a mid-sized vessel?* But of course, the steamship wasn't just going to Collingwood. It had begun this journey in Sarnia, made stops in Goderich, Port Elgin, Tobermory, and now Owen Sound. It would compete its circuit in Parry Sound then circle back. I wasn't sure if it would overwinter in Sarnia or in Owen Sound. The Owen Sound Harbour was a coveted wintering spot for ships, sheltered as it was by the huge bay. This would be its last passage for the season. I had been fortunate to secure tickets. Thomas and I would return to Owen Sound by train.

The ship sounded a warning blast. Thomas scrunched up his face as though to cry, then thought better of it and giggled, then shouted "hoot!" Damone and I looked at each other and smiled. He seemed almost as proud as I. We all looked out of the foggy window and we waved to the people bustling about the harbour. Thomas waved with all his might, so his entire body swayed. Damone's eyes sparked.

"If you like sailing so much, why did you never go before?" I asked him.

"Folks wouldn't take kindly to a Negro man travelling alone," he said. His voice was entirely devoid of bitterness. I flinched, looking at the whiteness of my own hand. We settled ourselves for our long journey.

"Why are we using both steam and sails?" I asked Damone.

"Most steamers do, the masts and sails help the engines in a fair wind and steady the ship when the water's rough," he said.

The water was choppier than I expected it in the bay. Thankfully, Thomas fell asleep in his pram. My stomach roiled but I breathed steadily and as calmly as I could, focusing on the horizon. I kept my seasickness at bay, but Damone was not so successful. He began to burp with distressing regularity and resonance.

"Shhh," I nudged him non-too-gently in the ribs. "Cover your mouth, you're a young *lady,* remember?" I passed him my lacy handkerchief. One gentleman looked over at us, shot me a look of disgust, then walked to the spittoon and expectorated with great gusto. He stuck another chunk of tobacco in his mouth, so large that one cheek bulged like a chipmunk and chewed methodically, all the while looking at Damone and me with a raised eyebrow.

At least Damone, Laura, *has a reason for her uncouth behaviour.* I kept my eyes studiously averted from our disapproving fellow passenger.

As we neared the mouth of the bay, the wind increased, howling like a banshee as it blew across the wide-open waters of Georgian Bay. The lowing of the cattle got louder. *The swells must be ten feet high.* My hands gripped the handles of the pram so tightly that my knuckles were white. Damone held his hand over his mouth then grabbed a bucket and was sick. My stomach churned and turned but somehow, I held on. It was all I could do to stay seated on the bench and make sure Thomas was not tipped from the pram. Damone was no help whatsoever. He lurched back to sit beside me and I straightened his bonnet to cover his cropped hair.

"I hope the cattle are penned securely," I shouted to Damone. I couldn't bear to think of how scared they must be, trapped and helpless, exposed to the brunt of the waves.

"Of course, they are," he said. He looked utterly miserable, but continued, "they know what they're doing. The captain has reduced power from the engines, and I'm sure he's taken in the sails. Don't fuss, Charlotte."

Thank goodness, the crashing waves made it impossible for the disapproving gentleman to overhear Damone's complete lack of respect for his supposed mistress. Damone put his hand over mine which was still tightly grasping the pram. We'd both heard of the *Jane Miller,* a 78-foot wooden steamer that sank November 24, 1881, just north of Owen Sound bay. Twenty-eight lives were lost, including all of the crew.

"She carried 28 passengers and nearly 10 tons of freight, including four bedsteads, and kegs of butter," one sailor had told me He had tears in his eyes, and brushed them away. "She was heading to Manitoulin Island in the middle of a terrible storm with blinding snow. After her last stop in Big Bay, she steamed toward Wiarton to take on a load of wood. About an hour later, the lights of *The Jane Miller* disappeared all of a sudden." The sailor, whose name was Ernie, seemed to have a compulsion to tell me the details of the disaster. He appeared almost without interest in the normal purpose of a visit to the brothel, as he continued,

"They organized a search party next morning, sent out the tugboat *Tommy Wright.* A little way out, they noticed a patch of water that was discoloured and had bubbles rising to the surface. On a nearby beach, they found a bucket rack, an oar, a flagstaff and two sailor caps, all from the ship. They dragged the area time and again, but the wreck was never found." He remembered who and what I was, and said kindly, "But don't you worry your pretty little head about that..." as he unpinned my hair.

My reverie was interrupted by yet another loud belch from Damone. His brown skin had a green tinge now and his breath smelled foul. I touched his hand. "I know you aren't feeling too well..." I said.

"That's an understatement," he groaned. Although the cabin was cool, and heated only by the sparsely spaced radiators, his brow was sweaty. I passed him my handkerchief yet again.

"Try to be discreet, for heaven's sake!" But most of the other passengers looked too ill themselves to be concerned with my maid. The ship tossed and swayed with a violence I'd not thought possible. The poor cattle. I could still hear their frightened cries. Somehow, miraculously, Thomas slept on.

Time passed, interminable. The ship heaved, swayed and pounded. Thomas awoke and shrieked with fear. I held him as best I could while maintaining my precarious balance on the cushioned wooden bench. Damone was no help at all and made use of the buckets provided a number of times. A harried looking crew member came around with extra buckets.

"Lift up your benches," he shouted. "Put on the life vests." I looked at him more closely, and noticed he was wearing an odd-looking vest. Incredibly, it looked like it was made of cork. I looked at Damone.

"It floats," he said. "It'll keep a person from drowning."

"Yes, so we can die slowly from hypothermia," my sour humour sounded false in my own ears. Then I realized. "Thomas? What about my baby? Is there one small enough for him?" I felt like an outsider observing this drama. I was part of it yet removed, as if there were no way my baby could be in danger. Damone and I lifted the bench but the cavity was empty.

"Our bench is empty!" I screamed at the crewman.

He went to a nearby bench and extricated something brown. He hurled it at me.

I caught it and put the cork vest around my neck. It was heavy and felt awkward. My daze ended when a wave slammed into the ship so violently that I could barely hold my head straight. The sailor picked himself up and said,

"I'm sorry Ma'am. We don't have any little ones. Best to put Baby inside your own vest."

He lurched off to attend to the other passengers.

"How will I ever put Thomas inside my jacket?" I asked Damone. Then I noticed. "Where's your vest?" He shook his head.

"Oh, for God's sake." It was more a prayer than curse.

I thrust Thomas into Damone's arms, then ran as best I could after the sailor. I tapped him on the shoulder, hard.

"You didn't give my maid a vest."

"They're for whites only, Madam."

I grabbed his arm. "Negros will sink just as quickly as we do, and she's only a girl."

He thrust me aside. "Go back to your seat. No life vest for the maid." I swayed and nearly toppled. Someone grabbed my shoulder, keeping me on my feet. I was surprised to recognize the passenger who had seemed so disgruntled by Damone's burping.

"Did he hurt you?" he asked.

"No, I'm fine." I wiped away the tears of frustration and he grabbed me once more to keep me upright when the next wave crashed into us.

"Go back to your baby," he said. "Crawl if necessary." Somehow, he caught up to the steward and cuffed him hard in the face. The wind howled, but I could just hear him scream,

"That's no way to treat a lady," I could barely hear his voice above the wind. I noted then how young the sailor was, a boy really. His face was dotted with angry pimples.

"Give me a life vest," said my unknown benefactor.

"They're for whites only," the boy said as he held the vest out of reach.

"Give me the vest!" The gentleman balled up his hand.

The sailor threw the cork vest. I tried to catch it but the ship lurched and it hit me on the head. My benefactor shouted with rage.

"Leave it," I screamed, and crawled back on my hands and knees to my little family and handed the heavy cork vest to Damone. Damone was holding a terrified Thomas. I took my baby and held him tight. Damone put on his vest, for once not complaining. His hands were trembling as he tried to tie a bow. "Just tie a knot!" I shouted into the wind, and he nodded and obeyed.

***

My gentleman friend returned. "Does it fit him?" he asked.

"Yes, thank you," I said. He nodded and returned to his seat. I tried to soothe Thomas, then the penny dropped. He had realized Damone was not a maid. The ship tossed and heaved, and I told myself that Damone was not my main concern at the moment. I focused on the non-ending struggle to maintain my balance, while keeping Thomas safe. Thomas and Damone both were wretchedly ill. The cabin smelled dreadful as most passengers were forced to make repeated used of the buckets. Time stood still and my entire world had shrunk to the tiny, cold, clammy, reeking cabin. I looked out the steamed window. A whitecap towered over the ship. The frothing water looked like carded wool. Wet carded wool. I realized that I could no longer hear the frightened cries of the cattle.

"Damone, what happened to the cows?" I shouted.

"They've probably pushed them into the water to lighten the load," he screamed back. I could see the whites of his eyes. He huddled into his cork vest.

"Charlotte, you'd better secure Thomas in your vest," he said. "Now."

I knew he was right, but I knew Thomas would hate feeling trapped and enclosed. I did it anyway. Thomas screamed and kicked, but somehow, I fastened the cork vest around both of us. The roaring lake was so loud that I could hardly even hear Thomas' cries. All I could think about were the cows, trying desperately to stay afloat in the icy cold swells. *Can cows even swim?* I prayed that they'd drown quickly and peacefully. Did God care about cows? Did God even exist? I shook my head. I couldn't let my mind wander. I had to stay alive. I had to keep Thomas alive.

By now we were marooned in the open water, miles away from the shelter of the bay, at the mercy of the southwest winds lashing across the vast expanse of the Great Lake. I could see on the distant shore that the trees were doubled over in the wind. It seemed that the whitecaps that slammed into the *Lady Macdonald* were ever higher. Damone stood. "I've got to see what's happening," he shouted. "Maybe I can help." From the look of him, he seemed too sick to remain upright, never mind be of assistance. But somehow, he made his way out the cabin door. I started to croon a lullaby to Thomas,

Rock a bye baby, On the Tree top; When the wind blows, the cradle will rock....I remembered how the song ends, and stopped singing. Thomas was crying and hiccupping now. I rocked him and soothed him as best I could. Damone returned and lowered himself beside me. His maid cap was askew and I couldn't be bothered to tell him to act like a woman. Everyone was too sick and preoccupied with staying alive to be concerned with my maid. He snuck his hand into mine, and we sat and tried to wait out the storm.

There was a tremendous thud, steel against rock, so jarring that I fell off my hated wooden bench on top of Thomas. Damone was on top of me. I could barely breathe, could barely move. The cork vest made things worse. Thomas screamed and shrieked and Damone took forever to remove himself from on top of me.

"Get off me," I screamed.

"I can't," he said, "there's someone on top of me."

Finally, we got ourselves upright. The ship was tilted and seemed to be listing, buffeted on all sides by the enormous waves. Damone swore and started to repeat the 23rd Psalm. Spittoons, spare cork vests, and loose chairs flew in all directions.

"What happened?" I asked.

"I think we hit Vails Point shoal. I've heard the sailors describe it. Just past Conallson's Harbour. It's a mile-long rocky bank in only a few feet of water. The wave troughs make it even more shallow. We must have been blown off course." He had tears coursing down his cheeks, mucous running from his nose. He was talking fast but still his teeth chattered.

"Are we sinking?" I kept on rubbing Thomas's head, the only part of him protruding from the ungainly cork vest. At least the ship wasn't tossing up and down quite so much.

"If we're not sinking now, we will soon," said Damone. He gripped my hand so hard that mine ached. I didn't pull away. "We're about to capsize or be torn to pieces. Maybe the bottom has been torn off, or the shoal will have torn a hole in the bottom. Either way, we're…." He cursed and I didn't reprove him.

A crewman came into the cabin. His skin was devoid of any colour. He screamed at the top of his lungs, "Proceed in an orderly fashion to the deck. The captain blew off steam to prevent a possible boiler explosion. You're safer on deck. Go now!"

Damone and I, still clutching hands, walked crab-like towards the door, wobbling and bracing with the swells. I noticed that most passengers seemed too ill to obey the instructions. Maybe they were so sick they didn't care if the ship sank or not. I didn't stop to try to help them. I had to save my baby, and Damone, if I could.

We stood, cold and wet on the deck. The ship tilted drunkenly, and we gripped the rigging to stay upright. The crew passed a life-line along and we held onto the line and to each other for dear life. The ship rolled for about twenty minutes. It seemed like every moment was our last. The waves rushed in like watery mountains and every few moments we heard the despairing shrieks of those unfortunates who were swept out to sea. The cabin soon gave way, and I don't know how many people were lost, washed off the boat with no hope of rescue. Some people seemed to go crazy and jumped in the raging water in the hopes of swimming ashore. Land was nowhere near, and I knew what their fate would be.

The electric lights went out. "Why are we standing here? Is anyone going to do something to save us?" I shrieked to Damone.

"They must be hoping the fishermen from Conallsons Harbour will come for us. The ship's doomed. They should get us into the lifeboats."

We were struck by an enormous wave.

"Hold on," Damone screamed, and I gripped the line and Thomas with all my might. The freezing wave soaked us even more and I could barely breathe. When it had subsided, I checked to make sure Thomas was still breathing. Thank God, he was. I think he was too scared to cry.

Finally, Captain Roberts came around. He alone seemed calm.

"All passengers remain where you are," he yelled above the wind. "Hold onto the lifeline! All crew, lower the lifeboats. We can't wait any longer for the storm to subside."

The crew rushed to lower the lifeboats. There were only two that I could see, and they looked in bad repair. I turned to Damone.

"Come with us? You are a maid, you're a girl, you can get on with us, please Damone?"

He shook his head and removed the maid's cap, and took off the dress, revealing his usual attire underneath.

"I'm a man. Women and children first."

"But you're like my brother. Please! I don't want to lose you."

"Man or maid, I'm a Negro. They'll never let me on. Go. Go now. Get Thomas to shore safely. I'll catch up with you."

I hugged him, clung to him. "God bless you. I'll still get you to Toronto. I promise."

He pushed me. "Go, Charlotte. They're lowering the lifeboat. You have to save yourself and Thomas."

I turned away and didn't look back.

***

"Women and children first," the sailor said, as men pushed their way to the where the lifeboat had been lowered. I was shoved so hard I almost toppled over, but I held onto the lifeline, and made my way to the side of the ship. The men let me through, some reluctantly, others with great grace and dignity.

"Do I have to climb down the ladder?" I was appalled. The ladder was made of rope and rough wooden pegs. It was blowing in the wind as the sailors fought to keep the lifeboat steady beside the ship.

"Of course, you silly cow. Go!" shouted the sailor. He held me so tightly that it hurt as I positioned myself. Thankfully the vest kept Thomas tight to my chest so I didn't have to support him as I lowered myself down step by step. One misstep, and Thomas and I would be lost.

My hands were freezing and I could barely move them. I had to force my fingers to grab each rung as I carefully lowered one foot after another. How many rungs? I tried to keep count but lost track after eight. The wind blasted me in the face. Thomas was shrieking. I slid, but held on for dear life, and cursed the choice of footwear I had chosen – my dainty lace-up boots with a two-inch heel, which added more difficulty to my descent.

Finally, I reached the end of the ladder. The lifeboat pitched and bobbed, and when it rode a wave close to the ship I jumped. A waiting sailor grabbed me, shoved me onto a bench, and turned his attention to the next passenger making her descent. She was not as lucky as I. A huge swell crested, and she was blown into the water. We all looked away as the next person began her descent. She was luckier or perhaps wore more sensible shoes and landed in the lifeboat beside me.

This process was repeated fourteen more times. We lost three more. Finally, the sailor said, "We can't take no more. Start rowing to shore." He signaled to the ship above, and we began our trip towards land. The rope ladder, now with no-one on it, swung dangerously close to my head as the men put their backs to rowing towards shore. Our little lifeboat was tossed on the huge swells, and I prayed every prayer I could think of that we not be overturned. Thomas' lips were blue, but he made no sound. All I could do was pray and say his name over and over, trying to tell him that we would get to shore safely, even though I was sure we would not. I put my head down to shield him as best I could from the lashing rain and wind. His dark hair was soaked.

We huddled and braced ourselves against the waves. An older lady was seated on the floor of the boat, in the fetal positon, rocking and crying. I thought of Damone and looked back to the ship. I couldn't see it. I searched the horizon frantically, then saw just the tip of the deck, and the smokestack still out of the water. It was sinking and sinking fast.

I redoubled my prayers, hoping against hope they were able to lower the other lifeboat and Damone would get to shore safely. But I had to focus on my son and myself as the swells continued to threaten our small boat.

The sailors battled the waves, seeming not to feel the bitter cold. Snow mixed with ice rained down on us. The wind was still blasting; the swells still mountainous. Thomas' lips remained blue and I huddled over him and cradled him as best I could in the ungainly cork vest. I could see the vague outline of the shore and realized with relief that we were making some headway. The sailors appeared to be aiming for a dock of sorts, and I tried to guide them, as of course they were facing out towards the open water. "Port," I shouted, but remembered that their left was opposite to mine. "Sorry, starboard." One of the sailors swore, and I apologized again, and was more careful with my directions.

It took a full 45 minutes for us to get to the dock. By that time, I could no longer feel my own hands, so numb and frozen were they. There were about ten women and children huddled into their overcoats and shawls waiting for us to dock. They caught the ropes the sailors threw and fastened the rowboat securely. I didn't even know if Thomas was still alive. I pushed my way to the side of the boat yelling, "I have a baby inside my vest." One of the men grabbed my hand and pulled me safely onto the slippery dock. A woman, undid the vest and took Thomas. I could see his lips were bluer than ever, and his eyes closed.

"Follow me," the woman screamed over the wind and crashing waves. I did as I was told and we walked and ran to the nearest building, a tiny rough-hewn log house. She ran in the door, and I followed.

"Take off your wet clothes, this is no time for modesty," she said as she rushed Thomas to a rocking chair beside the woodstove. She laid him down on the chair, knelt beside him and began tearing off his clothes.

"Martha," she said to a young girl hovering at her side, "bring all the blankets we have. And my Sunday dress. Hurry, hurry!"

"I don't want to take your best dress," I said. I knew from the rough cabin that my benefactor did not have much money.

"It's the only one I have besides the one I have on," she said, as she continued to unfasten Thomas' sodden clothes. He let out a cry, and I felt a wave of relief wash over me, as huge as the swells I'd just escaped.

"Leave the baby to me; you must get into dry clothes," my unknown friend said in a no-nonsense, commanding way. "What's the baby's name? What's yours?"

We introduced ourselves, and when Martha returned with a black silk dress, so worn it seemed burnished, I thanked her profusely and without any shame at all stripped out of my sodden clothes and put it on. It was too small for me, and I had to leave some buttons undone, but it was dry.

Mrs. Gillam bustled around. She prepared some soup for Thomas. "Are you still nursing him?" she asked.

I shook my head "no," ashamed.

She said only, "That's unfortunate; it would have been handy. But I have a good, nourishing beef soup that should fill him up. Do you want to feed him? Only if you are warmer, but I do think he'd be more comfortable with his Mamma."

I felt a surge of pride, and gratefully lowered myself into the rocking chair beside the woodstove and took Thomas on my lap. He ate and drank greedily, and I felt an enormous gratitude that we hadn't perished. I was lulled by the warmth of the woodstove and felt sleepy. I shook my head. Damone! His face flashed in my mind and I felt ashamed at my own happiness. Had he survived? Had anyone else escaped after our little craft had made it safely ashore?

"Will your husband return soon? Do you think there were any more survivors?" I asked Mrs. Gillam. I had barely noticed her appearance when I had first entered the house, due not only to my shock and near-hypothermia, but also to the poor light of one weakly flickering kerosene lamp. She lit a candle and brought it to sit near to me on the rough kitchen bench. I saw that although I'd judged her to be in her 50's, so weather-beaten was her face, she was probably only in her 30's. Life clearly had not been kind to her. *Why is her face so lined?* I was also surprised that she only had one child, but it wasn't my place to ask intrusive questions.

"From what I saw, there will be no more survivors, unless another lifeboat was lowered with lightning speed," she answered. Her voice was cultured. I must have looked surprised, and she smiled.

"My father was a schoolteacher, and he believed in educating women," she said in response to my unspoken question. "But he died when I was 12, and I had to go into service, as a maid. My Dougie is a good man, and has always treated me kindly, but it is so nice to have a woman to talk to. You sound educated, too. Come sit beside me, Martha." She motioned for her daughter to sit beside us on the rough bench.

I was so tired I could barely keep my eyes open, but I recognized the hunger in her voice for companionship, and I thought of how lonely and isolated she must be in this tiny hamlet, waiting for her man to return from his fishing trips, always worrying that he might not come home. So, when she asked me a little too eagerly, "Do you enjoy poetry?" I sighed, and said, "yes. I certainly do. I'm reading Wordsworth at the moment. I'm attempting to get through *The Prelude,* although some evenings, I find it puts me to sleep."

She laughed, a delightful, musical sound that made me happy I had made the effort. We discussed poetry for a while, and Martha evinced a real enjoyment of Emily Dickenson's fine work. I must have looked surprised at the depth and breadth of her knowledge, because Mrs. Gillam said a bit sharply,

"There's not much else for us to do in the evenings here." I looked down, then nodded. We continued in our literary discussions, until she said, "How selfish of me. You and Thomas are exhausted. Why don't you go to sleep? You can take my bed."

"No, I can't go to sleep until I know if my friend was saved."

She looked at me for a long moment. "Miss Evans, Charlotte, if I may call you that. It is almost entirely unlikely that there were any more survivors after your party made it to shore. I think you should retire and accept that your friend has perished. I'm not trying to be cruel, merely practical."

I started to weep. She took Thomas from me and said, "This little boy has been through too much today. Why don't you go into my bedroom and take some time to yourself? Martha can give you some warm bedclothes, and she will prepare the bed with the bed-warmer. Please, Martha."

Her daughter looked proud at the trust her mother placed in her. My mind was in turmoil but mostly I was exhausted and I did not argue further.

***

I don't remember much of the following twelve hours. I fell asleep and slept deeply, without dreams. Mrs. Gillam must have put Thomas into bed beside me at some point, because when I awoke, the sun was shining in the tiny bedroom window, and Thomas was sitting up beside me, clearly needing to be changed and fed. I took care of our basic needs, then left the sanctuary of the bedroom where I had been able to forget about the storm and shipwreck for half a day of sweet oblivion.

"Good morning," said Mrs. Gillam. "Would you like some oatmeal?"

I wondered if she had much food to spare, but didn't want to hurt her pride, so I accepted a bowl to share with Thomas. Daddy had insisted that I sew money into the hem of my coat, "just in case, my dear," so I had ample funds to buy my benefactor a new frock and repay her for any food we consumed. Still, she didn't know that, and I appreciated her generosity.

Finally, once I had fed Thomas and myself, I gathered my courage and asked, "Were there any more survivors?"

She sighed and looked infinitely sad. "No. My husband is out with the rest of the fishermen trying to find and recover the bodies."

I put my head down on the table and cried again. Mrs. Gillam once more took Thomas, bundled him into his coat, which she had hung to dry by the woodstove the night before, and shut the door quietly behind her as she left with Martha and my baby.

I cried for a long time. I could hear Damone's riffs on the piano in the back of my mind. *How can I face Mrs. Barrett?* I thought of the money he put aside for his mother and sister every month, and the degradation he subjected himself to earn that money. I thought of him taking off the maid clothing which was his ticket to survival and choosing a near certain death. *A death with utter dignity.* I would miss my friend, but I was also fiercely proud of the man he had become.

***

I dried my tears and cleaned up after the humble meal. I went into the bedroom and retrieved five dollars from the pocket I'd sewn into my skirt. I wrapped it in a bit of paper, and put it in the top drawer of

Mrs. Gillam's spotlessly clean but bashed up dresser. I was careful not to look at her undergarments, but I wanted to ensure that she and only she received the money. I had no knowledge of her relationship with her husband, and many men felt no compunction whatsoever at taking any and all of a wife's earnings.

There was a commotion at the door, and I hoped it was Mr. Gillam. I wanted to go back to the brothel; I yearned to see Jack. What would I tell Inspector McLaughlin? *I'll cross that bridge when it comes.*

I exited the bedroom to find that the time of my reckoning was now. Inspector McLaughlin was inside the tiny house, looking outsized in his police uniform, accepting a cup of tea from a clearly charmed Mrs. Gillam.

He looked at me. His eyes crinkled but he said nothing. He took out his handkerchief and blew his nose, a loud honking. I went to retrieve Thomas from Martha, and went over to him, using Thomas as a shield, I supposed. It was cowardly, but I was feeling low on courage at that moment.

Inspector McLaughlin patted Thomas' head, and stroked his cheek. His blue eyes met mine, and I remembered that I didn't have a bonnet on. What was left of my hair was unwashed, windswept, atrocious. I'd forgotten all about it. I felt heat in my cheeks but I stared at him steadily.

"Were you or Thomas hurt?" he asked. His voice was low.

"We were cold and scared, but we're remarkably unscathed. Thomas is still very quiet, not himself, but I guess that's to be expected…"

"Yes," he agreed. Mrs. Gillam and Martha looked on, curious.

"I'd like to speak to Charlotte alone," he told Mrs. Gillam. "Police business."

She looked disappointed, but she and Martha donned their cloaks and Mrs. Gillam said, "we'll go to the barn, and feed the chickens." They left, closing the door a little louder than necessary.

"Well, it is her house," I said. The inspector moved me away from the small window, and put his arms around me and Thomas, hugging me so tight I could barely breathe. He kissed the top of my head, where the hair was downy, like a baby's. *He really does care about me.* I couldn't accept this until today.

"I'm so glad you're safe," he said. "Tell me how you got to freedom."

I did just that, and he held my hand, and smiled at Thomas throughout. His smile was lopsided, and a bit goofy. His nose was crooked and huge. I liked him more than ever.

"Damone is dead," I finished. I withdrew my hand; happiness did not seem appropriate.

"What you did was brave, Charlotte. Foolish too. I need to get you back to Owen Sound before any of my colleagues arrive here and realize what you did. You could be incarcerated for a long time. Damone murdered Reverend Crudden, I'm certain of it. I have his clothes, and will have them tested for blood stains. If the blood matches the Reverend's, I will have proof of his guilt beyond a reasonable doubt."

"Yes, he did murder the Reverend. Do you want to know why?" Thomas was too young to understand, and I related the story, sparing no detail.

Inspector McLaughlin listened without comment, only occasionally asking for clarification. When I finished, he blew his nose again, hard.

"Let's sit on the sofa," he said. I obeyed; Thomas was heavy. I sat Thomas between us and gave him his wooden locomotive to play with. Of course, I had brought it from the ship – I'd tucked it into my cape pocket. A mother does not leave behind her child's favourite toy.

Once seated, the inspector shifted so that he could look at me. I leaned in as well, and Thomas, oblivious, shouted "choo-choo!"

"I understand why you did what you did," Inspector McLaughlin said, "but of course in my official capacity I must condemn your actions."

"I understand," I said. "Will I go to jail?"

"I'm going to do my best to make sure you are not found out," he said. "What you told me remains between us and must die with Damone. Your maid perished and you have no knowledge of Damone's whereabouts. Understood?" His voice was sharper than I anticipated, and I nodded.

"What about Mrs. Barrett?" I asked.

"I will deal with her. You must leave Owen Sound as soon as possible." I felt a stab at parting from him but I nodded my acquiescence. Thomas must come first from now on, and the upheaval of his being separated from an incarcerated mother was not to be thought of.

"I'm going to take you back to Owen Sound. There will be an

inquest, for which you'll have to remain. Are you going to stay in that godforsaken brothel?"

"Yes. But I only cook now."

"I'm aware of that! But it's no place for a child."

"I know. I can't stand the thought of living there now. As soon as the inquest is finished, I'm going back home to Galt. I'll live with my Daddy and his new wife, and hopefully become a chemist myself."

"You're returning to Galt?" he asked. His voice was soft and he let go of my hand.

"What choice do I have?" I knew that I loved this man, and it appeared, incredibly, that he cared deeply for me. "Hopefully no-one in Galt will be aware of my recent past, and I can pass Thomas off as Jane's child. Ironic, isn't it, that I'm back to the original plan, but encumbered by the proof of my sin?" I smiled without a trace of humour. Courage, or the pretense of courage, was the only way I could wrap my tattered dignity about me.

"Thomas will bring you great joy," he said.

"He brings me joy every single moment," I said.

"Have you heard from his father?" His voice sounded casual, but the look in his eyes was anything but.

"No, and I won't. I know that now. He is so under his domineering mother's thumb, he will never be a man. We are much better off without him," I said. I felt exhausted, the events of the past day and the loss of Damone, plus so many other passengers, weighed on me.

"Did they recover Damone's body?" I asked.

"No. I'm sorry."

"How many people died?"

"It looks like 21 passengers and crew are still missing."

I began to cry. He slid over on the sofa, put Thomas on his knee, then held us both.

There was a tap on the door, and we slid apart.

"Come in," he called.

Mrs. Gillam and Martha entered. "Will you be needing to eat? Only…"

We jumped to our feet. "Thank you, no," said Inspector McLaughlin. "I must get Miss, I mean Mrs. Evans back to Owen Sound."

I smiled at his delicacy and gathered up the meager possessions I had brought from the *Lady Macdonald.* I gave Mrs. Gillam a warm hug, and said,

"Give my thanks to your husband for such kind hospitality. I'm sorry I slept so much that I never met him."

We said our goodbyes, and I embraced Martha, then Inspector McLaughlin bustled me away. It was chilly, and he wrapped a rough blanket around Thomas and me in the somewhat primitive police wagon. We didn't speak much on the way back to Owen Sound. The ground was frozen but there was no snow, and the day was dreary and dark, barely windy at all after the mad extravagance of yesterday's storm.

Inspector McLaughlin opened the wagon door for me. It was too early for the men to have begun to arrive.

"Wait," I said, as he reached for Thomas. "I don't think I can stand another moment here. Can I stay with Bart until the formalities are wrapped up? Please, take me to Bart."

His eyes crinkled and he smiled. "Of course. Will you be warm enough while I explain to Mrs. O'Hara what has occurred?"

"I might be, but Thomas is very cold. We'll have to come in. Besides, I have to collect Jack and his food."

We went to the back of the house and entered the most innocent room, the kitchen. Jack was ecstatic at my return, and barked, jumped, and licked me. Mrs. O'Hara and the other girls rushed to greet us, marveling that Thomas and I had survived. Word of the shipwreck had clearly reached Owen Sound. Inspector McLaughlin pulled the keeper aside, and explained about Damone to her, and the need for extreme discretion. I passed Thomas to Eliza, and said to the other girls,

"Mrs. O'Hara will explain. I'm going to go to my cousin's house to recover." I went upstairs and gathered as many belongings as would fit into my remaining valise, the other having been lost in the shipwreck. I shut my bedroom door behind me with loathing. I would not, could not spend another night in this house. I walked as quickly downstairs as the ungainly valise would allow, and with muttered goodbyes, I retrieved Thomas and Jack and walked to the wagon, leaving the valise for the inspector to carry. Even Jack seemed overjoyed to leave.

We drove to the farm in silence. When we arrived, Inspector McLaughlin said,

"Are you warm enough to wait here for a moment while I explain the situation to Bart?"

I nodded, and he went inside while I held Thomas and Jack close.

Jack was still thrilled at my return and kept looking at me with such uncomplicated love in his brown eyes that it lifted me a tiny bit from my gloom. The inspector soon returned to the wagon, accompanied by Bart, whose homely face was split into a wide grin. He took Thomas from me and said in a matter-of-fact way,

"You've come back, Charlotte. You were always too good for that place. Come in and get yourself warmed up."

Inspector McLaughlin walked me to the door, then touched my arm.

"I have an awful lot of paperwork to get through."

"What about Mrs. Barrett?"

"You'll have to trust me."

I looked away. Did I trust him? But of course, I had no choice.

I stayed with Bart for three uneasy days. I told him everything. He tried to hide his shock, but his big, open face was easy to read.

"I'm sorry Bart," I said.

"It's not me you need to make amends to," he said.

I hung my head. "I know. I need to make it up to Thomas."

He squeezed my hands. "And you will. You're both so young. Go home to your Daddy."

"I'm going to. As soon as Inspector McLaughlin says I can leave Owen Sound. This place hasn't been good to me."

We both sat, side by side, by the woodstove, lost in our own misery.

After three days on the farm, I was going stir crazy. I had to get out. I helped Bart with the chores, then took Thomas and Jack and walked into town. No one paid me any attention whatsoever, although I felt like I had "sinner" stamped on my forehead. My feet took me of their own accord to Mrs. Barrett's tiny house, even though I knew Inspector McLaughlin would not approve. *He'd understand though.*

She opened the door before I had a chance to knock. The lines on her face were more deeply scored than I remembered, and her eyes were bloodshot. She practically crushed me in a hug. Trinity sat quietly on the shabby sofa, playing with a doll made from rags. She smiled to see Jack however, and at an unspoken command from her mother, came to the door and greeted us. She bent down and let Jack jump on her and lick her. Mrs. Barrett didn't object this time. I don't know that she even noticed.

"Would you like some tea?" she asked me as she took my cloak and Thomas' coat. "Trinity, please play with Thomas."

"You can play with Jack too," I assured the little girl. She had loved her brother and must be feeling his loss almost as much as her mother.

Once I had my chipped tea mug in hand, Mrs. Barrett could contain herself no longer.

"What happened? Inspector McLaughlin told me the bare bones, but you were there. I gotta know."

She listened without a word while I told her.

"He always was a brave boy. Oh, not in the fence climbing, tree climbing way, but in the way he faced his situation in life head on. He always knew he was different in so many ways. As if having dark skin wasn't enough!"

Her shoulders heaved and I hugged her close. She smelled musky, unpleasant, and I wondered if she had been taking proper care of herself.

"What will you do?" I asked her.

"Inspector McLaughlin is lending me enough money to go to Nova Scotia. My no-good husband lives there, and I have an aunt. He has promised not to reveal that Damone killed Reverend Crudden until Trinity and I are gone. He's given me a week."

I shut my mouth. I wanted to scream, this is your home! But I knew that the inspector was right; there would be no more welcome for her in Owen Sound once folks learned the truth about the murder. And the truth had to come out, or all of the women involved in the brothel would live the rest of their lives under a cloud of suspicion. Including me.

"Do you have enough money?" I asked.

"Damone always provided for us. I have some savings. I could probably pay the passage for us to go to Nova Scotia by myself, but I need some to start our new lives, to find a place to live, until I can find work."

"Here, take this." I opened my reticule and handed her a generous sum.

Her eyes opened. "No, honey…"

"Mrs. Barrett. My Daddy is prosperous. I've made a mess of my life. Let me do something good for a change. Please. It'll make me feel better. I feel wretched that I couldn't save him."

Now I was crying, and she comforted me.

"Better that he drowned a hero, than be hanged. You gave him the only chance he had. You're a good girl, honey. Now go, take your

Thomas, and make something of your life." She passed me a clean, rough handkerchief. I cleaned myself up as best I could and after I had pressed a dollar bill into Trinity's hands, we left. I don't remember the walk back to Bart's farm.

***

Time passed slowly as ever on the farm, although I threw myself into cooking, cleaning, caring for Thomas, and helping Bart with chores. After two long weeks, which seemed more like months, I opened the door one Sunday morning to find Inspector McLaughlin very much wanting to be invited in. After the tea and biscuits were served, we chatted while he played with Thomas and the train.

"Mrs. Barrett has left, and I'm optimistic that she is safely in Nova Scotia," he said.

"I hope she can build a good life there for her and Trinity. She told me how much you helped her," I said. I hung my head. "I visited her without your permission. I had to tell her what happened to Damone."

"Something else for me to overlook." He sighed. "In the future, I would like you to be honest with me."

"Yes, I promise, no more deception." I cleared my throat. "Sometimes I wish I had never disobeyed you at all, and left Damone to face his fate. I'm sorry. I truly am."

"He would have hanged. There is no worse death. Now that it's all over and done with, I can tell you, as a private citizen," he gestured to his civilian suit, "you did that young man an enormous favour. As well as his family. Very often loved ones don't recover from having a close relative swing. You've given them a chance to mourn Damone as a hero, not a criminal."

I felt the heat rise in my face. I looked down.

"You're free to leave Owen Sound now." He took my hand. "I think you should return to your father, let him help you. I'd like to come to visit you in Galt, if I may."

My face flamed hotter still. "I'd like that very much."

He stood up. "I must be going now. I am going to attend Mass today." He saw the surprise on my face.

"Of course, I'm Roman Catholic, surely that doesn't matter to you?"

"Of course not. I just can't imagine you in a church."

He smiled, kissed the top of Thomas' head, scratched Jack's ears and walked out the door with a jaunty step. He hadn't tried to hold my hand or kiss me goodbye.

That evening, after Bart had finished his chores and lit his pipe in his favourite chair by the fire, I told him that I was free to leave. He scowled, then said, "It's for the best, but I'll miss you and young Thomas."

"I'll stay until the end of the month," I said. My throat felt constricted, and my stomach had a knot in it.

"No, book your train ticket, and start your life again. Owen Sound has not been a good place for you."

I got up, went over and hugged him. He looked surprised but pleased, and after a moment, he hugged me back. He smelled of wood smoke.

"I'll miss you too," I said.

The next day, I telegraphed Daddy, booked my train ticket, and retrieved Jack's basket from where I had placed it in a dry spot in the barn. The day following, Daddy met me at the train station, and brought us home.

"What do you plan to do with the rest of your life?" he asked once we had boarded the train.

"If Lavinia will help with Thomas, I'd like to finish school. After that, what I really want is to be a chemist, like you."

He blushed bright red, said nothing, but hugged me tight. We didn't speak until we reached home, *Lavinia's home*, I supposed. However, she was more than welcoming to me and especially Thomas.

"Can he call me Grandmamma?" she asked me tentatively as we sat sewing by a roaring fire. "If not, I understand, Lavinia will be fine." Her face was red with the heat of the fire, and her lined face was beaded with perspiration.

I didn't answer for a moment, thinking of my beloved Mamma. How she would have doted on Thomas. But Mamma was dead, and Lavinia was not. And Mamma had been a kind and caring woman. She would want Daddy and me to be happy, and I thought that she probably would be pleased that Lavinia was taking such good care of Daddy.

"Grandmamma would be lovely. We're both lucky to have you in our lives." I realized that I meant it.

A month passed, and I immersed myself back into my Galt life. We told everyone that Thomas was my cousin's baby, and that my cousin had passed away. A lie is always easiest if it is mostly based on the truth, and although some matrons looked at me sharply, I held my head high, and Lavinia and I both cared for him proudly and openly. I tried to put my time in Owen Sound behind me. I missed the water; I yearned for the water. The Grand River, while beautiful, could not hold a candle to the ever-changing majesty of Georgian Bay. But I was grateful to be settled, and I began to think of returning to school.

I was on my hands and knees one day cleaning out the fireplace when I heard the doorbell ring.

"I'll answer it," called Lavinia, and I assumed it must be one of her friends, or a peddler flogging his wares. I was scrubbing hard with the wire brush when Lavinia came into the room and said, "You have a visitor."

I stood up and pushed a stray strand of hair from my eyes. I heard footsteps, then in walked Inspector McLaughlin.

"Hello," I stuttered.

We stood facing each other, smiling foolishly.

He walked over, kissed my cheek, then wiped my face with his handkerchief. I flinched at the sooty mark on the white linen.

"You always see me at my very worst," I complained. But he only laughed.

"At your worst, you are more beautiful than most women are at their best."

I closed my mouth. My bald spot was slowly growing in, and with clever hairdressing was almost unnoticeable. Almost.

"Where are my manners? Would you like to have tea and some biscuits?" I asked.

"I'd really like to go for a walk," he said. "Would your stepmother watch Thomas for us?"

"I'm sure she will." Of course, Lavinia said yes. Her eyes were wide with curiosity, but she said not a word, acting like having an Owen Sound policeman visit her step-daughter was the most natural occurrence in the world.

I put on my cloak and a stylish burgundy hat I bought myself when I returned to Galt. It was so nice to be able to wear colours again rather than the unrelieved black Mrs. O'Hara had demanded of us.

"I'll take you to the river," I said. He tucked my arm in his and we walked down Parkhill Road. It was icy in spots and we both slid a little, laughing. We had to walk briskly to keep warm, and I felt a nice cold flush on my cheeks. I knew I looked my best in the cold.

"Your eyes are sparkling," he said.

"Yes, well, I suppose I'm relieved to be back home. I'm actually enjoying Lavinia's company. I was such a foolish, stupid girl."

"A girl who learned many lessons," he said. He squeezed my hand more tightly.

"Is there somewhere warmer we can go to talk?" he asked. "Privately?"

I thought about it. "I suppose if we are quiet, we can sit in a pew in Trinity Church."

"Lead the way." And I did.

We settled ourselves near the back, and he did not relinquish my hand.

We sat in silence. The sun's weak light glittered through the stained-glass windows, leaving a dancing stain on the pew in front of us. I closed my eyes, allowing some of the serenity of the place to sink into me.

"I want us to get married," he said. His voice was too loud.

"Pardon me?" My face burned.

"You heard me. I think we should get married."

"But you know what I am. What a bad girl I am."

"Put it behind you. That's all in the past. You're still young, but you have matured. We can make a life for ourselves."

"But you're so much better than me. I don't deserve you."

"Look at me Charlotte." I raised my eyes. The sunlight was almost blinding; I looked down again at the pew.

"I helped kill a man in Ireland. He was a wealthy English landowner and enclosed some common lands while my people were dying from desperate poverty. My aunt and uncle and their seven kids had nowhere to go, turned out of their tiny home. They came to our house which wasn't much bigger. I was part of a lynch mob. We burned his house down with him inside. We let his wife go free. My father put me on a boat for Canada the next day. Now do you think I'm better than you?"

I leaned into him then.

ABOUT THE AUTHOR

Lee Johnston has a Bachelor and Master of Arts (English), and Certificate of Creative Writing from the University of Toronto. She is a long-time member of the Cambridge Writers Collective, and is the Literary Coordinator of the Cambridge Mayor's Celebration of the Arts. She was awarded an Arts Connect Cambridge grant in 2018. Damnation Corner is her first full-length novel.

Made in the USA
Lexington, KY
19 July 2019